ALSO BY TREVOR COLE

Norman Bray in the Performance of His Life

The Fearsome Particles

PRACTICAL JEAN

A Novel

TREVOR COLE

MCCLELLAND & STEWART

Library and Archives Canada Cataloguing in Publication

Cole, Trevor, 1960-
    Practical Jean / Trevor Cole.

ISBN 978-0-7710-2325-5

    I. Title.

PS8605.O44P73 2010   C813'.6   C2010-901558-4

We acknowledge the financial support of the Government of Canada through the
Book Publishing Industry Development Program and that of the Government of Ontario
through the Ontario Media Development Corporation's Ontario Book Initiative.
We further acknowledge the support of the Canada Council for the Arts and the
Ontario Arts Council for our publishing program.

The poem referred to on pp. 64-65 is "My Last Poem" by Manuel Bandeira, in a translation by
Elizabeth Bishop published in *An Anthology of Twentieth-Century Brazilian Poetry*, edited by
Elizabeth Bishop and Emanuel Brasil, Wesleyan University Press, Hanover, NH, 1972.

The line on p. 179 is from the song "Mele Kalikimaka," written by R. Alex Anderson.
© Bibo Music Publishing.

Typeset in Minion by M&S, Toronto
Printed and bound in Canada

This book is printed on acid-free paper that is 100% recycled, ancient-forest friendly
(100% post-consumer waste).

McClelland & Stewart Ltd.
75 Sherbourne Street
Toronto, Ontario
M5A 2P9
www.mcclelland.com

1   2   3   4   5   14   13   12   11   10

For Solana

PROLOGUE

YOU MIGHT THINK this a rather horrible and depraved sort of story. But that's because you're a nice person. The events of this story are not the sort of thing that nice people think about, let alone do. But that's speaking generally, and traditionally, because the truth of it is that this story is filled with nice people, and yet what happened could not be more awful. It's one of the quirks of our modern times.

Everything began when Jean Vale Horemarsh had to look after her mother, Marjorie, who was dying of a terrible cancer in one of the soft organs. It might have been the pancreas or the liver. It wasn't uterus or lung or bone or breast. Jean never said exactly, but when she talked about her mother and how much pain she was in, Jean would move her hand around her middle, a bit off to the side. People watched that hand floating around there in the squishy mid-range, and most got the basic idea.

Just to meet her, you would have liked Jean. There's no doubt about that, because everybody liked Jean. She really was the most likeable person, always smiling, always looking you straight in the eye, asking about you and your children. Her favourite adjective was "sweet," as in "Aren't you sweet?" and "Isn't that sweet?" And she liked the word "delectable," too, when it came to describing an enjoyable food or situation. "That was a delectable party," Jean would say. Charming, people called her.

You'll think, because of the past tense, that she's dead. She's not. It's just that now, most people in Kotemee keep their distance.

Pronounce that Ko-*teh*-me, by the way, please, not *Ko*-teh-me or Ko-teh-*meee*. A lot of day-trip visitors and TV reporters from the city get it wrong. Last May, Council almost voted to have the pronunciation added to the "Welcome to Kotemee" sign on Highway 18. But the motion lost by a two-vote margin. Some people don't adapt well to change.

Jean had – has – reddish blond hair, which she kept trimmed short because of her pottery and porcelain work, and that lovely pale, freckly skin that people with reddish hair often have. A lot of Hollywood actresses have that kind of skin and you'll only discover it when you see them in a really close-up picture in a magazine, but never in a movie because they cover it with makeup or make it disappear under hot lights. Which seems a shame. The other thing about Jean, physically, is that as she got older she struggled just a bit with her weight. You would never say that she was heavy, just heavier than she would have liked. But she was tall, about five-foot nine, so she carried it well. She had a nice, firm jaw line, and in public she made sure to wear little sweaters or linen jackets that gave her a good proportion. And when she stood talking to you, she would hold her arm casually across her stomach area, as if she were holding a glass of white wine, although usually there was nothing in her hand at all. It was just . . . there. You might have considered it an affectation, if you were being uncharitable.

Jean's mother was dying, then, of cancer, and Jean was taking care of her. While she did that, she lived at her parents' house on Blanchard Avenue, sleeping alone in one of the three guest rooms, which used to be her bedroom when she and her two brothers were children. It was quite a big house, with lovely olive-green clapboard siding, on one of the nicest streets in Kotemee, because Marjorie and her husband, Drew, had both been highly accomplished people.

Yes, accomplished is the word for Jean's parents. For most of her adult life, Marjorie Horemarsh was a veterinarian, and she looked so professional and dedicated in her white coat, with her auburn hair pinned tight, you would have gladly let her treat you for most any *human* trouble. And Jean's father, Drew, though he's been dead now for six years and retired for twelve before that, was the local police chief. His oldest son, Andrew Jr., went into the force as soon as he could and now he's the chief. There's no nepotism suggested; that's just how small towns work. Andrew Jr. took after Drew in lots of ways, including his size and his deliberate ambition, in this case to follow in his father's footsteps. "I'll be chief one day," Andrew Jr. would say. "That's a lock." And Drew didn't say any different. So everyone assumed that some day, Andrew Horemarsh, Jr., would be the chief of the twenty-three-man, five-car force, and for the last number of years he has been. And his brother, Welland, works with him in Community Services. Under him, technically, but most people in town say "with."

Neither of the brothers could spare time away from their police work to help Jean take care of their mother in the last stages, which was no surprise. Marjorie could have afforded special care, but no, she considered it Jean's daughterly duty. And no visitors, either;

Marjorie insisted on quiet. So there Jean was, alone, rambling about in the big house, attending to all the household and caregiving chores. She did it for three long, heartbreaking months – and she was able to do it, and it was expected of her, because she didn't work. Jean had what she herself called a passion, and some called a pastime, which, it was felt, she could put aside for the good of her family. Which was her ceramics. And now, get ready, because here comes the story of Jean's ceramics. Which is not the main story, only a side one. But it must be told.

Jean's ceramics, which she sold from a studio-showroom called Jean's Expressions, at the end of Kotemee's main street, were the loveliest, most ridiculous pieces of pottery you or any other living person has ever seen. She had an obsession with leaves, did Jean. For instance, if you were given a bouquet of flowers in a nice vase, and Jean came over, and you said, "Look at these lovely flowers that just came," Jean would give you an "Aren't they sweet?" and she would barely even look at the flowers. She would go straight to the leaves. The greenery. Which is really the filler. She would let them lie against her palm in the light, looking at them with her head tilted at an angle and a dreamy haze over her face. And if it was a leaf she hadn't often seen, she would lean in close and study the veins and the cell structure and the edges, which she called the "margins." And then she might sniff at the leaf, as if it had a fragrance.

And these leaves were what she tried to do in her ceramics. But she didn't simply paint leaves in pretty patterns on the usual plates and bowls and cups. No, she made the leaves – the leaves themselves – in various ceramic constructions, combined with tendrils and vines and ferns and shoots, the usual green elements. And her goal was to make these concoctions as lifelike and delicate and suspended in mid-air as the real thing. Which meant, as you would expect, they broke.

Half of the time they just shattered right in the kiln. And she would weep for every one. But if they survived that, then they broke as she moved them from the studio to the showroom. And if they endured that fourteen-foot journey, then they cracked or collapsed when someone bought one and tried to move it from the showroom to their car, or from the car to their house, or one day, a month later, when their teenager came home and slammed the door.

But Jean would not be deterred. She'd experiment with different clays, and glazes, and temperatures, because naturally people complained. When people buy a pottery cup, they want a good strong handle, and they expect that same kind of sturdiness in a ceramic anything. In their minds, that's the point of ceramics. But Jean's wish didn't seem to be to make something that would last; it was to make something exquisite, just to know that she had done it. She had always been like that, a different sort of thinker, an artistic spirit, you might say, ever since she was a child. And in a family of otherwise sensible, solid, down-to-earth sorts of people, real doers, as veterinarians and police officers are, that made Jean an anomaly. Her differentness bewildered her father and brothers, but it frustrated her mother deeply. So much so that whenever Jean, growing up, did or said something that was out of the sensible family norm – glued hundreds of Swarovski crystals to her fingertips, say, or married a substitute high school English teacher named Milt – Marjorie would sigh and exclaim, "Little girl . . ." or "Young woman . . . how can you possibly be a Horemarsh? You don't have a practical gene in your body!"

When she was young, Jean didn't know about genes, so she thought her mother was ruing the lack of another sort of girl inside the body of her daughter. Another Jean . . . a practical Jean.

And then came her mother's long, painful, debilitating illness, when there was no use for the exquisite in the face of the dirty, dismal certainties. When she had to summon the practical in her. Until Marjorie Horemarsh finally, blessedly, died. And then what happened after that . . . happened.

And here in Kotemee, all anyone can say now is, "*Thank God* I was never a good friend of Jean Vale Horemarsh."

Chapter 1

The sun was shining on the whole of Kotemee. Spangles trembled on the lake, shafts of gleam stabbed off the chrome of cars lining Main Street, and in Corkin Park the members of the *Star-Lookout* Lions, Kotemee's Pee Wee League team, swung aluminum bats that scalded their tender, eleven-year-old hands. But for Jean Vale Horemarsh, there was no light in her life but the light of her fridge, and it showed her things she did not want to see.

A jar of strawberry jam, empty but for the grouting of candied berry at the bottom. A half tub of sour cream, its contents upholstered in a thick aquamarine mould. A pasta sauce and a soup, stalking fermentation in their plastic containers. A crumpled paper bag of wizened, weightless mushrooms. The jellified remains of cucumber and the pockmarked corpses of zucchini and bell pepper in the bottom crisper drawer.

In the kitchen of her sun-warmed house on Edgeworth Street, Jean bent to the task of removing each of these abominations. The jam jar was tossed into the recycling bin. The putrid liquids were dumped into the sink. The zucchini, cucumber, and mushrooms became compost. The mould-stiffened sour cream would not budge from its tub, so Jean scooped it out with her hand. Anything suspect – a bit of improperly wrapped steak, a bottle of cloudy dressing – was presumed tainted and excised without mercy from the innards of the fridge. It was three o'clock in the afternoon and Jean still wore the black jacquard dress she'd worn to her mother's funeral. She had not found the will to take it off, although she had undone several of the buttons. So as she worked, erasing the evidence of time, destroying all signs of decay, her dress hung open slightly, exposing the skin of her back to the refrigerated air.

Watching her from a corner of the kitchen, Milt, Jean's husband, confessed that he should have cleaned out the fridge weeks ago, while Jean was still at her mother's. But it was a revolting chore, he said, and he kept putting it off; he didn't know how she did it.

"I have a strong stomach," said Jean.

It had been three full months since Jean and Milt had lived together. Marjorie had made it clear that in dying she required Jean's full attention, which left Milt to mind himself at home. Now, as Jean bowed and stared into the cool, white recess, he came up behind her. He reached over her for a jar of peanut butter and, with only a slight hesitation, touched his fingers to the unbuttoned region of his wife's back and began to draw them lightly downward.

"What a terrible, terrible idea," she said.

"Sorry." He retreated with the peanut butter and screwed open the lid. "I just thought, we haven't . . . I think it was snowing the last time. But you're right, bad timing." He set the jar and lid on the counter and reached for a bag of bread. "If you're hungry, I could make you some toast."

Jean straightened at the fridge, summoned tolerance and forgiveness, and gave her husband a sad, sheepish look. She folded her arms around him and set her chin on his shoulder. It was more a lean than a hug. "Poor Milty," she said. "Poor, poor Milty."

"Milty's all right."

"You can squeeze my breast if you want."

"What, now?"

"Nothing's going to happen because of it. But you can do it if you like and then disappear into the bathroom or something."

"Well, I don't think that's necessary."

"Suit yourself." She began to separate from him and before she did, he slipped a hand in and latched onto her left one, just holding it for a moment as she waited. "There," she said finally, and patted his cheek as she left him.

"I could take it out right here," he said from the kitchen.

"Don't."

He headed past her, toward the powder room in the hall. "It's not like I haven't."

A few minutes later, slumped on the matching green velour living room chairs in a room invaded by the late-afternoon sun, they stared at *Winter Leaves*, which Milt had set on the coffee table in honour of Jean's return. A clutch of hydrangea leaves ruined by frost it was meant to be.

"That looks nice there," said Jean. "Thank you."

"Thought you might like it."

She pushed herself out of the soft cushions and leaned forward, squinting. "Is that a crack?"

"Just a small one. I glued it."

"There's another one."

"Only two, though. Don't keep looking."

With a sigh Jean slumped back in her chair. "It is impossible for anything beautiful to last."

"But you made something beautiful. That's the point."

Jean stared at Milt. "That is the point, isn't it?"

"Absolutely."

She nodded and let her chin rest on her chest. Never had she been so exhausted, and yet so relieved. The exhaustion and relief seeped through her muscles and bones, a bad and good feeling all at once. *This must be the way athletes feel,* Jean thought, *after they've run a thousand miles and won the game.* She let the sensation slip through her like one of those drugs that young people take and allowed her mind to drift backward to the funeral at First United Presbyterian. Everyone had been there: Jean's brothers, handsome so-and-so's in their dress uniforms; Andrew Jr.'s silent wife, Celeste, and their two grown children, Ross and Marlee, sparing four precious hours away from their busy young lives, thank you so much for your sacrifice; her own good friends, most of them anyway, full of sympathy and support; and a hundred Kotemee folk who'd known Marjorie Horemarsh as the best veterinarian they'd ever brought a sick spaniel to, and not as a mother who'd praised only marks and commendations and money and prizes and never beauty . . . never, ever beauty for its own sake, and not as a patient who moaned in pain seventeen hours a day and smelled like throw-up and needed to be bathed and fed and have her putrid bedsores swabbed and dressed . . .

"It was nice to see your friends there," said Milt. "Louise looked good, I thought. Or –"

"Louise looked good, did she?"

"Well. So did Dorothy. We should have them all over some day."

Jean stared at the ceiling and sighed. "What's the point, Milt?"

"The house has been pretty quiet. You could play bridge, like you used to."

"No, Milt, I'm not talking about that. I'm saying what's the point of anything?"

"Oh." Milt tossed his head back against the chair cushion as if to say, *Wow, that's a big one.*

"Exactly," said Jean. "You know, you think about a lot of things when you're taking care of your dying mother."

Milt leaned forward in his chair. "Do you want a drink?" He rose and steadied himself. His tie was askew, and the end of it rested against the mound of his belly, a little like a dying leaf against a pumpkin, Jean considered.

"I will have some white wine." She lifted her voice to talk as Milt made his way to the kitchen. "You think about things, Milt," she said. "You ask yourself questions."

"What sort of questions? No white, I'm afraid. Red?"

"Fine. Big questions, like, what's the point of anything?"

"Right."

"You live, and then you die, Milt. And whatever you had is gone and it doesn't matter any more. Nothing matters for ever and ever."

"Wow," said Milt on his way back with the glasses.

"So what is the point?"

He handed her the wine. "You want me to answer that?"

"I don't think you *can* answer that. I don't think anyone can."

"I think the point is to live the best life possible, for as long as you're able."

Jean, still sunk into the cushions and drugged with exhaustion, sipped her wine and picked at the threads of ideas and formulations and fantasies that had occupied her mind for the last couple of months, while she'd fed her mother unsweetened Pablum, while she'd stared at her thick, unweeded garden, while she'd kneeled alone in the en suite bathroom, cleaning the dried spray of urine from the floor where her mother had slipped.

"Beauty is the point, I think."

"There you go. You answered it yourself."

"A moment of beauty, or joy, something exquisite and pure." She made a face. "I hate this red wine. Did you open it a week ago?"

"About that."

"I'm not drinking it." She set it on the coffee table. "That's it for bad wine."

"Did you want me to drive and get some white?"

"Yes, but not now. Not while we're talking." For a while she stared at the coffee table, at the wine yawing in the glass, at *Winter Leaves*, without really seeing any of them. "More than once, Milt," she said. "More than once, when I was feeding Mom in bed? And she would lay her head back and fall asleep? I thought about pinching her nose and her lips closed and just holding them like that. Holding them tight."

"Until she died?"

"Until she died."

"Wow," said Milt. His eyes went wide as he shook his head. He looked, Jean thought, as though he were really taking it in.

"Because what is the difference?" She shifted to the edge of the cushion. "Whether you die now or die later, it's the same thing, but one way has less suffering. They do it for animals. My own mother did it. I watched it happen." Even now her mind filled with bright images, sudden whites and reds. In the very early days of her mother's career, when she'd had few clients and couldn't justify the cost of a clinic, Marjorie had used their kitchen table, spread with sheets of white plastic, to perform operations. She had allowed little Jean, who was the oldest of her children, to observe – this was real life, she said, no need to hide it – as she sliced open neighbourhood cats and dogs to pluck out their ovaries or spleens, or to reattach bloody tendons. Many times before she was seven Jean had watched her mother stick a hypodermic into the fur of some aged or diseased animal, watched her press the plunger and wait out the quiet seconds until its eyes closed. That was the simplest act of all, and the kindest, it now seemed to Jean.

"It's called 'mercy,' Milt. That's what it's called. Don't let a living thing suffer. I should have done it. I hate myself for *not* doing it."

"Don't hate yourself, Jean."

Jean stared at *Winter Leaves* and lost herself in a scene that had come to her several times before, projected like a movie against the backs of her eyelids while she slumped in the chair in Marjorie's darkened room, listening to her mother breathe. She saw her hand reaching down – in her imagination it was always morning, daylight filled the room, and everything was a pale pink – and squeezing her mother's soft nostrils between thumb and forefinger, the way you might seal the mouth of an inflated balloon. With the other hand she held her lips closed, too. Then the image changed, and she was pressing down on her mother's mouth; yes, that would work better. Squeezing her nostrils, and clamping down hard on her mouth. It wouldn't have been difficult; her mother was weak, and Jean's hands were muscled tools from years of working with clay. Marjorie's eyes would open, she'd be terrified, staring up at her daughter, fighting for her life, not realizing Jean's way was so much better. But it would only last a moment, that struggle, unlike the pain of her lingering disease. And afterward there'd be no recriminations, no feelings of betrayal, no abiding resentments. There'd be nothing, because that's what death was.

"I should have killed my mother, Milt." Jean felt the tears pud-
dling in her eyes. "I should have killed her before she got so sick.
Then she wouldn't have had to suffer at all."

He came to her and put his hand on her knee. "You were a
good daughter to her, Jean. You took care of her."

"Not like I should have."

She reached into her sleeve for the tissue she'd tucked there
and used it to dry her eyes. Though it was painful to believe that
she had failed her mother by not taking her life, her conviction in
that belief was, in an odd way, comforting. Certainty energized
her. She took a deep breath and looked into Milt's sad, grey eyes.
Such a sweet man.

"If you wanted to screw me," she said to Milt, "I'd be game."

Milt looked down at his hand on her knee, and off to the
powder room. "I don't think I *can* now."

She sighed. "That's annoying."

"I can try."

"No, never mind." She patted his hand. "I'd be just as happy
with some white wine."

Chapter 2

J ean was so glad to get out of the house. Relieved, simply to be able to venture into the blue-bright day, equipped with a purpose. She stopped the topaz Hyundai in front of 426 Marlborough Street, walked up the path to the wide bungalow owned by Gwen and Phil Thindle, long-time clients of Marjorie's, and dropped a card in the brass mailbox.

Your thoughtfulness was very much appreciated.

It had felt odd, being back in her own home. Unfamiliar, not having the desperate needs of her diminishing mother to consider every moment of every hour. Not having Marjorie's wavery moans filling the hallways and stairwells, or the smell of Pablum and boiled carrots, the only things she would eat in the end, heavying the air like the faint, sweet whiff of decay. It had been peculiar, in particular, having Milt there with her. Watching her.

"Milt," she'd said. "Please stop watching me."

"I'm not."

She'd been sitting at the dining table, with thank-you cards piled in front of her and Milt behind her in the living room, set in his chair by the iron standing lamp. He had a view of her from there and he hadn't had a magazine or book in his lap, so of course he'd been watching her.

"I can feel your eyes on me," she'd said. "I don't know what could be so interesting."

"What are you doing?"

Jean wheeled the car around the corner onto Sedmore Avenue and looked for number 157, where Judith Bell lived, an old friend of her mother's who had sent a very ordinary bouquet of gladioli and carnations with only a frilly thatch of plumosa, the most non-descript greenery. It wasn't really Judith's fault, Jean supposed. But what some florists tried to get away with was criminal.

My brothers and I appreciate your kindness.

She'd explained to Milt that she was writing thank-you cards to everyone who'd sent flowers and donations to the funeral. Some of them, for the people who lived out of town, were going to be mailed, and some of them, for the Kotemeeans, she intended to hand-deliver. "People have no idea how much work there is after a funeral," she'd said. "I'm sure it will remain a mystery to my brothers."

Milt, behind her, hadn't responded to that. Milt hadn't said anything at all. And it was his *way* of not saying anything at all that had prickled at Jean. She'd been writing, *It was so sweet of you to remember Mother's love of hydrangeas*, in a card to Marjorie's former colleague Millicent Keeping – though her mother had never given a second's thought to hydrangeas, or flowers of any kind, ever, and Jean was only writing it because Millicent was in a nursing home with no hope and it was the least she could do – and she hadn't even been able to reach the end. She'd had to slap down her pen after she'd written *hydr*.

"Milt, what?"

Milt had shifted sideways in his chair. "I was just wondering . . . well . . . when you were going to really let go."

"Let go of what?"

"I mean show some grief."

She'd sighed and picked up her pen – *angeas*. "I cried yesterday, didn't I?" *Best of luck in your remaining years*, Jean had finished, signing it the same way she signed her ceramics: *Jean V. Horemarsh*.

"That was more like the sniffles."

Jean had sealed Millicent's card in its envelope, risen from the table, and begun to gather her thank-yous. Milt's eyes had followed her as she'd dropped the cards into a green cloth shopping bag.

"You were kind of stone-faced at the funeral."

"Oh, that is just . . ." She'd stopped to look for her keys.

"You were like that at your father's funeral, too," Milt had said from his chair. "And right after, you tried to make that fire bush."

Milt had been referring to the time, six years before, after Drew had died of a heart attack and the funeral had come and gone like a blink, when suddenly Jean had been seized by the idea of making an enormous ceramic Burning Bush. Five feet in diameter, she'd thought, and equipped with some sort of everlasting flame that she had not quite figured out. There was no intention of making a religious statement; Jean was not at all religious. It had just seized her, like so many of her best ideas, that a huge ceramic Burning Bush was exactly the right piece to be working on the minute her father was in the ground. First she would have to make the little leaves. So she'd spent three solid days – that is, three days entirely without sleep and with almost no food – fashioning and firing smooth peltate leaves the size of her thumb. She'd finished about twenty-two hundred of them, which was possibly two or three times as many as she needed, before she lost her will and crashed to a deep sleep on the studio floor. The little leaves were still stored in a box somewhere, set in layers on stiff paper, like green ceramic cornflakes.

"That's not going to happen this time," Jean had declared to Milt from the front hall. "Nothing like that is going to happen." Then she'd just shut the door on her husband's watchful silence and got in the car.

The day told her to venture out and breathe, and she obeyed.

Her deliveries took her all over town, and she plotted her course precisely so she wouldn't waste gas doubling back. That was the sort of practical thinking her mother would have appreciated, Jean thought with some pride. And it was easy, too, because she knew the town so well. Other people might have thought of Kotemee as weightless and "quaint," the sort of place an ambitious person would skip in and out of like something hurled. But that didn't matter to Jean because all of her important memories were lodged in the crevices of the town. At some point in her life, she had walked or driven down nearly every one of Kotemee's wide streets, had been in dozens of its pretty, wood-sided houses. Some of these held more resonances than others, naturally. And with her mother's pain and death still reverberating in her head like a bell, Jean found herself running into those moments from the past more than usual as she drove. A part of her felt as if she had been exiled for years, banished to some strange, cruel atoll, and had just returned to the land that had made her who she was. She felt a need to reacquaint herself.

On Calendar Street, Jean relived the time she was nine years old and had walked home barefoot all the way from Bonner's Shoes. Marjorie had paid for new Converse runners and insisted on leaving the old, filthy pair at the store. But the new runners had precious, Chiclet-white soles and Jean had wanted to carry them for fear of getting them dirty. Hearing that, the saleswoman had held out the old shoes for her to put on. Jean's mother waved them away.

"She's got shoes," said Marjorie. "It's her choice not to wear them."

At the end of the woman's arm, the old runners hovered in the air. "She might hurt her feet."

"Then I guess she'll learn."

She did learn. Jean learned that she could walk for a half an hour with a box of new shoes in her arms and blisters rising like gumdrops on the balls of her feet, and not cry or stop even once.

On Mott Avenue, Jean slowed past a tiny park with dogwood trees and a stone fountain. When she was six years old that fountain had seemed so huge Jean was sure it had been made by God, because she'd believed in God then. And she'd imagined that when the fountain shot streams of water skyward, those streams were wishes being whooshed to Heaven. She remembered sitting alone on the pebbly edge of the basin, her feet in the cold, green water, and sending wishes on the streams.

On Falling Crescent, Jean passed in front of Dorothy Perks's old house, a simple four-square painted a browny grey now, though it used to be margarine yellow. It was in the basement of that house when Jean was sixteen that a twelfth-grader named Ash Birdy had slid his hand into her underpants, because he'd been watching Craig Veere do it to Dorothy and Ash felt a lot of pressure to keep up with Craig. Jean, on the other hand, didn't feel much pressure to keep up with Dorothy, so Ash was disappointed. Very much so. Dorothy and Jean were still great friends – she had a thank-you card for Dorothy in her bag – but what had happened later with Ash was another of those memories that stuck in a crevice.

As it usually did, thinking about Ash made Jean think of Cheryl Nunley. Sometimes it was the other way around – an image of Cheryl made Jean's mind leap to the boy. Either way, Ash was only a 10 percent part of the memory; Cheryl got the rest.

Hill Street was next. At the top Jean pulled up in front of Louise Draper's house. Louise taught Grade 9 and 10 English at Hern Regional High School, where Milt sometimes substituted. Years before, back in the ancient past of their marriage, Jean had been aware of a snag in the thread of her relationship with Milt, and she'd discovered that he and Louise had had the briefest, barest fling. It was hardly an affair at all, more like a friendship with glimpses of partial nudity, as a movie rating might have put it. But when she went to confront Louise, Jean had found herself far more charmed by the woman than threatened by whatever designs she might have had on Milt. She had an odd, abstracted air and a scattered sort of sincerity, so it took Jean no time at all to forgive Louise, and before long they were good friends.

Jean went up the steps with the card in her hand and was about to plunk it through the mail slot when the door jerked open and Louise burst into view. It was mid-morning on a weekday so that was a surprise, and Jean sort of jumped back. Louise did almost the same jumpy thing when she saw Jean.

"Oh, Jean!" she said. "I saw the car through the window and I thought . . ." She glanced from Jean to the car and bobbed her head down as if to see inside, looked back at Jean, and smiled. "It's great to see you!"

Louise was wearing a white blouse and shapeless tan skirt, which seemed like the sort of outfit she would wear to work. Her long, tarnish-coloured hair was combed as usual, high off her head. It was a style quite unconnected to modern fashion. It seemed stuck in a vague Other Time, which fit Louise because her mind often seemed drawn to some misty Other Place. All things considered, knowing Louise as she did, Jean thought it possible that her friend had just forgotten to go to school that day.

"Louise, you look so nice," said Jean. "Is that a teaching outfit?"

Louise giggled in the rolling, girlish way she had. "It's a P.D. day, Jean."

That was a relief, and Jean handed Louise the card. The two women chatted for a while, with Louise showing true concern for Jean's feelings regarding her mother's recent death, and Jean not knowing what to say because Louise expected her to be sad and sad was a draggy, wishful emotion – that's how Jean felt whenever she thought of Cheryl – and the way she felt about her mother's death wasn't like that at all. But apart from that, talking to Louise really was refreshing, and Jean decided that Milt's idea of having all her friends over was a good one. She invited Louise then and there to come for a little party on Wednesday night.

Framed by the doorway behind her, Louise looked happy and lost at the same time.

. "That's . . ."

"Not tomorrow," said Jean, "but the next night."

"Okay, sure!"

The trees and hydro poles cast charcoal cut-outs of themselves onto the lawns and sidewalks as Jean made a few more thank-you stops. There was a quick one to the tiny house owned by her good friend Natalie Skilbeck, who was working, so Jean wrote a note on the back of the card about coming over Wednesday. *It'll be fun!* And there was another to the minister who'd performed the funeral service for Marjorie. Jean couldn't quite remember the service because in her mind the entire funeral was such a dark, inaccessible blur, but she thought a thank-you only polite. *We very much appreciate your effort on behalf of our mother.* The minister came to the door in a rumpled plaid shirt and jeans, looking much less formal than Jean expected of a member of the clergy. He was an older man with large, flat glasses, like little windshields on his face, and when he saw Jean he immediately started talking about grief and how important it was. He went on and on about it. Jean listened as politely as she could for a while, and finally started backing away toward the car. By the time she was at the curb the minister was almost shouting at her to be sad. It was all a bit much.

She also delivered a card to Tina Dooley, even though Tina hadn't really earned one. *So nice of you to attend.* Tina, who owned the home accessories store Tina's Textures, was on the committee for the Kotemee Business Association and made a point of knowing the this and that of everyone in the Main Street Business District. By tomorrow she would know who had gotten a card and who hadn't, and Jean just did not need the trouble.

The next minute Jean was approaching Douglas Avenue. Nobody on the thank-you list lived on Douglas; if she had wanted to, Jean could have driven straight by it. Normally she probably would have. But today she found herself making a right turn and stopping the car in the crook of the road, in front of Cheryl Nunley's old house, number 242. After a while, she turned off the engine.

Of all Jean's friends, Cheryl had been the one most like her. Not in her artistic inclinations; Cheryl had scant few of those. But she was a girl who worked for her marks, who dressed neatly, about a year behind the trend, who preferred not to keep people waiting, who tittered rather than laughed out loud, who liked a treat once in a while – something with pastry – and who usually dated boys too shy to ask out the girls they really wanted.

So Jean had always been comfortable around Cheryl. Nothing chafed. Whether it was their opinion of *American Graffiti* (really wonderful) or Richard Dreyfuss (weirdly cute) or Home Ec. teacher Mrs. Woodenshantz (scatterbrained) or girls who smoked (disgusting), she and Cheryl agreed so much they might have been astrological twins. They never treated each other cruelly to gain favour with someone else. They stood together at dances watching Dorothy Perks get the best boys. They were each other's reliable backup plan, in case something more exciting fell through.

And on the matter of sex, well, if expressions of horror were a badge of identity then Jean and Cheryl belonged to the same anti-sex club. Oral sex: *gross*. Doggy-style sex: *gross*. Putting it in your butt: nobody really did that except in places like New York but, anyway, just *gross*. True, in some part of Jean's mind the thought of Ash Birdy doing some of those things, the first two anyway, didn't seem *so* bad. He was seventeen and had a jutty chin and thick, scrunchable sideburns and Jean could imagine being married to Ash one day and letting him do those things if he wanted to. But that one day was meant to arrive in the future, not suddenly in Dorothy's basement. So when Ash got his fingers under the elastic of her panties and started nudging into her hairs, Jean was so startled she squirmed and pushed his hand away and Ash got mad and left.

He ignored Jean after that, just as if she'd moved away or dropped dead. Which was awful. For a while Jean went over to Cheryl's every day to cry about how rotten Ash was, and Cheryl, like a good friend, always agreed. But about four months after that night in the basement, Cheryl and Jean were alone on Cheryl's porch eating Peek Freans Digestives. And it was strange because Cheryl was acting as if she wasn't hungry. Usually she loved Digestives because even though they were cookies it seemed like they were almost good for you and you could eat as many as you wanted. But Cheryl was just fiddling with the cookie on her plate and crumbling little bits off the edge, and Jean had to ask:

"Cheryl, is something wrong?"

She said nothing, didn't even look up, so Jean knew something *was* wrong and thought maybe Cheryl was mad at her. For what she couldn't imagine, unless it was forgetting to say something nice about the turquoise barrette in Cheryl's hair. That seemed like such a petty thing to be mad about, but Jean thought that was probably it. Cheryl could be a little sensitive sometimes; it was one of the few things about Cheryl that wasn't so great.

"I forgot to say," began Jean, "that's a really nice –"

Before she could finish Cheryl covered her face with her hands and started sobbing. Sitting across from her Jean was thinking, *Oh, for Heaven's sake. It's just a barrette!* But she leaned over and put her hand on her friend's shoulder and said, "Cheryl, I'm really sorry. It's such a pretty –"

Cheryl lifted her glistening face from her hands and bawled out, "I'm pregnant!"

Jean yanked her hand away as if it had been bitten. Even as she did it she wasn't proud of herself. And immediately Cheryl's sobbing grew and Jean felt ashamed. Her friend was so distraught, smearing her makeup with the edge of her hand, she began to reach out again. "Oh, Cheryl," she started to say.

"It was Ash!" blurted Cheryl. "Ash did it."

On the front lawn of the Nunleys' house there was a big weeping willow, which Jean had always considered the most beautiful kind of tree. When she heard what Cheryl said about Ash, the news didn't hit her the way the word *pregnant* had, instead it settled into her, like the feeling of becoming cold. She didn't flinch or gasp, or lash out. She simply stopped reaching for her friend, sort of froze in the moment, and turned her face toward the tree. Cheryl's crying changed from something that made Jean feel bad to something that didn't matter to her at all. It was as if Cheryl had become a strange new person, someone she'd just met. Sitting outside on the porch, staring like a doll at the willow, Jean thought back to all the times Cheryl had been so supportive and commiserated with her when Ash was treating her as if she were dead, and she decided that must have been a different Cheryl. The one beside her, the one with Ash's baby in her belly, that was somebody she didn't know. And when this new Cheryl became inconsolable, apologizing and clutching at Jean as if grasping for forgiveness, Jean stood up and walked away from her, down the steps of the porch and toward the willow. She had always loved to walk through the feathery boughs, letting them brush against her arms, and she did that as she walked toward the road, until Cheryl's crying behind her became too faint to hear.

Jean avoided Cheryl in the halls after that, and within two weeks she was gone. The Nunleys had relatives somewhere south and it was said that Cheryl had gone to live with them. One day a few months later, when there was a foot of snow on the ground and Jean was starting to think that boy Milt Divverton with the checkered shirts was kind of okay, Margy Benn rushed up to Jean after math class. She had news and she delivered it breathlessly. *Did you hear about Cheryl?* That was when Jean learned that Cheryl had had a miscarriage. It was a hard one, apparently, because the fetus was about five months along. *Some girls don't get all the way better when it happens that late*, Margy said.

When Jean got home, her mother was doing paperwork at her desk in the office she kept downstairs. She had taken off her smock and wore an old grey T-shirt, loose at the neck, and playing low on her stereo was a record by Chicago, which was her favourite band because of the horns. So she seemed more approachable than she sometimes did. Jean stood in the doorway of her mother's office waiting for the song that was playing to end, and then in the silence she repeated Margy's exact words and asked if what she'd said was true.

Marjorie glanced up at Jean and back to her papers. "Depends on what you mean by *all the way* better," she said. She pushed back from her desk and went to the stereo, shaking her head as if with disappointment or disgust. It was a terrible idea, completely impractical, she said, for a sixteen-year-old girl to keep a baby. Marjorie flipped the record over and threaded it onto the spindle. As it started spinning again she set the needle down. "Cheryl should have aborted it months ago," Marjorie said to a splurge of horns. "She should have aborted it when she had the chance."

Parked in front of 242 Douglas, Jean admired the gorgeous old willow, grateful that successive owners of the Nunleys' house had never cut it down, and thought about her friends coming over on Wednesday night. Louise and Natalie would be there, certainly, and Dorothy too, she hoped; maybe Adele would drive in from the city. She was letting her gaze linger on the tree's long, slack limbs, shivering in the warm breeze that filtered in off the lake, and doing her best to avoid glimpsing the garish pink bench someone had parked beneath it – just a terrible addition – when a wave of swelling melancholy hit her. Oh . . . the sadness flooded in so strong it took her breath away. She felt her face flush and squeezed shut her eyes. All the emotion everyone had been telling her to feel for her mother, it came at Jean now. And she felt it not for her mother, but for *Cheryl.* Because Marjorie had been in awful pain and now she wasn't; what was sad about that? But Cheryl . . . Cheryl had been through something just awful, and as far as Jean knew she was still alive.

She held her hands against her face. She breathed into her palms. That moment . . . walking away . . . she relived it now and felt such shame. She had been a terrible friend to Cheryl. Despicable. In fact, in fact – it came on so full and black, this thought, like a sort of eclipse – what had she ever done for *any* of her friends? Oh . . . behind the wheel of her car Jean squeezed her face and gave a little moan. All she'd done, for years and years, was receive their support and encouragement, accept their appreciation of her art and her pleasant company. She had opened her arms and welcomed what came. She was a *taker*, that's what she was. And in return . . . she handed out thank-you cards.

This new truth, this fresh awareness, this sudden, hard bolus of insight pressed itself into Jean and she breathed slowly as it came. Eventually, and with a sense of resolution, she released her face and gripped the wheel of her car. *Jean Vale Horemarsh*, she said to herself, *you've got to do more.*

Chapter 3

An idea, or – what came before an idea? – a *pre*-idea, a vague
and smoky intuition, was beginning to form in Jean's mind,
gathering and condensing into something potentially powerful,
potentially great, like a mob massing before a riot. And she was
excited by it, was Jean. Because this advancing storm of perception reminded her of the feeling that unfailingly came over her in
the days leading up to some breakthrough in her work, some new
and deeper understanding of clay, or tool, or leaf.

She marched into the Kotemee police station, past Melissa at
reception, whose wide face first lit up at the sight of her – "Hi there,
Jean!" – then collapsed into woe. "I'm so sorry about your mom."

"Don't be sorry, Melissa," Jean said as she went. "Be glad, be glad!"

"Oh," said Melissa. "Sure."

As Jean continued down the hall she cradled in her hands,

and kept at a precise verticality, *Mississippi Spleenwort* – three slender and towering ceramic fronds on a rectangular onyx base, entwined and reaching skyward, each one laddered on two sides by tiny, triangular leaves and looking like the backbone of some prehistoric serpent. It was a piece that she'd done years ago, that had taken seven tries, breaking five times before she'd managed to set it in the kiln, and once in mid-firing. When it was finally finished, when she'd been able to pull it out whole and gleaming, she'd given it to her mother, who had immediately set it on a dresser in the smallest of the guest bedrooms, the one that never had any guests, which had been Jean's room growing up, and left it there. It was as if her mother hadn't accepted *Mississippi Spleenwort* as a gift at all, but was merely keeping it in storage, for Jean.

Now Jean was bringing it to Andrew Jr.

"Hey, Jean!" said Suzy Felter, hanging up the phone at her desk outside of Andrew's office. Her face went long with sympathy and she started to rise, her arms spreading as if she were aiming to give Jean a hug. "How're you doing, hon?"

"Just fine, Suzy." Jean offered her cheek to Suzy like a shield as she held *Mississippi Spleenwort* out of harm's way. "You know, Mom's not in any pain any more."

"That's a good way to look at it. She's at peace."

"Well, she's dead. I think that's what matters."

"Okay," said Suzy, as if she was thinking about that. "By the way, have you thought about grief counselling at all?"

"Why would I think about that?"

"Oh, because grief works in mysterious ways. We in policing understand that better than most people."

"Hmmm," said Jean. "But you're a secretary."

Suzy looked at the ceramic in Jean's arms as if it had appeared just then. "Pretty sculpture!"

"Thanks, it was Mom's and now I'm going to give it to Andrew Jr. Is he in?"

"He is for sure. Just in a meeting. Here, is that heavy? Do you want me to put it down somewhere while you wait?" She came toward Jean with both hands outstretched.

"No, it's probably better if I hold it."

While she waited in one of the barely padded chairs set along the wall, next to the filing cabinets, Jean watched Suzy Felter work at her desk, answering calls and attacking her keyboard with a raptor-like efficiency Jean had once disdained, but now admired. With her bronzed hair and professional nails and twin, Eagle Scout sons, Suzy had been one of those practical people that, to Jean, seemed to have life too planned out, too squarely ordered to allow in even the slightest splinter of spontaneity and beauty. She was the sort of person who would say an impossibly difficult-to-achieve ceramic sculpture was "pretty" but would never think to buy one.

But practicality, even of the sort that Suzy represented, was no longer an evil in Jean's mind. She had come to what the French call a *rapprochement* with practicality; she finally understood it. The fact of the matter was that you could not deal with your mother's soiled sheets and bedpans and one particularly grue-some ingrown toenail, every single forsaken day for three months, without drawing upon your own practical resources – resources that you had never known existed within you, resources that you had been told all your life were entirely and shamefully absent, but that were in fact there, hidden and boiling, like something molten in the heart of a mountain that was actually a volcano ready to spew.

So that was one thing. And the other thing, the other awaken-ing for Jean, had to do with death. Not its inevitability, which was certainly no surprise, but its utility. It was one thing as a child to witness death over and over so that it nearly became part of the everyday. It was another to see, with the wisdom of experience, what a difference it could make. The strange thing about sick or aged animals was that by the time Jean saw them they rarely revealed their pain. They were simply quiet, and death made them quieter. But humans who were suffering could express their pain in any number of ways. In the contortions of their face, their body, and their voice, in the panicked pace of their breathing, in the vicious things they could say, about a person being an oddity and a disappointment, about being not loving and not good, when you were doing your best to help them and it wasn't enough. Pain was different for humans, and so was death. Jean had seen this so clearly that last night, standing desolate by her mother's bed; one moment Marjorie was twisted in agony, and the next moment she wasn't. The purity of the effect, the sudden tranquility, was almost heartbreaking.

Suzy's professional nails began to snap and claw at her keyboard. "Jean, he's ready for you now."

Jean hadn't seen anyone come out Andrew Jr.'s office door. "I thought he was in a meeting."

"Well, a phone call. That's sort of a meeting."

Inside the chief's office, which Jean still thought of as her father's and remembered from the days when she would run in as a child and drape herself in the silky flags in the corner and play with the ceremonial Colt 45 mounted on a marble plinth, Andrew Jr., heavy and square as a plinth himself, sat at his imposing chief's desk in his imposing chief's uniform staring at a computer screen. When she approached he began to rise – "Jean," he said – and reached out his thick hand as if he were going to shake hers, as if she might be a politician or a reporter or just a regular citizen, and not his sister. She ignored it.

"Look what I brought you," she said.

Andrew Jr. dropped his hand and stared at the sculpture, his head and body at a slight angle, like a tall gravestone dislodged by vandals. "Okay," he said, slow and uncertain in the manner of someone presented with a dilemma.

"It was Mom's and now it's yours," said Jean. "It's called *Mississippi Spleenwort* and it's a gift from me to you."

He considered it at an angle for another second or two, then straightened. "Maybe that's something for Suzy's desk."

"No, it's for you. Look, there are three fronds, and you can say they represent the three of us. Where should I put it?"

"The three of us?"

"You, me, and Welland. See? We're entwined like a family and reaching upward together." She smiled at him with her customer smile, the one she kept on whenever and for as long as anyone browsed through her shop. "I want you to appreciate how hard this was to make," said Jean, "and what a sweet gesture it is on my part to bring it to you as a gift, even though you barely said a word to me at the funeral."

Andrew Jr.'s meaty face went pink with embarrassment or quiet, incomprehensible rage. "Mom just died, Jean. Not really a time for chit-chat."

"I *know* she died. I was *there* when she died. In fact I'm *happy* she died."

Andrew Jr. pinked up even more, if that was possible. "You can't mean that."

"I do. Not that I didn't love her. Of course I did, but –" Jean closed her eyes and shook her head, a resetting. "You know? We'll just drop it. I don't think you'd understand. I think we'll just find a place for this and leave it at that." She looked around, toward the wall where hung a framed and matted picture of Drew and Andrew Jr., taken the day her brother joined the force. Full uniforms on, the two men stood shoulder to shoulder, stiff and proud in the sunshine, the beaks of their caps sending hard shadows diving across their unsmiling faces. Jean looked past the picture and in the corner, by the Colt 45, saw that the end of a low bookshelf was unoccupied. She set down the ceramic with great care and admired how sweetly it caught the morning light from the window.

"There," she said. "And if you ever want that moved, you be sure to call me and I'll come and do it. If you try I expect it would just disintegrate."

For a moment Jean stood opposite Andrew Jr. in the middle of his office and adjusted the sleeves of her short linen jacket. They came just past her elbows and seemed to accentuate the thickness of her arms and she wished now that she had worn something else. Something more flattering. Andrew Jr. was so imposing, the way he just stood there saying nothing, just embodying a great, hulking, tree-like masculinity that he was probably proud of but that was really just a shell to keep out anything true and real and meaningful. Any other brother would have hugged his sister just then, to express their shared sense of loss, or to thank her for such a lovely gift, but he just stood there. Hulking and rooted. Like a great, giant, pink-faced redwood.

"Actually, there was one thing I was hoping you could do for me," said Jean. She fairly flung her hands to her sides in an effort to leave her sleeves alone. "I was hoping that you could track down Cheryl Nunley for me. She wasn't at the funeral and I haven't heard from her in years and years."

Andrew Jr. started to move toward his desk. "Who's Cheryl Nunley?"

"Cheryl Nunley," Jean repeated. "My very best friend from high school." She smoothed the fabric of her skirt around her hips. "You once tried to spy on her when she was going to the bathroom."

Andrew Jr. dropped his bulk into his leather chief's chair. "I never did any such thing," he said. "And that's a lock!" He started to roll away from her, in the direction of his computer screen. "Anyway, how and why should I be trying to track this woman down?"

"You're the chief of police!" exclaimed Jean. "I'm your sister! Add it up!"

He hunched over his keyboard and began to type single-fingered, punching down on the letters like a hydraulic press. "I can't use official police resources for personal business."

Jean gripped the sides of her head. "I have never once asked for a favour from you. I took care of Mother for three months with no word of thanks. And now I ask for one small thing and you say no. What is the point of enduring life in a family of policemen if you can't, one day, have somebody found when you need to?"

Perhaps it was the note of torment in her voice, perhaps the mention of their mother and all Jean had done for her, but Andrew Jr. paused in his key punching and half turned. "I said I couldn't do it. I didn't say it wasn't doable. Go ask Welland. I'm sure he'd jump at the opportunity."

"Welland," said Jean, because that was all that really needed to be said.

"He's always pestering me for some real police work. Tell him I assigned him to this." Andrew Jr. grinned. "Tell him I 'put him on the case.'"

"Can he use the equipment?"

"What equipment?"

"I don't know!" exclaimed Jean. "I just assumed there'd be equipment involved. Welland will want to be able to use the equipment . . . What?"

At his keyboard, Andrew Jr. was staring at the ceiling and

shaking his head. "I'm trying to imagine what sort of equipment that would be."

"You know . . ." Jean began, her voice quivering.

"The 'Person-Finding equipment'?"

"Just never mind." She wheeled, marched to the bookshelf, and carefully picked up *Mississippi Spleenwort*.

"This goes to Welland," she said.

Welland's office resided on the other side of the police station, where his single window faced Tucker's Car Wash and the scrub brush beyond. He had no secretary, and no flags, and the picture on his wall showed a uniformed Welland on his first day, standing and smiling next to the staff sergeant; Chief Horemarsh had been otherwise engaged. Welland was taller than Andrew Jr. and not as bulky, and since he had been in the force practically as long as his brother it might have been assumed that he would be just as advanced in his policing career. But although Welland possessed a handsome approachability that made him good for charity calendars and traffic safety presentations, it was plain to anyone who knew both Horemarsh brothers which one was better suited to the hard knuckle work.

"Really?" said Welland.

"He said, 'Tell him he's in charge of the case, and tell him I said so.'"

When Jean had walked in, Welland had been busy calling local musical groups to see if he could interest one in performing at the annual Police-Fire-Library Picnic to be held in three weeks in Corkin Park. He had no budget to pay them, he said, but he had managed to negotiate the loan of a flatbed trailer they could use as a stage. So far so good; the stumbling block seemed to be that the group needed to supply its own generator for the power, and most groups appeared not to own one. Until Jean had walked in, Welland told her, his biggest concern had been where to track down a fairgrounds band that could play Carrie Underwood, Garth Brooks, and a little Elvis Presley, and also happened to have in their back pocket a six-horsepower, three-thousand-watt, diesel Briggs & Stratton.

But now Welland was up and pacing in a tight space defined by his desk, the wall behind, the filing cabinet he had within reach of his chair, and the coat stand in the corner near the door. As he paced, he shoved a hand down his back, inside the collar of his blue policeman's shirt, scratching and clawing at God knew what.

"Why didn't he call and tell me himself?"

"Oh, that's simple," said Jean. "I was bringing you my ceramic – do you like it, by the way?" There wasn't much space in Welland's office, but Jean had found a spot for it on top of the standing safe where Welland kept the receipts from charity raffles and other community events the police got themselves involved in.

"Yeah," said Welland, eyeing it more than a little suspiciously. "It's kind of scary."

"Well, it's ferns," said Jean. "They're prehistoric. So, I was bringing this to you and Andrew Jr. said, 'Since you're there, tell Welland.' And because it's a favour for me, also, it makes sense that I tell you. But he was adamant this was his order."

"Adamant."

"Absolutely. He could have had anybody do it, and he said you."

Outside, in the Tucker's lot, Jean could see one of the Birdy boys – Jeff it was, Ash's oldest son. He had two, Jeff and Gordie, from his marriage to Ruth Donoghue, a girl who had taken mostly technical classes in high school and likely never complained no matter where he put his hands. Jeff had the same jutty chin as his father, and he was out there hosing down his Popsicle orange 1972 Plymouth Barracuda. The whole town knew what that car sounded like – they got an earful of it just about every evening. Jean was a little surprised to see Jeff working so hard, soaping and spraying. Occasionally, a fleck of suds hit Welland's window and began its slow, sliding descent.

"Because this is the kind of work I've been wanting to do," Welland was saying, still scratching.

"I know. For a long time."

"When Dad hired me in '87, he never said I'd be stuck here in Community Services. I don't think it was his plan for me. But then Andrew Jr. got on his rocket and just – zoom!"

"Well, now it's your turn."

Welland stopped scratching and stared in thought toward his window. A soap bubble the size of a walnut clung there on the glass, holding its ground, without popping. "But why this assignment? Why now?" He squinted at Jean. "Maybe it's impossible. Maybe he's setting me up to fail."

Jean pressed her hands to her eyes. "No, Welland. Listen to me." More than any man she knew, more so even than Milt, Welland was like a piece of too-wet clay that would not hold its shape. "This is not going to be hard for you. This is like a warm-up. Like when you go golfing? This is your practice swing. Just find Cheryl Nunley for me. And then you can show Andrew Jr. you deserve more real police work."

Welland rolled his chair away from his desk and eased himself down into it like someone trying out a new lounger at Sears. "Okay," he said. He patted the edge of the desk in front of him. "Okay, I'll give it a go."

"Good."

"There's probably some tracking devices I'll need, or some such. Maybe tie into the computer surveillance networks." He was staring off, talking mostly to himself. But he turned back to Jean. "Why do you want to find this woman, anyway?"

"Actually, Welland, I don't know. That's being honest. I just –" Jean looked out to the sky through the soap-flecked window. "I feel some big new understanding of life coming for me. Something that's going to change everything. And I just want to gather around me all the people that I love most in the world."

Welland nodded. "I understand."

Jean was reassured and she smiled and took two steps toward the door. As she opened it, she turned and pointed toward the ceramic. "Don't ever try to move that."

Chapter 4

A ction had always seemed the proper response to death. It wasn't something Jean went about deliberately; it just happened. Milt had a rather right-wing brother, Albert, who died in November 1989 – he had a wonky heart and got much too excited about the Berlin Wall going down – and the next day Jean started a campaign to have pretty, wrought-iron street lamps installed along the busiest section of Main Street. As it turned out, the town had only enough money for one lamp. But up it went, long and black with a handsome ornamental curlicue, at the corner of Calendar and Main.

When her cousin Sarah Fulbright, who was living in the city and married to Dr. Dick Fulbright, steered into a sycamore one night at eighty miles an hour, Jean immediately decided to take swimming lessons. She went every day to the

Hern Regional Recreational Centre and built up a very nice backstroke until she developed an ear infection from the inadequately treated water.

Having an artistic outlet was often very useful in situations like these, because Jean could dive into her work. And it almost never went haywire, as it had after the death of her father. In the early Nineties, for about six months, there was a run of deaths among her former public and high school teachers, and she amassed quite a collection of shelf-sized pieces dedicated to various sorts of mint.

Where these surges in the wake of death came from Jean couldn't have said. She had never been very troubled by a sense of her own mortality. She didn't consider herself prone to other manias. And what happened that spring day when she was six . . . well, that was such a long time ago.

Marjorie had been away for almost two weeks, helping to take care of her own mother, Jean's Grana, after she had snapped her tailbone on a flight of polished stairs. Her mother had taken Andrew Jr. and the baby, Welland, with her, but Jean had had to stay for school. While Marjorie was gone, their German shepherd, Mona, which was really Drew's dog, delivered a litter of five grey-and-brown puppies. Marjorie had known this was going to happen, and she had not seemed very happy about it. But Jean was delighted, of course. She watched, entranced, as Mona licked and nudged the whelps in the box, situated in the far corner of the garage under a halo of coiled hose.

The puppies were odd in some way that Jean didn't understand. She knew it only by the way half of her father's face went squinty when he looked at them the first time and muttered, "I guess your mother was right." But whether or not they were odd didn't matter to Jean. Within days she had named them after storybook characters – Flossie, Alice, Sam-I-Am, Rapunzel, and Horton. She'd cleaned out the puppy mess with a plastic beach shovel, and she had surrounded the box with "friends," which were her collection of stuffed animals. The friends, of which there were eight, in various sizes and fur types, were meant to protect the puppies from anything that might threaten or hurt them, and also keep them company in the sullen loneliness of the garage when Jean could not be there.

Every day when Jean came home from school she filled Mona's water bowl and carefully petted each puppy with seven long strokes. Because she loved them all equally and wanted no puppy to get more or less affection than the others. And she gave each of the friends time in the box so they could become closer to the puppies, especially Sam-I-Am, who wasn't moving very well, or much at all, except for his little grey rib cage. And every day, Jean made another attempt at pleading to keep the puppies, bopping her father's knee with her fist as he sat watching Walter Cronkite. But Drew made no promises about the puppies. He said only that he wouldn't be giving them away at the station like he'd planned, that was for damn sure. As far as he was concerned, he told Jean, it was her mother's decision.

That spring day when Jean was six, she arrived home from school wearing the yellow cotton dress she had picked out that morning to find her mother had returned. Jean knew it as soon as she opened the front door, even though the boys were nowhere to be found, because the air in the house felt thinner somehow, pulled taut as if the air were a string. She ran to the garage and found Mona whimpering and scratching at the base of the door that led to the backyard. She saw her stuffed animals in a circle on the floor, surrounding an empty space where the puppy box had been.

Jean's heart began to bump in her chest. She gripped the sides of her dress by her legs. "Mommy?" she called through the door.

"Don't let the dog out," came her mother's voice from the yard.

She dashed back into the house. There was another door to the backyard at the top of the basement stairs and she ran toward it. She ran as fast as she could because now she could hear Mona scrambling over the kitchen linoleum after her. She jumped down the short flight of stairs to the landing, her dress flying up to her waist, and she managed to get herself mostly through before Mona arrived and tried to squeeze and squirm past. It took all of Jean's six-year-old strength to keep Mona inside, pushing on her furry, twisting head and scrabbling paws so she could close the door.

Outside, under the sprouting elms of the backyard, Jean found Marjorie, her auburn hair pinned back, hauling a bucket of water across the patio to the picnic table. On top of the table sat the puppy box. Jean could hear the faint squeals of the puppies inside.

"Mommy," said Jean. She tried to breathe more slowly so she could speak. "What are you doing?"

Marjorie sighed. "Dealing with this situation your father left for me."

Jean approached the table with care.

"I told him this litter would be bad," said Marjorie, "but he wouldn't listen."

Jean wanted to ask her mother if she could keep the puppies, the way she had planned to, but when she opened her mouth to ask, her lips began to shiver, and asking seemed the most impossible thing. So she watched as her mother lifted one of the puppies out of the box. It was Sam-I-Am, the smallest of the litter, about the size of Marjorie's hand. At the back door Mona scratched furiously and her whines reached a higher pitch. Jean watched her mother put Sam-I-Am in the bucket and she had to speak, she had to speak, even though her lips were buzzing.

"Mommy, are you washing him?"

Marjorie looked up from the bucket at Jean, her mouth pressed flat.

"Are you washing him, Mommy?"

"No, Jeanie, I'm not."

"What are you doing?"

Her mother looked down in the bucket again. "I'm putting him –"

"Are you drowning him, Mommy?" Jean's lips were bubbling so much she could barely complete the words. Her vision began to sparkle with tears.

"Yes." After a few seconds more Marjorie lifted Sam-I-Am out of the water and set him, limp and dripping, on the picnic table. She used her wet fingers to smooth a bit of hair behind her ear, and took another puppy from the box.

Jean began to jiggle her hands at her sides. There was no air in her lungs. "But not Alice, Mommy," she said. "Not Alice, Mommy." The back of her throat stung. She grabbed and pulled handfuls of her dress. Her tears fell into her mouth. "Sam-I-Am was sick but not Alice, okay, Mommy? Okay, Mommy?"

Marjorie held Alice squirming in her hand. "These puppies aren't right, Jeanie. They won't live. They shouldn't even have been born. But your father refused to have that dog spayed."

Jean watched as her mother drowned Alice. In the house, Mona cried and raced between the door at the top of the basement steps and the green door to the garage. Jean stood and stared, her body shuddering with hiccups, as Flossie, and Rapunzel, and finally Horton went squirming into the bucket and came out sleek and limp as livers. At some point Mona stopped running and from behind the green garage door let out a sound that made Jean put her hands over her ears.

And why, Jean wanted to know between hiccups, didn't her mother use the needle to put the puppies to sleep? Don't be silly,

Marjorie told her. That drug was expensive and no one was paying her to do this. Drowning was the most practical solution.

Two hours later, after her mother had showered and gone back to Grana's to get the boys, but before her father had come home from the station, Jean went to the garage. Mona lay in the corner, quiet and motionless in the dim light, and Jean put an oatmeal cookie on the concrete floor within a few feet of her. "I'm sorry, Mona," she said. After a moment, she went to the spot under the coiled hose where the puppy box had been. She sat there on the floor, surrounded by her stuffed animals. There were three brown teddy bears. There was a panda, one Snoopy, a plush lion, a floppy beanbag kitten, and a tall, hard-packed giraffe. They were named simply, for their attributes – Bear, Big Bear, Floppy Kitten, and so on – because Jean had been given them when she was much younger, when words themselves were novelties. Now she read stories, she knew about life and death, and she believed in things she couldn't see, such as ghosts, and fairies, and princesses, and Heaven. She was much more grown up, and she could undertake difficult tasks.

As she sat on the floor of the garage, Jean wasn't angry at her stuffies for failing to protect the puppies. Not under the circumstances. But she was worried because now the puppies were alone in Heaven, which she was told was nice but was certainly huge and probably frightening for puppies who "weren't right" and had been sent there so young.

She had to do something. Some action was required, to make sure the puppies weren't scared and alone. Jean had thought up what she was going to do as soon as her mother was gone. But she spent a moment on the floor of the garage, petting Giraffe and Panda and Lion, trying to decide whether to make it a surprise.

Yes, she decided, a surprise was best. It gave less room for worry and fright. She gathered up some of her stuffies, as many as she could carry, set them outside the green garage door, and went back for the rest. Once she had all of her friends out of the garage, she closed the door to keep Mona inside. She took her stuffed animals to the picnic table, set them in a careful row on the bench seat so they could watch the sun sinking in the sky, and at the tap she filled the bucket her mother had used.

Once full of water the bucket was too heavy for Jean to lift, so she dragged it slopping over the patio stones and got it as near to the table as she could. From the picnic table she brought down Giraffe, because he was the youngest and most easily scared. Giraffe was from Africa and ate the leaves of acacia trees. She kissed him on the side of his long neck. Said, "Good Giraffe." And plunged him headfirst into the water. She held him under for a minute or two, her hands turning numb from the cold. When she was sure the air bubbles had stopped, she put his sopping body aside on the patio and took the next in line, which was Lion. Lion who roared, but always obeyed when Jean told him to be quiet because she needed to sleep.

"Thank you, Lion," Jean said. "I liked you very much." And she pushed him to the bottom of the bucket.

One by one, and without tears, Jean drowned seven of her stuffed animals so they could be with the puppies. By the eighth, which was Bear, the sun had fallen to the top of the fence that separated the Horemarsh backyard from the Peltiers' next door, and Jean had had to fill up the bucket twice, because the animals swallowed so much of the water.

Bear was the hardest to drown, because Jean had known him the longest. He was not very pretty, because some of his stuffing had leaked from a foot before Grana could mend him, and his left ear was quite a bit chewed. But he had always slept with her, from the first day she could remember, and she knew she would miss the cushion of him against her body, and his curly brown fur against her cheek. That was being selfish, though. So after she had hugged him close for a long, long while, Jean pushed him under the water and drowned him, watching the bubbles rise.

When she was done, Jean took the soggy animals out to the side of the house, by the eaves spout, and dropped them into the same tin garbage can in which her mother had disposed of the puppies.

She had needed to do something. She had done what she could.

Chapter 5

In her studio-shop at the end of Kotemee's Main Street, under a hanging tungsten light pulled low, Jean worked on *Kudzu Attack!* It was to be one of the biggest ceramics she'd ever finished, perhaps four feet tall, on a three-foot-square base. She'd been inspired to create it after watching a TV documentary about the invasive and virulent growth of the kudzu vine in the southeastern United States. Kudzu could grow up to a foot a day, Jean had learned, and was amazingly versatile: you could eat it, make tea from it, make baskets or fences from it, bale it like hay and feed it to cattle, or watch as it choked the life out of an entire precious forest. But what Jean loved about kudzu more than anything was its leaf. It was completely unremarkable. There was nothing jagged or menacing about it. Grouped in threes, with gentle, rounded lobes, it seemed the friendliest, most innocent leaf in the world. But when you knew what it could do, you looked at it differently. To Jean, the kudzu leaf looked like a stingray slicing through the water. While she was at her mother's, Jean had thought often about *Kudzu Attack!* She imagined a tall, swarming wave of kudzu leaves and vines curling over a small, crouching, innocent miniature oak, majestic and tragic and serene all at once, like the hand of Doom.

Just now she was working on the leaves. She pinched off cherry-sized pieces of porcelain clay and wedged them with the heel of her hand to press out the air, then worked and shaped them between her thumbs and fingers until each piece was three inches wide and paper thin. Then she selected a trim knife from her wall of tools and cut each leaf precisely, made ribs with threads of clay rubbed between her palms and laid them in, then etched in the veins with a pin tool. Each leaf took her seven or eight minutes and she figured she'd need about a hundred and sixty in all. After that she'd work on a hundred feet of vine. She had to keep the leaves under plastic so they wouldn't dry out entirely, so they'd get leathery but not crisp. And when she was ready she'd build it all without wire – she hated wire because it seemed like cheating. She thought if nature could construct something without wire, then she could as well, even if it took her five, or ten, or fifty tries.

Jean knew that once she had finally completed *Kudzu Attack!* she would never be able to sell it. The piece would sit in her show-room, on its own dedicated table, for as long as she owned the shop. Probably for as long as she was alive. People would come in and admire it, or gawk at it, or snicker. But nobody would be able to imagine it as a thing in their home. So it would be with Jean until she died. And then someone would try to move it, and it would crumble to pieces.

But it didn't matter.

Growing up, Jean had learned never to tell her family about her plans for projects. She'd made the mistake a couple of times, letting out a hint of her idea, like a wisp of smoke, and whoever she had told would scoff and say it was impossible, and not only impossible but pointless. They'd blow the smoke away from in front of her eyes and the idea, or Jean's will to realize it, would vaporize. And so she never spoke of her ideas in anything but generalities – something big, something new, something exciting – until she had accomplished whatever she'd imagined. Then they could laugh all they wanted. That was the singular sort of practicality that Jean had always embraced.

And with that experience, she knew she could never tell anyone about the other idea that was beginning to form in her mind, the "new understanding" she had hinted at to Welland in his office. It was still just a strange, exhilarating swirl of smoke, and until it was solid and real she could never say a word. People just would not understand.

The bell above the shop's front door jingled and Jean looked up to see Natalie Skilbeck floating in like a bit of dandelion fluff on a breeze.

"Hey there, hon," said Natalie. She held up a little brown paper bag. "I brought you a cupcake."

"Oh, gosh. Aren't you sweet!"

Natalie closed the door and stepped wide around a blue-glazed piece set on the floor that Jean called *Night Stalker* – a flaring sheaf of wormwood plants with reaching herbaceous fingers that tended to catch on nylons and skirts and tear a nice big hole. She dropped the paper bag on Jean's work table. "Chocolate," she said. "I hope you approve. They just put out a fresh batch at Dilman's and I said, hey, I'll bet Jean needs a treat."

"You are a mind reader." Jean dug into the bag. "I was starting to get woozy."

"That's what I'm here for," said Natalie. "One of these days I'm going to buy their Butter-Pistachio No-Conscience Torte. I just have to get up the nerve."

Natalie owned a dog grooming shop over on Kanter Street, which came perpendicular to Main, and she'd been good friends with Jean for twenty-three years, ever since Jean had taken Milkweed, the Bichon Frise she'd once owned, for a trim. Of her Kotemee friends, Natalie was probably the one Jean trusted the most, because of the shared experience of being Business Association members, because Natalie unfailingly said what was on her mind, and, to some small degree, because Natalie was a smidge over her ideal weight, just like Jean.

Natalie looked at the sleeve of her mauve knit top and *tsk*-ed. "Collies," she said with disgust and brushed at the hairs with sharp chopping motions of her hand. It was with a similar sort of gesture, Jean imagined, that Natalie had divorced her husband, Sandeep. "So how's my girl doing?"

"I'm doing just fine!" said Jean, and she bit into the cupcake. "Mmm, oh, this is delectable." She caught a crumb as it tumbled from her mouth. "Really, I thought I was going to faint."

"Hon, you can't let your blood sugar get so low. I swear that's why so many women slam their cars into telephone poles."

Jean paused. "I didn't know it was so many."

"Oh, it's a lot."

"Well, I just get so focused when I'm working."

"You're really going to town here," Natalie said, surveying the table. "What's it going to be?"

"Oh, you know. Just one of my silly contraptions."

Natalie pursed her red lips until they looked like a smushed raspberry and gave her a disapproving look. "Jean, don't talk like that. You're always so disparaging of your own talents. I wish I had half your skill with sharp objects. I know a couple of

Pekinese bitches who could use a nice, quick behaviour modification." She made an elegant stab-rip motion as she said it.

Jean shielded her eyes with a chocolatey hand and felt herself blush. She had long ago stopped feeling odd about the fact that she blushed more around Natalie than she normally did. In some way she had accepted that Natalie's role in their friendship was to be mildly shocking, and hers was to be mildly shocked. It was almost an arrangement, a negotiation that suited them both. "The way you talk sometimes, Natalie," said Jean, "I feel like I'm in one of those gangster rap videos."

"Bitches is a technical term, Jean. I didn't say they were ho's. Although it would be completely and entirely fitting."

Jean leaned away from the table and knocked the crumbs from her hands. "So, did you read my message? Can you come tonight? It's just casual, for drinks."

"Of course." Natalie touched the corner of her mouth to indicate a smudge of chocolate on Jean's, and Jean attended to it with one of the stiff paper towels she always kept near a bucket of water when she was working. "It's understandable you might want some company after everything. Did I tell you I thought the funeral was lovely? Although the minister was a bit wordy, I thought, a bit God-ish."

"It's not that I need company," said Jean. "It's just that seeing so many of my friends at the church, I thought, gee, we haven't all been together in one place for so long." Talking about the funeral brought to mind what Milt had said, about being stone-faced. Looking back, she realized she probably hadn't been at her best; a little numb, maybe. A bit hollow. Natalie was kind not to mention it.

"Did you want me to bring anything? Apple pie? More cupcakes? I'll march right back up to Dilman's. I mean, the smallest excuse will do."

"Actually," said Jean, "Adele mentioned she might bring some treats from a place she knows in the city. She says their butter tarts are the work of the Devil."

Natalie breathed in deep and slow in a way that suggested she was displeased or annoyed, and Jean knew what was on her mind even before she said, "Adele Farbridge?"

"Yes, you remember her."

Natalie hummed a small note of assent and nodded, looking off at the half dozen pieces in Jean's *Bleeding Heart* series set on display shelves along the wall. "I know she's an old friend of yours and everything, and you invite who you want. I just find her a bit condescending, that's all. She's got this whole city attitude, like we're hicks living in a quaint little tourist town and she's Miss Queen of the Urban Realm. Like if she wanted to, she could fuck her choice of our husbands without a word of protest. Except she couldn't be bothered."

"You are terrible."

"Well, doesn't she act like that? The way she drops names and gossip as if she's got everybody you read about in the morning paper on speed-dial."

Jean shook her head and waved her hands. "I don't see it and I don't want to hear it. You're my friend and she's my friend and everybody should just get along, and if you loved me at all you would."

"Hon," Natalie batted her lashes and pouted, "what says 'love' like a chocolate cupcake?"

"I think you two don't like each other because –"

"She said she doesn't like me?"

Jean hesitated, and then lied. "No, no. But there's obviously an atmosphere around you two, and if anything it's because you're too much the same." Natalie made a scoffing sound that Jean thought it best to ignore. "Anyway, Louise will be there and you like Louise."

"Yes, Louise is fine. A little . . . no, she's fine."

"Maybe Dorothy Perks, too. If she can find somebody to take care of Roy."

The bell above the door chimed and Jean and Natalie watched as two elderly women made their way into Jean's shop. They looked to Jean to be in their late seventies at least, wearing their day-trip attire – smart khakis and blouses, with sunglasses on chains around their necks and little cotton hats on their white heads – and when they saw they weren't alone they trilled, "Hello," and Jean said, "Come on in!" They advanced tentatively on their comfortable shoes, keeping their hands and purses close to their sides, the way they might have while walking through a crowd of grasping slum children in Mumbai. But Jean knew that they were only being careful; they respected the fragility of the things around them, they understood it, because they themselves were just as delicate, their lives were filled with fragility – Ceramics "R" Us – and they were going to take their time.

"Just have a look around," said Jean. "Let me know if you have any questions."

"Thank you," said the lady in the sea-green top, speaking for her companion in yellow.

Jean made sure to smile, but watching these women, she felt a profound unease. The force of the feeling surprised her, and held her. She couldn't shake the idea that these women considered themselves the lucky ones – existing without debilitating pain, unlike so many their age – and yet even they were surely living diminished lives. Jean had only to look at them to know their limbs were stiff and sore, their eyes were weak, their skin had gone papery and lax, the internal systems of their bodies were no longer reliable. They were faint remainders of what they once had been, mere impressions left in the sand, and the things in the past that had made them feel vital and alive were now beyond their reach. Every day for them was another accounting of all that had been lost, and as they walked about in their clean cottons, the threat of imminent disease and distress followed them like a black hound on a leash, and they could never be rid of it. They would argue, if anyone said this to them. "Oh no," they might protest. "We're quite capable and content." But Jean knew what she knew. The signs of change, the incremental deficiencies, were already showing up in her own body; there was no doubt where things were headed. So she was distressed for these women, as they ventured toward the wall of display shelves. She felt worse for them than for her mother. The truth of it was, Jean thought, her mother was the lucky one now.

And then the woman in yellow picked up a piece that Jean called simply *Rosemary* – her realization of the spindly herb: a foot and a half tall, spiky with tiny blade-like leaves, and so realistic it almost wavered in the breeze. Before Jean could warn her, the woman tipped the piece over looking for a price on the bottom, and it snapped off at the stem and smashed to dust on the floor.

"Oh, no!" gasped the woman, a hand to her mouth.

"What an old twat," Natalie whispered.

At the house that night, before the women arrived, Milt busied himself in the kitchen, cubing cheese, uncanning olives and smoked almonds, dishing out tortilla chips, and mixing up a big batch of Mojitos. He was wearing his favourite blue shirt with tiny black checks, Jean noted. And over that he wore his charcoal-grey sweater vest, which he liked because he thought it made him look "trimmer." The fact that it was a fall-winter accessory didn't seem to register.

"You're going to be hot in that vest," Jean warned him. "You should just take it off."

"I won't be hot," said Milt. "I'll be drinking Mojitos."

He had a buoyancy about him that contrasted his side-combed hair and buttoned sleeves, and Jean realized that having endured three months of forced abstinence from any female presence in the house, he was now about to go on a bender.

Natalie was the first to arrive, blooming in a summer dress, her lips freshly fruited, and Milt got to the door first and greeted her. "Well, don't you look extra spiffy," she said. She caught Jean's eye and waggled a paper bag. "More cupcakes, Jean. I say you can't have too many."

Milt was still beaming from the compliment. "I'm drinking Mojitos," he said, brandishing his glass. "Want one?"

Natalie pursed her lips until they rose up red like a welt, and winched them left and right in contemplation. "You know, I think I'll start with a straight-up scotch."

Dorothy Perks arrived next, in a loose black tank top and bunched shorts, her long dark hair gone netted in the humidity. She came up the walk with a phone to her ear and silvery bangles in the crook of her elbow; from her other hand, her large leather purse hung by the straps like a melee weapon ready to be slung.

"I don't know how long I can stay," were the first words out of her mouth, as she hugged Jean one-armed in the foyer.

"Is it Roy?"

She dropped her phone into her purse with an exasperated sigh. "No one knows how to handle him. People intimidate so easily. He's a teddy bear if you show him who's in charge." She reached into her bag and pulled out a bottle of Shiraz. "Here. Sorry. It's what we had."

Roy was not Dorothy's child, although most people overhearing her conversations about him might have assumed that to be so. No, Roy was her husband. In high school, Dorothy had always been attracted to the manliest boys, and so it had been no surprise to Jean that a few years after graduation she had started dating, and eventually married, a cruiserweight boxer by the name of Roy "Big Boy" Lundquist.

"Big Boy" had his run in the 1970s and ended up with a record of eight wins, forty-two losses. His trouble was that cruiserweight was a fairly unpopular division, and he had a hard time finding appropriate matches. If he'd been able to knock off some pounds he could have competed one rung down in the middleweight division and might have won his share. But Roy, who was Swedish by heritage, had too great a love for *surströmming*, a putrid-smelling fermented herring that he bought and consumed by the crate, and so his only option had been to bulk up and compete in the heavyweight division, where stronger, better boxers more or less spread him on toast. Now, in his late fifties, "Big Boy" had a classic case of *dementia pugilistica*. He was punch drunk, permanently impaired, and Dorothy was more his nanny than his wife.

Milt appeared from around the corner. "Hey, Dorothy," he said, lifting his glass. "Mojito?"

Dorothy looked at Milt and shook her head as if she were startled, distracted, as if this were far too much input to process. "Mojito," she repeated, squinting. "No, uh . . . what is that, rum? No . . . God . . . Don't you just have some club soda or something?"

Jean looked at Milt as they passed him. "I told you none of my friends like those drinks."

Milt watched them go. "You wait!"

A few minutes later, as Jean and Milt entertained their two guests in the living room, they heard the rumble of a high-performance engine from the street and Natalie said, "Quick, Jean, where's your red carpet?"

"Natalie," said Jean, "you be nice."

In the foyer, Adele Farbridge, still as thin and sharp as a stiletto heel, smiled with her large masculine teeth and cleared strands of ironed hair from her face with the arms of the sunglasses she pushed back on her head. "Jean!" she said, as if her sight had just now been restored, and pressed her cheek-to-cheek. "Oh, it's so good to see you. How are you? Can I say, again, how awful I felt not making it to the funeral?" She spoke in a deep, cello-ish voice, mouthing each phrase as though applying salve to the wounds of the dispossessed. "It was simply impossible because we were making a substantial bid for a Herbert Mense property on Monday. He's heading to divorce court, desperate for money, and so our opportunity was upon us and we needed to have all our ducks in a row."

"Well, it's so great to see you now!" said Jean, who found herself suddenly swaying to follow the path of Adele's gaze because Adele, holding a black, lizard-skin briefcase in two hands, had begun to look down at the floor around her tiny, silver sandals. "Adele?" said Jean. "Can I – ?"

"Jean, is there somewhere I can tuck this for safekeeping?" Adele held the case out before her. "I didn't want to leave it in the car."

"Good thinking," called Natalie from the living room. "We've got so much street crime in Kotemee."

Adele swivelled her head in the direction of the voice. "Is that Natalie Skilbeck?" she said. "How wonderful."

Jean and Adele had met during their first year of art college, back in 1975. For nearly a year they'd roomed together, and Jean had been rather enthralled with Adele's offhand way with men and wine and money. Adele came from an established family, had gone to a private girls' school, and told Jean at the time she had no intention of becoming an artist. She'd chosen photography as her major only because her financier father had given her a Leica for her seventeenth birthday, and she told Jean she wanted to "live the artist life" for a while. "To scratch around," she purred. "To think and fuck and drink and get a bit dirty from it all." After that first year she quit, made her teary goodbyes, and went on to economics at Cornell, but Jean had felt a need to keep the friendship going ever since.

In the foyer, Milt jostled his glass and rattled some music from his ice cubes. "Mojito, Adele?"

"No thank you, Milt," she said, reaching out to touch his cheek. "But a Fumé Blanc, or whatever you have that's dry, dry, dry would be lovely."

Louise Draper was typically late to arrive. Jean saw her through the sheer drapes of the front window, coming up the walk with a bouquet of something in her hand. She was dressed in the same white blouse and tan skirt Jean had seen her wearing two days before. According to Milt she often wore the same outfit in class two or even three times a week, and it was only because she was such a good teacher that her students weren't merciless. It always gave Jean an uneasy feeling on Louise's behalf, to think that she was working with a strike against her because she was a tiny bit odd. People had no tolerance for difference, even in one's own family. Maybe especially there.

As Jean watched through the window, preparing to open the front door, Louise stopped suddenly on the walk and turned as if to go back to her car. But then she lifted her right arm and seemed startled by the purse dangling from her shoulder, and resumed her advance to the door.

"Oh, jeez, I'm late, aren't I?" she said, giggling as she entered. "D'you know what? I thought it was last night and I'd missed it. Really, seriously, I'm such a loser sometimes." Looking off into the living room she slipped out of her pumps as if she were stepping off a log and then studied with apparent confusion the bouquet in her hand. "Right. So I saw this bouquet at that little shop on at the corner of Cumner. You know those two old gay men?"

"Aren't they lovely?" said Jean. "So personable."

"I know, I know, they're great, they're so great. And I saw this bouquet, and you can ignore all the flowers" – Louise made spattery gestures with her free hand at the many coloured blooms – "because they're just, well I know you're not into those. But I just thought, you know, the leaves were nice." She giggled again.

Taking the bouquet, Jean knew there was nothing interesting about the leaves. They were just more of the typical florist greenery – a few cuttings of leatherleaf fern and cocculus – and she'd long ago exhausted any artistic potential there. No, it was Louise thinking of leaves at all that touched her. "That's so sweet," she said.

"Hey, Louise," said Milt from the limits of the foyer. "Can I interest you in a Mojito?"

"Oh, sure, that'd be great."

"Really?" said Jean. It was easy to believe that Louise might not be clear on the nature of Mojitos. "It's sort of a resorty cocktail with sugar."

"Yeah, yeah. Well, actually," she paused to wave at Natalie in the living room, "uh, Milt and I were both in the liquor store when they were giving out samples of this mix they had and it was pretty good."

Jean turned toward her husband. "Is that right, Milt?" she said. "Is that what gave you the idea for Mojitos?"

Milt went somewhat still and nodded to Jean with a certain care. "Yes."

Jean glanced back at Louise, who was staring at the flowers in Jean's hands. "Well, good!" she said to Milt with a light laugh. "At least you won't be drinking that whole pitcher yourself."

———

For an hour or so, they just chatted, Jean and her friends, and Milt, of course, staying rather quiet now with his tall, tinkling glass. Seeing all of them seated in her living room, comfortable and well served with drinks and snacks, Jean let herself enjoy, for a while and to the degree that she was able, the fun of having everyone together. Dorothy quickly dropped the pretense of soda and moved to wine, which allowed her to talk about men she found attractive, and that was always fun. Louise did a masterful job of mining the woeful ignorance of her students for everyone's entertainment. Natalie was her usual feisty self. On books: "You know what burns my ass? Novels that try to teach me something. I want a story, not a goddamn textbook." On Hollywood: "Political movie stars make me puke. Hey, Bozo, your opinion on gun control is an assault on my pleasure." On Adele: "Farbridge, where are those butter tarts you promised, warming on your manifold?" And Adele had to stop talking about foreign exchange risk and who got drunk at Davos and give her apologies. Apparently there'd been a line at the tart shop that would have delayed her arrival for thirty minutes. "That's how marvellous their tarts are," she insisted. So about the tarts, at least, everyone understood.

But it wasn't quite the usual gathering for Jean. She felt an urgency in the midst of her friends that had to do with more than making sure their glasses were filled, an urgency that seemed both familiar and new. Since the funeral she'd worked hard to keep thoughts about her mother and what her mother had endured at bay. But now, surrounded by the women she was closest to, those thoughts hovered behind everything she said and heard, colouring it all, darkening it like a bruise. She looked around the room at these women and saw how life had marked them. Their worries and misfortunes sat with them like shadows. To her left was Natalie and Natalie's hypertension and sadly crumbled marriage. At the end of the couch sat Dorothy and the awful burden of her uncrumbled one. Beside her was Louise and . . . well, Louise was perfectly healthy and had no burdens as far as Jean knew. But she was slightly odd, and that was its own kind of trouble. And over in the mahogany armchair sat Adele and Adele's mastectomy, which she had suffered five years before after finding a lump during her getaway to Antigua. And beyond those trials, all the things that Jean as a friend had been helpless to prevent, she knew there were more to come. Vicious, ruthless time was grinding away like a jackhammer, pulverizing bit by bit the foundations of their contentment. It was coming down, inevitably. In her urgency, Jean could see what her friends could not: the room was crowded with warning.

She tried to keep up a cheery front, smiling and laughing and doing her best to participate, but it seemed that no one was fooled. Milt was the first to act, joining Jean in the kitchen when she went to get more cheese and asking if everything was all right. She assumed he was asking because she'd found out about the Mojito tasting with Louise and he was feeling guilty, so she told him it didn't matter. She hoped never to get upset over something so insignificant, now or ever again.

But after that, one by one, each of the women made an attempt to connect with her. Was she all right? Was anything bothering her? They did it subtly, with eye contact or a light touch on her arm, or more forcefully by other means. Natalie asked Jean at one point to show her where the bathroom was, although she knew perfectly well, and when they were alone she cornered her in the hallway.

"Jean, I want you talk to me," she said, staring into her eyes. "You're upset. I can tell. I felt it earlier in the shop. It's no good sitting on feelings, you know. That's how things just explode."

Jean did what she usually did, which was to make a joke about it. The only problem, she laughed, was having to manage all the personalities in the room. Everyone was "so much work." Getting drinks, getting snacks, attending to every little remark. "It reminds me of waiting on my mother." And of course she wasn't serious at all – she was glad everyone was there – and Natalie didn't take it that way. But something about confessing to a friend, even in that small way, about the ordeal of the last three months put a small chink in Jean's wall of defence. It was the smallest of fissures, the merest hairline crack, and the emotion that leaked through it was barely a dribble compared to the vast lake still pressing against the dam. But it was enough to start her crying.

She felt like such a child, blubbering in front of a friend. Natalie led her to the bathroom so as not to disturb the others, Jean apologizing the whole time. "I'm so sorry. This is so silly of me." There seemed to be torrents inside of her trying to come out. But in the midst of her tears Jean glanced up and, seeing the worry in her friend's face, she just put a clamp on things, just shut it down and composed herself. "That's enough of that," she said, blinking. She washed her face; the cool water against her cheeks felt calming, just like Natalie's comforting words. And when she'd patted herself dry with a soft towel, and the two of them had come back into the living room, everyone appeared to believe that Jean had had a good cry. Jean knew better, of course; it hadn't been good at all. Nothing had been assuaged or released. But still, the belief seemed to make it easier for everyone to talk a little more openly than before.

With the light outside fading, and the living room settling into darkness, Milt switched on the iron standing lamp by his chair. The glow caught the wine in Adele's hand as she swirled it and sent golden baubles scooting across the carpet.

"Losing someone close," said Adele, "it's very hard. Can be."

"Oh," said Natalie, finding a seat on the couch. "Can it?"

"Mmmm," said Adele.

"But," said Jean, and she cleared her throat, "it's not losing my mother that was hard. I was saying this to Milt the day I got home, after the funeral. I was just happy she was out of pain. Do you remember, Milt?"

"Yes," said Milt. He was only saying yes.

"There was no reason for her to suffer like that," said Jean. "I mean, the pain she went through, the indignity of it, the cruelty . . . it was inhuman." Jean put her hand to her forehead. She wasn't about to cry again, that crisis had passed. But her heart was racing, and her thoughts were going smoky again, swirling in confusing ways, and it seemed comforting, somehow, to press her eye with the heel of her palm, even as she felt everyone watching her. She pressed and willed her heartbeat to slow.

"I don't think any of us can imagine," said Natalie. She was concentrating on the fabric of her skirt, brushing at it softly with the tips of her fingers, the way she might brush flies from the sores of a starving child. "My only hope, when it comes time for me, is that something else takes me. Something fast."

"Maybe you'll choke on a cupcake," offered Adele.

"Well, you know what?" Natalie leaned toward her. "It would be better than going through what Jean's mother went through."

"I envy guys," said Dorothy.

Jean blew her nose with a tissue. "How so?" she said.

"It just seems they go quick. Soldiers . . ." Dorothy made a shooting gesture with her thumb and forefinger. "Accidents. There was a guy Roy fought against once. Bill Powell. It wasn't the next fight but the one after, he died in the ring. One punch." She made a fist and held it to the back of her jaw, showing where the fatal blow had landed, as everyone took in a breath. "But if you're talking about natural causes, usually it's a heart attack, right? I mean, look at all the guys who go out shovelling snow and –" She snapped her fingers. Then she glanced at Jean. "Isn't that what happened to your father?"

Jean nodded. "It was something like that." She didn't actually know what had caused her father's heart attack. One winter's day her mother had simply announced that it had occurred.

"Have you noticed," said Adele, "only men seem to die in the act of sex?" Everyone seemed willing to wait for Adele to elaborate. "If they're our age," she continued in her low, vowelly tones, "they'll go off to a hotel room to cheat on their wives with their secretaries, and then keel over as they orgasm." In her chair, Adele pantomimed a man so violently thrusting his hips that her hair bounced, and then she suddenly grabbed her chest and collapsed with a choking sound. Everyone laughed. "Poetic justice, perhaps," she said, "but not a bad way to go, I should think."

"Why can't women have that?" demanded Natalie. "Fatally penetrated by a six-foot-four bricklayer."

Milt caught Jean's eye and motioned to his empty glass, then eased out of his chair and began to edge toward the kitchen.

"Why don't you pour Louise another one of those," said Jean, nodding toward the empty tumbler at Louise's feet.

"Oh, sure," Louise giggled. "Thanks."

"And I'll have one too," Jean said. "Just to see what the attraction is." She held out her wine glass and waited for Milt to take it.

"You know what I think would be nice?" said Louise.

Milt hesitated in the midst of retrieving glasses, sort of crouching on the carpet like prey hiding in the tall grass.

"I'd like to die with someone reading poetry to me," she said. "Maybe something by Elizabeth Bishop. Or that translation she did of that Manuel Bandeira poem."

Everyone waited, except for Milt, who resumed his flight to the kitchen.

"Do you know it?" said Dorothy.

"Well, the one I'm thinking of, it's called 'My Last Poem,'" said Louise. "It's about a poet who wishes his last poem could be as beautiful as a scentless flower, as ardent as a tearless sob, and have the passion . . . What was it? . . . The passion of a suicide who kills himself without any explanation."

For a moment the only sound in the living room was that of Milt stirring Mojitos in the kitchen, his spoon knocking ice against glass.

Jean, sitting in her chair by the window, wiped her eyes with the crumpled, snotty tissue she gripped hard in her hand. "Everyone should have a last poem," she said. She said it more to herself than to anyone else. But then she looked to see if the others understood. "I mean, as a metaphor, not literally. I mean, everyone should have a last moment of beauty in their life. Because life can be so hard and dismal, why can't we end with something absolutely pure and sweet? Something wonderful? We earn that, don't we? I mean, that should be our right, as human beings." All her friends nodded, watching her. "My mother deserved a last poem," she said.

"Sure she did," said Natalie.

Jean's hand felt stiff, rusty; her muscles seized as she wiped her nose again with the old, balled-up tissue. She was alone now. She hardly noticed Milt setting a tall green glass on the little table beside her; he was merely a shape in the shadows. Sitting by the window, she was all alone when her mind filled with an image, sudden and unstoppable, like gas being pumped into a chamber. She could tell this was what she'd been waiting for, since the day of the funeral. This was how the best plans and most intricate designs came to her; they rushed in at her, fully formed. She'd been waiting for just such a revelation. She knew to let it come.

She saw her mother lying in bed, head wrenched back, neck roped with pain, and the vision caught her breath in her throat. But then . . . then . . . as she watched her dying mother, she imagined something quite fantastic. Oh, it was quite wonderful, and terribly sad, too, as a truly artistic vision can often be. She imagined offering her mother a last . . . sweet . . . moment of beauty, a last poem, in exchange for the pain she'd been given. Who could resist such a trade? Oh, it was so tragic, Jean thought, to know it had been within her power to grant her mother that gift, if she'd only thought of it in time. Because she knew how it could be done now. She looked at her friends gathered about her in the room, her friends and their shadows, and she could picture it clearly. And how tragic it would be for her mother – though her mother was dead and beyond knowing – to see her daughter giving that gift to someone else. Someone else and not her. Yes, that would be tragic, in its way. But now that she knew, Jean thought, what kind of monster would she be, what kind of friend, to deny that gift to these people she loved?

Death didn't have to be slow and agonizing and bleak. Suffering was not a given. A person could have a last poem. And it wasn't something that had to come by chance. That was the revelation. It could be guaranteed. Jean breathed deeply, deeply, and felt her muscles relax. This always happened when she was sure of her vision, before she started work. She became calm.

And it was an added joy for Jean to know that this vision she had, this gift, this plan, wasn't ridiculous or scoff-able at all, but entirely practical. Exquisitely practical. Had she not been dead, had she not been buried and beginning to rot, Marjorie Horemarsh would have been so proud.

Chapter 6

Jean gave her mind over to thoughts of blood. It was the morning, and she sat drinking English Breakfast tea across from Milt in their bright dining area, with a daisy light from the bay window painting the far wall and the antiqued china cabinet. She watched him eat his crusty toast with marmalade – an oddly bitter taste with which to begin the day, she'd always thought – and knew that blood was not going to be a problem.

This was the great benefit, the singular one, really, of having been raised by a veterinarian mother wholly oblivious to a young daughter's sensitivities. Watching Marjorie in her white coat cut into tabbies and Labradors, even once a Great Dane – anaesthetized and splayed out larger than either of her little brothers on the kitchen table – had inured Jean very early on to the sloshy, lurid aspects of organs and vessels and bodily fluids.

She was more accustomed to it, at the age of seven or eight, than the first-year veterinary students who were sometimes assigned to work with her mother, who would often observe Marjorie slicing open a pink, shaved belly and faint with a crash at the first scarlet trickle.

"That was nice last night," said Milt. "Everyone seemed to have a good time."

"Mmmm," said Jean. Her eyes were set without seeing on the first done button of Milt's Lacoste golf shirt, which had been purple when she'd bought it for him twenty or so years before and had since faded to a lavender-tinted grey. Milt wore this shirt when he had no substitute teaching assignments and planned to idle the day away in the house, reading how-to books he'd bought at the hardware store, as if reading about how to do something forgave never managing to do it.

And he had never once golfed.

"What are you thinking about?" he said.

She wiped splashes of red out of her mind and lifted the teapot to freshen her cup. "Nothing to concern you." He was still nervous about the night before, Jean could tell. Worried about her mood or her attitude regarding his encounter with Louise. Husbands, she thought, or hers at least, monitored their wives for trouble the way pioneers once watched their dry goods, checking for mould in the wheat flour, weevils in the corn. But the fact was that she couldn't have been less concerned about anything happening between Milt and Louise. She almost wished something would happen, if that's what would make Louise happy. Because that was all that mattered to her now, the happiness of her closest friends. That was the vital thing. That was the point.

"You're not thinking about Louise, are you?" said Milt.

"No, not Louise. Not specifically."

"I mean Louise and me. Because there's nothing to think about there, Jean. That's all over. That's history. The whole Mojito thing was just a total, weird coincidence."

"Stop worrying about it, Milt. It's not even in my mind."

"Okay." Frowning, he began to spread marmalade on a second piece of hard toast, dry, the way he preferred it lately. "So is it to do with your work? That kudzu piece?"

She lifted her tea. "It's an idea. Something a little different."

He bit into his toast, watching her, and began jabbing at the air with his half-eaten slice. "Yeah. I should've figured it out. You've got that faraway idea thing happening in your eyes. Oh, jeez, sorry."

A bit of marmalade had flicked onto her cheekbone, and Jean wiped at it with a finger and then licked it off. Foul, bitter, rindy taste. No, marmalade was not for her.

Milt kept his head down for a while, chewing his crust, his mouth emitting sounds of walking on gravel. When he looked up he said, "Is it something I could help with?"

"I don't think so."

"Remember I used to help you? Remember that time you needed a bigger kiln and I helped you build it?"

She sipped at her tea. "I think I hired someone to do that."

"But I read up on it."

Jean set down her cup, reached across the table, and laid her hand on his wrist.

"I took out all those books from the library so I could advise you."

"Milt, darling," she said, smiling as sweetly as she could but letting him see her eyes. "I'll slice my wrists if you don't stop talking."

"Okay, you're concentrating, sorry. *Artist at work.*" He popped the last bite of toast into his mouth. "It's nice to have you home, though."

She had so much to do. So much to think about. Jean took their little Hyundai to the Sobeys for a shop, partly because the house was low on just about every staple – Milt's own shopping while she'd been gone had apparently centred on milk, bread, and a rotation of frozen stir-fry dishes – but also because she knew it would help her. Ever since living as a student on her own she'd found that walking up and down the aisles of a supermarket, when it wasn't too busy, really cleared her head.

Inside the store she grabbed a cart, picked out the old flyer that was lying in the bottom, and made her way into the produce section. There she felt the ceiling's full cathedral height above her, and let the cool, humid air hit her face and neck like a breeze off the lake and bring goosebumps to her sleeveless arms. She went slowly through the mixed greens, the herbs and packaged salads, the fennel and snow peas showered with mist. And then, finally, past the tomatoes, amid the citrus and the pineapples, Jean nudged into the question that was plaguing her most at the moment. The question was: *Who should be first?*

That dilemma sat on her as something stressful and fraught because, having had the vision, she had to act. She was compelled. An idea unexecuted was no better than a daydream; it did nobody any good. Yet acting on her vision required making a choice, and to choose one friend before the others suggested she liked one best, while the others would have to follow in some sort of ranking, next to least. To Jean that didn't seem right at all. It was possible to have a best friend, she supposed, one who resonated in one's experience more deeply than anyone else. But after her experience with Cheryl she had always tried to avoid making judgments like that. Even when girls in her class wanted to be granted that status, wanted exclusive access to her secrets, or sole rights to the cafeteria seat beside her. No, she wouldn't do that. She loved all her friends equally.

It was another reason for her mother to shake her head in exasperation. "You have to find your strongest allies, Jean," she would say, frowning at the irritation of her as she scratched through her paperwork. "You have to form a circle of support. It's ridiculous and unnatural not to. If you try to make everyone your friend you won't have any real friends at all."

Well, somehow she had managed, and she had cultivated a group of friends that she cared about deeply. Through the years, of course, the numbers had diminished. People got busy with their careers, raising their families. Some of them died – Margy Benn getting her head split open by a mare's hoof at thirty-two had been a shock. (Quick for her, though, Jean now considered; so much better than Jane Tiller and her cervix. Oh, if only she had thought of this *sooner.*) And of course, saddest of all, she had lost Cheryl's friendship – not just lost it but thrown it away.

That was a mistake she couldn't take back, Jean knew. It was a piece that had shattered in the kiln. But what she could do, what she *had* to do, was try again. She could do the best thing now, for all of her friends. And pushing her cart past the baskets of peaches, Jean realized that meant she had to find a way to put an order to her plans. Someone had to be first, and someone last. That was just how it was.

"Oh, Jean!"

Jean turned to see Fran Knubel hurrying a cart toward her and felt a weight press the air out of her chest, because this was exactly the sort of encounter she didn't need at the moment. Fran lived with her retired husband on Jolling Crescent, which was one of Kotemee's better streets. Some said "the best" but Jean preferred to avoid those distinctions. Fran had obviously just had her hair done; it was all wisps and waves. She'd decked out her hip-heavy frame in summery-designery things, from fashion houses Jean had never heard of and didn't care to, and presented herself in full makeup, with opal earrings. Oh, and Jean could see now an opal dolphin brooch. All this for a morning trip to the grocer's.

"Jean, did you see they had California oranges on sale back there?"

"No, Fran, I wasn't looking for oranges." Jean glanced into Fran's cart and saw several flimsy plastic bags stuffed with fist-sized vine-ripened tomatoes and Chilean peaches and some disturbingly large zucchini. But no oranges. "Looks like you weren't, either."

"No, I never buy those," said Fran. "Jim loves them, but they're all skin as far as I'm concerned. Peel them and there's nothing left. I prefer the satsumas, you know, those little mandarins? They're really, really nice and you can get them in those big organic stores but they hardly ever stock them here. This is such a terrible grocer's. Terrible. I wish we had one of those organic stores, don't you? But they'll never come here. Why would they? Nobody in this town would appreciate them. Well, besides us."

Jean nodded and looked off toward the breads. Implicit in Fran's helpful alert about the sale-priced, all-skin navels was the understanding that Jean-and-Milt had less money than Fran-and-Jim, and might appreciate a heads-up on the opportunity to save a few precious cents on produce. Fran Knubel was just full of the sort of help and counsel that made you feel like a total fool who'd stumbled into all the wrong choices in life. It was one of the few drawbacks of living in the sort of pretty, small town to which people retired that once someone like Fran arrived, as she had some years before, you could never fully be rid of her – every time you turned around she was at the grocer's, at the book store, at your mother's funeral – and every year was one more year of wishing that she and Jim would unretire and move back to wherever they had come from. And what made it that much worse for Jean was the fact that Fran did genuinely seem to like her and enjoy her company. She would come into the studio-shop two or three times a week, apparently just to chat. The curse of having a shop open to the public was that the public could be anybody; you couldn't jump up from your stool when she was about to walk in and rush to shut the door going, "Oh, sorry, Fran. Not you." Although she had also, over the years, bought several expensive ceramics by Jean and seemed quite delighted with them, which made Jean feel even more guilty. Really, the dismay of seeing Fran was always multi-layered. Maybe that was why it felt so heavy.

"So," said Fran, "are you doing a full stock-up or are you just getting something special for dinner? We could go 'round together. And by the way," she leaned in and touched Jean on the wrist, "I read they have chicken wings for two dollars off a pound."

"I'm so stupid," Jean blurted.

"What?"

"I left my wallet in the car."

"You have your purse, though," said Fran, helpfully pointing.

"I know." Jean leaned her cart into a hard U-turn around a barrel of dried figs. "But when I paid for gas I left the wallet on the seat. Isn't that dumb? You go ahead and maybe I'll catch up."

The morning sun wasn't that hot, but Jean thought she would bake sitting in her car in the parking lot, so she rolled down the two front windows before she pulled out her phone. Then she punched in Welland's direct number. It rang only once.

"Constable Horemarsh."

Jean knew it killed Welland to have to say *constable* when his brother got to say *chief.* Even *sergeant* would have been better. "Hi, there," she said. "It's Jean. Just calling to see how are things coming on finding Cheryl Nunley. Any luck yet?"

"No, no luck yet. No. Sorry. No." Welland's voice had the tone he got when he was saying only part of what he wanted to say, and the part he wasn't saying was the much bigger part. It was a quality of compression, as if his voice were a grilled cheese sandwich being pressed into the pan.

"Oh, well, is there any trouble? I mean, is there something you need from me? I tried to tell you everything I know but maybe . . ."

On the other end of the phone Welland sighed, and through the phone it sounded like a sudden windstorm in Jean's ear. "I haven't even started looking yet."

"Oh, but –"

"No, I want to look. I wish I was doing it right now, instead of packing up Billy Walker for one more kindergarten cookie bang." Billy Walker was Welland's little dummy boy, made out of foam and clothes from the Goodwill, which he stored in a suitcase and took into classrooms to talk about traffic safety. The younger children loved Billy, and they always got to eat cookies when he and Constable Horemarsh visited; that's what Welland was referring to with the mention of *cookie*. As for *bang*, that was just Welland expressing his frustration. "But I can't," he continued. "Before I start working on this I have to get trained on the system, and they haven't had time to train me yet."

"What system?" said Jean.

"It's a system. Does it matter what system? Do you need to know the name of it? CPIC. There, does that help? Does that make things clearer? I haven't been trained on the CPIC system, which ties into the RMS and the PIP and the NCIC. All those are cross-border data-archive and info-retrieval systems. And I haven't been trained on any of them, and I'm not doing anything until I'm trained. Because this might be my only chance to *get* trained."

Jean watched people coming out of the Sobeys in case one of them happened to be Fran Knubel, although it probably wasn't time just yet. "Isn't there anything you can do, though? Until you get trained, I mean."

"Like what – checking on the Internet like some fourteen-year-old kid? That's not really police work, is it? That's not what I've been waiting all this time for."

"No, I guess not."

"If I'm going to do this I'm going to do it right, okay?" At the end of the phone Welland said nothing for a moment and then he sighed again. It was a long, deep sigh but not nearly as loud this time, more of a surrender sigh, which was heartbreaking to Jean. "I'm sorry to be harsh with you, Jeanie. 'Cause it's not your fault. I'm just a bit aggravated because he said he'd train me yesterday – I need two sessions but that was supposed to be the first one – and then he called and said he had to push it off, and now I'm just waiting."

"Who said? Who's supposed to train you?"

"Ted Yongdale. He just made inspector so I guess he's all of a sudden busy."

Jean knew Ted Yongdale. He was a perfect sweetheart who'd once tried to date her when Milt was off at teacher's college. That was nearly thirty years ago but he still smiled at her whenever they crossed paths. It was one of those little inconsequential things that lifted Jean's spirits every now and again, and she knew it did something for Ted Yongdale, too.

"Okay, you just keep hanging in there, Welland. And how's everything going with finding a band for the picnic?"

Welland sighed. "I'm still looking. No one plays Garth Brooks any more."

"Well, that's understandable."

After they said their goodbyes, Jean closed her phone and opened it right back up, called the Kotemee police reception, and had Melissa connect her with Ted Yongdale. While she was waiting she gazed out her window and noticed a bronze Cadillac SUV that looked a lot like Fran Knubel's parked three spaces over.

"Inspector Yongdale."

Jean heard the faintest chuckle in Ted's voice, as though he was awfully pleased with himself. "Ted," she said, "it's Jean Horemarsh. I'll bet it feels real good to say *inspector* now, congratulations."

"Oh, hey, Jean. Yeah, thanks. Been a while coming, for sure. Sorry to hear about your mother, by the way."

"Are you supposed to be training Welland right now on the CPIC?"

That seemed to bring Ted up short. "On the what?" he said.

"It's called the CPIC system. I'm sure you've heard of it."

"Yeah, I'm just surprised to hear it coming out of you, is all."

"Oh, well, you'll get a real earful out of me if you don't get down to training him like you said you would. Here all this time I thought you were the nicest man in Kotemee, and now I don't know."

It didn't take long for Ted to promise to get Welland up to speed on the CPIC and whatever else he needed, pronto. And before she hung up, Jean did her best to bat her eyelashes through the phone with her voice, just to make sure Ted knew there were no hard feelings. Then, as she was putting her phone in her purse, Jean saw Fran coming out of the Sobeys and heading right for her with her cart. She twisted the key in the ignition just as Fran saw her and waved.

"Hey, Fran," she called as she backed out of her spot, "I just came out myself, I don't know how I missed you." Then Jean accelerated out of there, cursing under breath because now she was going to have to drive nine miles to Hillmount and shop in their dinky little A&P.

———

Natalie Dorothy Adele Louise Cheryl
Cheryl Louise Adele Dorothy Natalie

Jean sat at a picnic table in Corkin Park, on the west side of Kotemee, with little strips of paper on which she'd written the names of her friends, trying them in different orders to see if that would help make things clear for her. She'd finished shopping and knew her groceries were gradually warming in the car, the frozen juice going soft and the red leaf lettuce wilting, but this question of who first and who next was plaguing her, and she knew she couldn't move forward with anything until she'd sorted it out.

The slips of paper weren't working, though. It was becoming clear to Jean that solving this problem wasn't going to be a matter of feel, the way she so often worked when she was trying to decide on this or that arrangement of leaves in a ceramic, or the name for a piece, or whether it would be glazed in green or white or vellum grey. She was going to have to be more commonsensical and put aside her qualmish worries about being fair. Jean gathered up the strips of paper and mushed them into a tiny ball between her fingers.

So . . .

Natalie seemed an obvious person to start with, because she was such a dear – no, thought Jean, that was thinking emotionally. Was there any practical reason to consider? Handiness – Natalie lived four blocks away – was all she could think of. No less significant a consideration could there possibly be. But it was also no reason to rule her out. So, for the present: Natalie was an option . . .

Louise was arguably just as handy as Natalie; five blocks east or four blocks north, it hardly made any difference. But Jean could see a very obvious reason not to do Louise first. It was the whole matter of her affair with Milt. People who knew about the goings-on between those two – she imagined there were certainly a few still working at Hern Regional High School – would be asked if they knew of anyone with a motive to harm Louise. *Harm* would be how they would think of it. And Jean's name was sure to come up. It would be difficult, she thought, to convince suspicious people that she hadn't even really thought about the affair in years, even though the very fact that Louise was her good friend should have been evidence itself. And if the police started nosing around (she couldn't assume favours just because she was the chief's sister; that wouldn't be fair to Andrew Jr.), there was a chance she wouldn't be able to finish what she'd started. So, under the circumstances: Louise might have to be last.

The fact that Adele lived in the city was a mark both for and against her, Jean thought. For her, in that the element of distance would obscure any connection between the two of them. Against her, in that it was such a bother to have to drive into the city and deal with all that terrible traffic. Honestly, it was a full-day ordeal. And Adele was always so busy, it was hard to fit into her schedule. Sitting at the picnic table, Jean rolled the ball of names between her fingers and thought, well, inconvenience was hardly a good enough reason to exclude Adele from consideration. So: Adele, an option . . .

Now Dorothy, thought Jean. Dorothy . . . Living out along one of the rural concessions, not right in town, not too far a drive. Working hard to take care of Roy; now there was a bad situation that was only going to get worse. Oh, she put on a brave, no-nonsense face, but Jean could tell from Dorothy's eyes that she was starting to despair. "Big Boy" was close to three hundred pounds now. He could still dress and feed himself, but for how long? And when he got angry he was like one of those movie monsters tearing up everything in his path, except there was so little left now because their money was running out and he'd already smashed or torn or kicked so many of their nicest things. Poor Dorothy deserved to be rescued from all of that. She deserved to be treated to a special, joyful, passionate experience, and then freed . . . All things considered: Dorothy was a definite possibility.

Last, Jean put her mind to Cheryl Nunley. She thought that if she *could* choose someone for purely emotional reasons, it would have to be Cheryl. Because there was so much Jean felt a need to make up for. The abandonment of her friend at the darkest moments of her life. The subsequent decades of neglect. The hateful lack of curiosity about what had become of someone with whom she had shared so much formative teenage experience. It was as if she had worn Cheryl like a favourite pair of shoes and then kicked her to the back of the closet.

And yet, it was hard to imagine Cheryl being an option in the immediate future because Jean had no idea where she lived, and there was no telling how long it would take Welland to find her. The possibility existed that she wasn't even alive, which was just awful to think about. So Jean had to accept the facts: Cheryl was on the back burner . . .

As she sat at the picnic table, Jean let her eyes drift over to two men who stood chatting by the southern edge of the park near the line of scrub brush while each of their dogs, a boxer and a retriever, rolled around and chewed on sticks for lack of any organized activity. It was irritating for Jean to watch. The men had gone out to take their dogs for a walk and here they were standing. They were having a nice *stand*. Maybe it was just her mood talking, but it seemed to Jean that if you were going to do something, you should just get on with doing it.

She stood up from the picnic table and tossed her little wad of names into a garbage bin. The decision was made: it was going to be Dorothy first. Jean just hoped that somehow she could make it up to Cheryl, if she ever saw her again.

Chapter 7

It was grey. It was grey. Oh, God, it was grey. Another miserable, malicious grey day. *Oh, God, not another one*, she thought. Couldn't take it. Couldn't take any more of these grey days. Thought she would die. Wanted to die. It was unfair. God, it was so . . . oh . . .

Sheet.

It was the sheet pulled over her eyes.

With a vague swipe, Cheryl Nunley armed the sheet away and fell back to sleep.

Jesus was not in her wine glass. Of course he wasn't. It was the late afternoon, or the early evening, and for a minute there in the winery's big tasting room – for one bedazzling, unbelievable, oh my Holy Lord moment – Cheryl had been convinced that Jesus was staring at her from her glass of Cabernet-Franc. Of all the people, dead or alive, who could have been staring at Cheryl from her wine glass, Jesus was the one she would have wanted most. Jay Leno would have been nice too, because his smile was gentle and comforting. But Jesus, on the whole, was better. Cheryl blinked at the image in the glass. Her eyes were somewhat numb and she had to work to focus. "Hello, Jesus!" she shouted. "Say something, Jesus!" Cheryl clamped onto the stem of her glass with her two trembling hands and stared down into the wine, into his blood, the blood of Christ. "Talk to me, Jesus!" she shouted. "I'm listening!"

But it wasn't Jesus at all. Cheryl stared at his face, watching him saying nothing, which wasn't like Jesus, and she saw that it wasn't his face. It wasn't any face. It was just the reflection of some stupid . . . there . . . the stupid light fixture over her head. That's all it was, a light fixture. Not Jesus.

And nothing to cry about either, so just . . .

Cheryl smeared her cheeks dry and pushed her hooded gaze around the room at all the empty tables. She thought, it was a good thing Mr. Binderman wasn't there.

Oh, *great*. Cheryl raked through her purse in the parking area. She dumped the contents out onto the pavement in the dark and got down on her hands and knees and picked through the lipsticks and cigarettes and lighters and . . . corks and . . . button and . . . receipts for some stupid thing and . . . and what was that? That wasn't hers, that stupid metal hook thing, whatever it was. Throw that away. She had to find the ring of keys and . . . there was the ring of keys but there was. no. car. key. on. it. She swayed and stared at the keys and then she remembered, oh, they took that key away from her. That was her key and they took it. Okay, so now she couldn't go into town. And that meant she couldn't get more birdseed. And that meant Buzzy was going to die. Buzzy her cockatiel. From starvation. Buzzy, Buzzy, Buzzy. Buzzy who whistled and warbled like a telephone and other whistly things. She laid her head down, mourning Buzzy, who wasn't dead yet but surely would be soon because there was no food and he would be silent forever and that was sad. Buzzy, Buzzy, Buzzy, oh Buzzy. Nothing she could do. Her eyes were closed. It was okay to sleep here, on the pavement, Cheryl thought.

"Mrs. Yoon?"

Mrs. Yoon was not her name. That was someone who no longer lived here. That was someone she used to be, but that person was not her any more.

"Mrs. Yoon?"

Someone was still saying "Mrs. Yoon." How could a person keep calling another person by the wrong name? What was that? *Misidentification.* Probably a crime of some nature. Determined to make that stop. Tried to open her eyes but the sun poured in like lemon juice, so she kept them shut.

"I'm not Mrs. Yoon."

"Mrs. Yoon, you have to get up."

"What's my name?"

"Mrs. Yoon."

"No it's not."

"Mrs. Yoon, you are on the pavement. Please get up."

"Why don't you listen? I am not, not, not Mrs. Yoon."

"I'm sorry, Mrs. Yoon. I can't really understand you. I don't know what you are saying. But you have to get up now."

Mr. Binderman took hold of her arm and pulled her into a sitting position. She knew it was Mr. Binderman because no one else was here now, and also because he smelled like the vineyard, sweet and green, and because she recognized his voice, his old-mannish, Austrian voice – not German – which was kind and imperious and afraid all together. It was Mr. Binderman pulling her into a sitting position, from which she wanted to throw up. So she did throw up.

"Oh, Mrs. Yoon, no, that's not good. Not good. Here, I'm sorry, you take this. Please, you take it."

Mr. Binderman shoved a cloth into her hand. A flimsy cloth. A handkerchief. What was she supposed to do with it? Wipe her nose? Be that as it may, she had to throw up again. She did throw up again. All this was best done with eyes closed, Cheryl thought.

Buzzy was her only friend. Buzzy, the cockatiel, had been there from the beginning, arriving in Cheryl's life eighteen months before as a grand, angelic gesture, white warbling proof of Tam Yoon's affection. Cheryl was then just a divorced claims adjuster living in Syracuse, New York, who liked to go on winery tours and sometimes got a little silly and snuggly with well-dressed men she happened to meet. From his perch in his white wire cage, Buzzy had seen it all – Cheryl's sudden, swooning love for fifty-seven-year-old Tam; the determined effort to defeat the lifelong temptation that could undo her; the fervid plans for a future with someone a foot shorter and many, many times richer thanks to Tam's very astute investments in the cellphone industry; the campaign to convince Tam to use just a bit of that money to buy a little winery and retire in the very setting that had brought them together; the early, giddy excitement when Cheryl thought she had finally secured everything that mattered and could matter in a life like hers; the gradual weakening of that certainty, and the steady disintegration of everything that had been sweet and new and possible; the shouting and the crying and the horrible, angry accusations; the "you're pathetic" and "ridiculous"; the slammed door; the nights of Cheryl on the phone, begging Tam to forgive her; the anguish and remorse; the self-hatred; the days of lost hours; the months of lost days.

The surrender.

Throughout the formless, shattered days since Tam had gone, Buzzy was Cheryl's steady comfort. At noon, or thereabouts, he sat perched in his cage on a table in the living room, watching his circumscribed world with black-marble eyes. He never spoke but made a series of chirping and warbling and whistling noises that could sound like the kettle or the telephone or the fax machine or the alarm clock. Some of those ringing noises sounded very much like a phone call from Tam wanting to apologize and come home. But they weren't Tam calling. There was a dent in the side of Buzzy's cage to remind Cheryl.

By about five o'clock every afternoon, Buzzy had stopped sounding like phone calls and often seemed, to Cheryl, to have acquired the power of rudimentary speech. But he used it to utter only warbly nonsense words that Cheryl found indistinguishable from the Chinese curses Tam had sometimes hurled at her, his mouth contorted, his black hair flying.

By nine or ten, many nights, Buzzy was conversing emphatically with Cheryl about her failed marriage. Buzzy had a harsh opinion of the cellphone industry that had fuelled Tam Yoon's fortune, and of Tam himself, and of the New York wine industry, opinions which he was only too happy to share, and which resonated with Cheryl and seemed to confirm every qualm and misgiving she had had and ignored before committing herself to the life that now consumed her. Once in a while Buzzy said something so right and true that Cheryl would hug the cage. She would press her face against the wire bars so fiercely they left imprints that took hours to fade.

But by three and four in the morning, in Cheryl's experience, Buzzy had typically risen above such petty concerns. By then, most nights, Buzzy had convinced Cheryl to free him from his confinement, and he was flying about the living room and the dining room, the foyer and the stairwell, the kitchen and the solarium, his great white wings outstretched like the reach of a divine herald, lighting now and then on a chandelier or a curtain rod or a banister, delivering God's message in white, glistening packages.

By nine or ten in the morning, whatever heavenly force had imbued Buzzy with the power of speech and argument and transcendent grace had dissipated, and he was returned to the form of an animal, indeed, a menace. One who made unholy, piercing noises no pillow could block out. And in these bewildering, terrorized hours Cheryl often found herself shouting at Buzzy thinking he was the phone, or at the phone thinking it was Buzzy. There were times when things would get so cloudy and confused she would pick up one of these ringing, warbling things and fight it, bash its head against the wall, strangle it, while growling the bird's name. "*Buuuzzzzzzzyyyyyy.*"

And late the next morning when Cheryl pried open her eyes, Buzzy would still be there, perched and happy in his cage as if the world had not come undone.

Chapter 8

Young Jeff Birdy's orange Barracuda throbbed and gurgled at the corner of Calendar and Main while he waited for the light to change, and Jean could see him pointed across her path as she slowed to a stop. When the light turned she got the full spectacle of that boy easing his car into the intersection and curling left just in front of her. He took it nice and slow, like he was riding a show horse around an arena full of people who'd come to watch only him, letting the sunlight flash off his chrome and not seeming to care that there were cars behind him with drivers impatient to get somewhere, not seeming to care about anything at all in the world. Jean watched him in his dark T-shirt and Labatt's baseball cap, one arm dangling limp out the window as if it viewed disdainfully the task of gripping the wheel, and she wondered at the influences that must have led to such a display of . . . *arrogance* was the word. Ash had never been like that, had he? Jean didn't think he had. So how could this boy of twenty-two, who had accomplished no more than a clean car – a car that, as it made that clotted, back-of-the-throat noise sounded bronchially infected to Jean's ears – how could he smile with such enormous self-assurance at people he hardly knew? It was a paradox.

The paradox of Jeff Birdy's smile.

But he rounded the corner and he was gone, and Jean pushed the image out of her mind, because on this bright day she had before her a bit of a challenge. She needed to convince Dorothy to leave Roy at home for an evening and come out to dinner with her. They hadn't really had a heart-to-heart in a long time, just the two of them, and as Jean set herself the task of making a lasting experience for her – or, not lasting, but exquisite – she was feeling a little under-equipped.

Over the past few years she had lost track of what made Dorothy deeply happy. Her friend had become someone who personified resilience and endurance, someone you admired for facing a hardship you were grateful to have avoided yourself. It had made her a little severe, though. There were walls around Dorothy, and whatever sense Jean had of who was inside, the woman of secret joys and wishes, came from her memories of the Dorothy she'd known in high school so many years before.

That Dorothy, the regal seventeen-year-old with a fall of chestnut hair, had loved track and field, and swimming in cold, cold water at the lake. November wasn't too late for Dorothy Perks to dive in, so it was said; and one October 31st, after a Hallowe'en dance, Jean had actually seen her splashing away from that showoff Frank Rennick (and who's to say they weren't still in the water when people lost track of them long after midnight?). Dancing, of course, that was another thing she loved to do. Jean used to envy Dorothy for having her choice of tall, covetable partners for the "Stairway to

Heaven" finale of every event, and the way she so smoothly managed the song's awkward transitions from slow to fast to completely rhythmless. During those last fifteen seconds, when everyone else stood around motionless like a closetful of poorly hung clothing, Dorothy zeroed in on the eyes of whatever boy she was with, draped her long arms behind his head, and pulled him forward so that their lips touched for the first and only time the instant Robert Plant eased out the word "Heaven." For Jean, who was usually standing against the wall with Cheryl, it was like watching the end of a famous romantic movie you'd seen over and over and over, predictable and unavoidable but still a little enthralling.

Swimming and running and toying with boys: there were surely now more depths of joy to survey in Dorothy Perks than that. But when Jean had called last night, Dorothy had insisted that she couldn't come out for dinner, or that if she did she needed to bring Roy along because she said there wasn't anyone left willing to sit with him. And Jean knew that if Dorothy brought Roy, then she'd be forced to invite Milt, because he was acting so needy lately it wasn't worth the aggravation and pouting to leave him behind. So she pulled the car to the curb and tried again.

"Dorothy," she said when her friend answered the phone, "I know you've said no already but I want to insist on you coming out with me this evening. We deserve a girls' night out, just the two of us."

There were some strange sounds that Jean couldn't quite place coming through the earpiece, and when Dorothy spoke she seemed distracted. "I'm sorry, Jean," she said. "I'd love to, but I can't. Do you want to know what I'm doing right now?"

Jean was fairly convinced she didn't want to know, but Dorothy was a friend, so the word "yes" came out of her mouth.

"I'm watching my husband tear the stuffing out of his favourite chair in big handfuls."

"Why is he doing that?"

"He says the chair is against him. It's making his ass sore, because he's been sitting in it all day, so now he's teaching it a lesson."

"I see," said Jean, and she waited while she heard Dorothy yell at Roy to clean up the mess he was making because she was sure as hell not going to do it. "Well, then – Dorothy, are you there? – I guess we could have a couples' night out." In the background, Roy was shouting something unintelligible. Jean tried to make her voice bright. "And we'll go someplace casual."

They went to Ted's Big Catch, which was a fish and chips place way up on Main at the corner of Primrose that was nicer than it sounded, with wood panelling and heavy varnished tables and those big captain's chairs that gave a big man lots of support and had only a little vinyl padding for the back.

The two couples arrived at almost the same time, and they settled around a table in the big dining room where there were lots of hurricane lamps and seashells and fish netting, and it was a lovely picture, Jean thought, reassuring herself. She said, "I wish I'd thought to bring a camera!" probably a little too enthusiastically. Dorothy looked much less frazzled than she had a few nights before at Jean's house. She had on black slacks, and a thin black cardigan over a peach jersey top, and she had her hair tied back to show off her long neck. She looked very slim, almost pert, and not at all her age, and Jean made sure to compliment her.

Roy had on a sports jacket, which he filled out with an impressiveness bordering on the grotesque, and his thinning hair was gelled and combed back in silvery strands, like a wire grille. When he spoke, his words came out slow and ponderous, and he seemed very calm, if a little confused, not knowing quite why they were there, or who Jean and Milt were, even though they had met many times before. Dorothy had encouraged him to wear a tie, she said, by which Jean felt she meant to explain the jumbled knot bunched against his thick neck. And Milt was Milt, wearing his usual checkered shirt and khaki pants with the black running shoes that Jean absolutely hated. "They're comfortable, and they look just like dress shoes," he insisted, even though that last part was not even close to true.

When the waitress came and asked for drink orders, Roy said, "Beer." Dorothy tried to whisper to him that he could only have milk or juice (she caught Jean's eye and mouthed the word "med-i-ca-tion"), but he bunched up the heavy features of his face until they looked like folds of pork and seemed about to cry or make a scene and it was a relief when Dorothy relented.

"Are you having a Mojito?" Jean said to Milt.

"No, I thought a beer."

"Fine, and I'll have a Chardonnay. Dorothy, are you joining me?"

"Well I'm driving, so . . ."

"Oh, just have one."

"Don't worry," said Milt. "The fried batter will absorb the alcohol."

They got their drinks and ordered their food, and then Jean raised her glass to toast Dorothy, saying, "Here's to my friend who has shown such grace and endurance in the face of everything." Jean knew it wasn't the best toast ever, but as she brought the glass to her mouth it seemed a little odd to her that Dorothy didn't seem pleased, and that she had looked immediately at Roy. But then Jean turned and saw Roy looking back at her with a suspicious glower and put her glass down.

"'Everything,'" Roy said. His eyes were squinty and he seemed to be chewing agitatedly on his lower lip. "What you mean, 'everything'?"

"Just everything," Jean said, trying for a chuckle. "Everything life throws at us."

"So why you didn't say to the whole table, 'everything'?"

Dorothy put her hand on Roy's forearm. "It's okay, hon. Jean was just being nice."

Jean felt the blood rushing to her face. "I was just being nice," she said, her voice reduced to a little girl's chirp. She looked at Milt, who was looking at Roy and seemed just as confused as she was.

"Roy doesn't like to feel like a burden," said Dorothy, focusing on Jean now with a great intensity.

"'Everything,' you mean me," said Roy, still glaring at Jean, still chewing his lower lip. "For what she needs 'endurance.' It's me."

"No, hon," said Dorothy gently.

"Oh, no," said Jean. "No, I wasn't talking about you."

"No," Milt contributed, shaking his head.

Roy's eyes squinted menacingly at Milt and back at Jean, and for a moment it felt to Jean as if the whole table, in fact the whole evening, were being dangled over the side of a cliff. And then she had a sudden inspiration.

"I meant growing old!" she exclaimed. "Because Dorothy looks so good! She's the same age as me, but I could be her older sister!"

Roy's eyes compressed even more, and the dark irises rattled back and forth like marbles in a matchbox between Dorothy and Jean. For a second or two he appeared uncertain, wavering, and it seemed that anything might still happen. And then a grin broke across his face like splitting skin. "Her mother!" The corners of his eyes crinkled and his grin widened until he showed pink gums and the brown ridges of teeth. He slammed the table, clattering the cutlery and plates. "You look like her mother!"

Dorothy's eyes were on her and Jean thought she noticed a flicker of pity in her face, pity stirred up with gratitude, like a sour-sweet Mojito. She chuckled. "That's right." She lifted her glass. "Here's to you, Dorothy!"

Roy slammed the table again and lifted his beer high. "To Dorothy!"

And Jean smiled at Milt, because after the poor man raised his glass he seemed unsure whether he should take a sip.

For a good hour or so, everyone seemed to enjoy themselves well enough. Milt munched happily on his burger and salad. Dorothy ate one of her fish pieces with the batter and one without, and the batter that she left on the plate looked like a little brown snowsuit for a tiny baby. She lit up a cigarette, too, even though smoking wasn't allowed, because she seemed to be aware that, with Roy sitting there so massively, no one would come to the table and ask her to put it out. And for his part, "Big Boy" ordered two plates of fish and chips, and piled them into his mouth, sometimes with his fork and sometimes with his fingers. Every once in a while if he started to pick up a big piece of fish – or his coleslaw, he tried that also – Dorothy would give him a sharp little smack on the wrist so that he would drop it. It seemed to Jean that Roy didn't like that very much, being smacked like a child, but otherwise he seemed to be quite content, laughing sometimes when he thought someone had made a joke, wiping his greasy mouth with his napkin or his sleeve, burping with deep satisfaction after his third beer. A couple of times, Jean tried to address a question to him, just to be friendly, such as, "How are you enjoying living in the country?" and "Do you ever watch boxing on TV?" But he would only look at her the way a toddler might, as if she were talking nonsense and just interrupting his fun. In fact, after the blow-up over the toast to Dorothy, the only words he said to anybody were, "I want the ketchup." And he didn't have to say that twice.

But despite the fact that the evening was proceeding as well as anyone might have reasonably hoped, Jean felt herself getting more and more frustrated. Because this wasn't supposed to be just a friendly get-together, this was supposed to be a fact-finding mission. And it turned out, as Jean had expected, that a dinner for four in a busy fish and chips restaurant was a terrible time and place to find out anything about a person that was of any value whatsoever. Every time she tried to open up the subject – "So, Dorothy . . ." – of what made her friend really, truly happy these days, Dorothy would get distracted by something Roy was doing, like pretending to eat the end of his tie, or she'd shrug and give some meaningless answer such as, "I just like to veg in front of the TV with Roy."

After more than an hour of this it was starting to occur to Jean, and frankly it was a surprise given that she had been friends with the woman for nearly forty years, that maybe Dorothy was not a very deep or thoughtful person at all. That was the sort of thing you'd think one person might have discovered about another person at some point, she thought, but apparently all their conversations for years and years had only skirted the surface like water beetles, not even trying to reveal any deep, dark, inner truths. She tried to put it down to the situation, which really was not ideal, but even so, by the end of her second glass of wine, Jean was feeling a little sad about her friendship and starting to lose some of the fire for her cause, at least where Dorothy was concerned.

And then something happened that put everything back on the right track.

Milt was doing the talking, going on as he liked to do about the differences between Grade 9 students and Grade 10 students, the two grades he tended to teach – in their maturity levels and tendencies toward aggression or insolence or overt sexuality, that sort of thing. Because he was a substitute teacher and wasn't able to form relationships with the kids in the classrooms, he believed he had a unique and "scientifically useful" perspective. He was like a "test rat" being dropped into different cages, he said. And of course all of this was going completely over the head of Roy, and Dorothy as well, and Jean was a little annoyed at Milt for discussing a topic that held so little interest for half the people at the table (three-quarters of the people, if the truth were known). But when Milt mentioned the part about being a "test rat," Roy thought that was hilarious and began to laugh so that his shoulders shook. And then, possibly because his mind was caught on the image of Milt as a small furry creature, he went to grab a handful of food from the wrong plate. It was Dorothy's little suit of batter. And when he picked it up with his fingers, laughing, Dorothy slapped his wrist, and that's when Roy hit Dorothy in the mouth.

It happened so quickly – the back of Roy's left hand flying up to Dorothy's face with a wet, splatty sound, Dorothy's head snapping back with the blow as she emitted a small, high-pitched "Oh!" – that for half a second it seemed no one was quite sure whether they had seen what they had seen. Then blood started to bloom from Dorothy's lower lip, which began instantly to swell, and tears came to her eyes. And Jean shot to her feet.

"You brute!" she shouted with all the air in her lungs. "How dare you hit my friend."

She rushed around the table to Dorothy, who tried to push her away, insisting she was all right. But Jean could see that her face was pale, and that she needed air or water or just a sense of safety. So she told Milt, who was sitting in his chair like someone at a magic show, paralyzed with amazement, to "watch that animal," pointing to Roy, who was quietly feeding batter into his mouth. And she helped Dorothy to her feet and led her outside, around the tables and past the waitresses and waiters, who seemed to be at the same magic show as Milt.

Out on the street, Jean set Dorothy against the front of the building, brushed the hair off her forehead, and used the cuff of her blouse to wipe some of the blood from Dorothy's mouth. It was still light outside and she could see the age in her friend's face better now, the lines around her eyes, the fragility of her skin, the soft, pouchy places that once had been flat and firm. Dorothy's mascara had begun to run in black tributaries over her cheeks, and Jean whispered, "Stay here and I'll be right back." She went into the restaurant, where Milt was now gamely sitting next to Roy and talking to him in a calm voice like an older, much smaller brother (she was so proud of him in that moment), and got a clean, damp cloth from the manager. When she returned through the door, she found Dorothy trying to light a cigarette with her trembling hands.

"Here, let me," said Jean. She gave Dorothy the cloth and, as her friend pressed it against her face, Jean put the cigarette to her lips, flicked the lighter, and inhaled. She hadn't smoked since she was sixteen and now, with her heart already racing, the act of lighting a cigarette, and feeling the rush and the urge to cough when the smoke hit her lungs, seemed daring and illicit.

The sun hung fat and buttery over the roof of The Granary bulk store on the far side of the street, and the light was beginning to take on that summer evening glow. Jean handed back the cigarette, and Dorothy straightened.

"I should go inside."

"Oh, no."

"He'll be worried about me."

"After what he did? Let him be worried." Jean took the damp cloth, wrapped the edge of it around her finger, and cleaned a smudge of makeup from the corner of Dorothy's eye. "Here's what we're going to do," she said. "I'm going to get Milt to take Roy home in your car. And you and I will have our girls' night out."

"Jean –"

"Don't worry about Roy." She kept her voice quiet, but Jean felt within herself a rising tide of purpose. Her will was inexorable, like the flight of a magnificent bird, or the march of a whole field of kudzu. She had never felt more sure of herself, of her plan, of what she could do for her friend. For all her friends. "You have every right to think of yourself and your needs right now. Tonight is about Dorothy Perks. Roy will be just fine with Milt."

"Are you sure?"

"I couldn't be more sure. Now, what I need to know is, can Roy show Milt the way back to your place?"

"Of course he can." Dorothy frowned. "It's not like he has Alzheimer's."

"That's terrific," said Jean, patting her arm. "I just wanted to check."

She went back inside, where Roy was now sitting quietly watching sports people on the TV screen hanging from the ceiling in the far corner of the dining room, with Milt in the chair beside him looking backward toward the door. Life in the restaurant seemed to have returned to normal, with the usual motion and chatter; people so easily moved on from dismay. When Milt saw Jean he seemed deeply relieved. And because he had been so quietly helpful, so reliable, she felt bad when she had to tell him he would be driving Roy home.

"No, I am not doing that," he said, thereby completely erasing in Jean's books all of the goodwill he had built up. "He's a total wild card. What if he clocks me while I'm driving?"

"That's absurd. He won't clock you."

"How do you know?"

"I'll have a word with him. You pay the cheque."

"The whole – ?"

Jean fixed him a look, and Milt sighed and slumped off to the waitress area. Then she went to the chair where Roy was sitting and tapped on his shoulder. His huge head turned and, seeing Jean, he started to cry.

"Dotty?" He reached for Jean's hand and swallowed it in a mitt of soft, blood-warm flesh. "Is Dotty okay? She be mad at me?"

"I should hope so," Jean said. "That was a terrible thing you did."

Roy's face crumpled even more than before and he nodded fiercely, sending plops of tears onto his knee and the floor below. Then he let go of Jean's hand, wiped at his eyes with a fist, and began to push himself up out of his chair.

"No, no," said Jean.

"I go to my Dotty."

"No, you sit down," she commanded. It was like ordering a giant cooked ham to sit. But there was enough force of will in her, she thought, to make even that happen if need called for it. And Roy sat. "Now listen," she said. "Milt is going to drive you home. You know Milt?" She pointed at Milt, who was slowly handing his credit card to the waitress. When Roy nodded she continued. "You be nice to him, you hear me? When you get home, you can watch TV together."

"With Dotty?"

"Don't worry about Dotty." She patted his hand. "Everything is going to be fine."

Outside, Jean tucked her arm into Dorothy's and led her up the street for half a block, past the print shop and the vintage clothing store, and under the ornamental street lamp with the wrought-iron curlicue that marked the start of Calendar, and Jean turned them down this street to get them out of view of the restaurant before Milt and Roy emerged. They walked for a while without talking. Calendar was lined mostly with modest two-storey houses, built before the war, but people cared for them as well as any mansion. Some of the gardens were lovely, and several times Jean had to resist the urge to stop and study the leaves she saw: clumps of lemon thyme with leaves like green grains of rice rimmed with gold, purple Persian shield, pretty catbells the size of dollar coins. At a house on the corner, someone had set out a pot of Angel Wing, which was as beautiful as any caladium plant she had ever seen. Jean made a mental note to come back for a closer look, when all this was over.

"I think it's going down a bit," said Dorothy, touching her lip.

"Oh, let's hope it stays for a while," said Jean. "You look like one of those bee-stung Hollywood starlets."

"I want you to know, Jean, he's never hit me before. Sometimes I thought he might, but he never has."

"It doesn't matter," said Jean.

"He's getting worse, though. His mind seems to work best when he's feeling paranoid. Maybe that's the fighter in him. Otherwise he's just a little boy."

"Don't think about it any more." As they walked, Jean put a light hand on Dorothy's back and rubbed her gently. "Don't think about it any more," she repeated.

Eventually, led by Jean, the two women circled around, across on Mott Avenue and down Primrose, as the sun dropped behind the buildings and the light turned bluish-grey, then darker still, until they were back at Main and it was feeling very much like evening. For now, Dorothy seemed content to go wherever she was taken, but Jean was aware that at any moment she might stop in her tracks and insist that it was time to go home. They came to the corner, where the light was red. Jean slipped a foot out of her shoe and rubbed it – she wasn't used to walking so far in pumps – and began looking around for another restaurant, or just a place for them to sit and talk. Then she heard a familiar sound.

The deep, clotted, throat-phlegmy noise of Jeff Birdy's Barracuda came toward them along Main and the car pulled to a stop just over the white line of the crosswalk, its juddering engine heating and vibrating the air around them, its headlights carving out bright swaths of the intersection and making everything else shrink into darkness. Across the street the walk sign flashed and Jean tried to nudge Dorothy forward off the curb, into the spray of light, toward the other side. But for some reason it was harder to get Dorothy moving than she'd expected. Her hand against Dorothy's back met the resistance of someone holding her ground.

"Who's that?" she said. She was squinting from the lights, and at the corner of her mouth – hard to tell, it might have been the squinting effect – seemed to be a tiny, puffy smile.

"Nobody to worry about," said Jean. "Just Jeff Birdy." She tried to make the nudge at Dorothy's back a touch more insistent, without turning it into a shove.

"Ash's boy?" said Dorothy, actually batting Jean's arm away. "I haven't had a good look at him since he was ten." She bent down and shielded her eyes, trying to see past the glare into the Barracuda's interior. Above them the traffic lights changed and Jean waited for Jeff Birdy to drive on. But he didn't drive on. He just sat there with the green light, throbbing.

"Why doesn't he go?" Jean said.

"I think I see him," said Dorothy, peering into the depths. "Oh, I think he's handsome."

Behind Birdy the driver of a Toyota honked his horn, and out of the side window of the Barracuda came a hand that twirled lazily in the air to wave the car past. The ground under Jean's feet shook with the Plymouth's pistons, she smelled its raw exhaust, and she clutched Dorothy's arm as if they were two virgins standing at the lip of a volcano. Then, like a dentist's drill lifted off a tooth, the noise and shuddering just stopped, the headlights of the wide, orange barge went dark, and in the shimmer of silence Jeff Birdy swung open the driver's door and stepped out. Dorothy straightened and drew a hand down the edge of her hair.

"Hey," said Birdy, grinning.

"Hey," said Dorothy. She flicked a hand at the car. "Seventy-three?"

"Close. Seventy-two." He lifted off his ball cap by the brim, rubbed his hair with the heel of his hand, and set the cap back down securely.

"I like the paint job."

Birdy nodded, as if he judged the comment reasonable. "Looks better in the daylight."

"Morning light," said Dorothy. "About five or six."

"Maybe." Birdy grinned. "I wouldn't know."

Jean cleared her throat and adjusted the purse strap on her shoulder.

"This is my friend, Jean," said Dorothy. "I'm –"

"Nah, let me guess," said Birdy. "I'm good with names."

Dorothy let out a high, girlish laugh and Birdy leaned against the roof of his car, studying her. After a few seconds he said, "Roxanne."

A smile spread wide over Dorothy's face. "You're a mile off."

Birdy shook his head. "No, I'm not." He opened his driver's side door and his body began to disappear into his car, legs first. Before he was fully gone, he paused. "Get in," he said.

"Oh," said Jean. "Well, no. We were just –"

Dorothy turned to face her. "Tonight is about Dorothy Perks," she whispered. "You said."

She was standing close enough that she could smell the cigarette smoke on Dorothy's breath and see the glimmer of excitement in her eyes. Jean looked over her shoulder at Jeff Birdy. She wasn't sure what faith she could have in that young man to make Dorothy happy, but she knew that she probably couldn't do it by herself.

"Why not?" she shrugged.

The inside of Jeff Birdy's car smelled of stale beer and burnt motor oil, and there was a chance, Jean thought, that if she had to stay in the back seat long enough with the windows closed she would wind up with a terrible headache. Birdy had rolled up the windows because he wanted to show off his stereo but thankfully, after about twelve ear-splitting seconds of Toby Keith, Dorothy had managed to get him to turn it down. Or maybe she had turned it down herself. Jean couldn't really hear at the time, and she couldn't see much from the back because the springs in the ripped vinyl seat seemed to be mostly broken and she was sitting lower than she was used to sitting. She could see, however, that Jeff Birdy was steering the wheel of his car with only the heel of his left hand, and that Dorothy was leaning over toward him, half out of her own seat. Jean thought that somebody probably had a hand on somebody else's leg.

"So what are you girls up for?" said Birdy.

"I dunno," said Dorothy. "Anything, I guess." She looked back at Jean. "What are you up for, Jean?"

"Anything sounds good to me," said Jean, in a way that she hoped sounded joyful and adventuresome and not middle-agey. She had decided she was going to say yes to whatever Dorothy wanted. This was her night. And the truth was, Jean was a little excited herself, although it was funny to her how familiar it all seemed, sitting in a loud old smelly car driven by a cute Birdy boy who seemed to think he could have whatever he wanted. It wasn't a very pleasant feeling, really. More wistful, all things considered. But anyway, that didn't matter. It was just important that Dorothy have a good – no, not a good – a *wonderful* time.

"You want a beer? I got some beers in the back."

"Sure!"

Birdy reached a smooth, muscled arm into the back and pointed to a battered plastic cooler on the floor, shoved into the crevice between Dorothy's seat and the bench of the seat into which Jean was sinking. "You wanna pull the lid off that and grab a coupla cans for Roxanne and me?" He said this without looking around at Jean. "Help yourself while you're at it."

Jean considered asking him whether he should really be drinking while he was driving, but she abandoned that idea on the grounds that she knew what sort of answer she would get from him, and what sort of look she would get from "Roxanne." She bent down and had to use all of her strength to pry off the lid because it was so snugly wedged between flanks of vinyl. At a certain point in her struggle down there, among the gum wrappers and fragments of straw, Birdy turned on the car's interior light. Jean thought he was doing it to help her. But when she finally managed to sit up straight with three wet cans in her hands, she realized that Birdy was examining Dorothy's face while he drove. His eyes stared hard at her, his jaw muscles flexing. Dorothy was facing straight ahead, and Jean could feel the tension radiating off her like sonar.

"So how old are you, anyway?" said Birdy.

As far as Jean could tell, Dorothy didn't flinch. "Why don't you guess," she said, her voice a small, tight version of itself. "Are you as good with ages as you are with names?"

She kept staring straight ahead. In the back seat, Jean held the cold, slippery cans to her chest, hardly breathing.

"I know you're north of forty," he said. He looked forward and snapped the wheel to avoid something in the road ahead, then went back to staring. "But you're not as old as my mom ... I guess that's all that matters." He reached up to the ceiling and flicked off the light.

In the back seat, Jean marvelled at the cold calculus of young Jeff Birdy, and she silently cheered for Dorothy. Because Jean was acquainted with Jeff Birdy's rather plus-sized mother, and she was a good four years younger than either of the women in her son's car.

"I got the beers," she sang, and passed two of them to the front. As she did, she gave Dorothy's shoulder a little squeeze.

They drove with Jeff Birdy in his rumbling Barracuda along two-lane highways and across gravel concessions as the darkness settled around them. If Birdy was "between jobs," as he explained at one point, he also seemed to be between ideas as to what to do with two mature women willing to be taken wherever he intended to go. It didn't seem to matter to Dorothy, who leaned her head onto Birdy's shoulder and held his arm as if it were a vine keeping her from sinking into quicksand. In the back seat, Jean helped herself to another beer and silently mouthed the words to Birdy's country tunes.

The roadside landscape was turning grape-coloured in the darkness when Birdy abruptly hit the brakes, and the gravel beneath the car shotgunned the floor under Jean's feet. Dorothy lifted her head.

"What is it?"

He threw his car into reverse and looked over Jean's shoulder as he began backing up. After about fifty feet he crunched to a stop again and rolled down his window.

"You see that lane?" said Birdy.

Dorothy leaned across him to look out his window as Jean slid over on the back seat and rolled down hers. In the dim starlight, on the side of the road, Jean could see the shape of a huge oak or maple tree on a knoll and, beside that, the beginning of a lane that was not much more than two wheel ruts worn into the dry earth. The lane seemed to lead nowhere but down, toward some place beyond view that was even darker and more remote than the place they already were.

"I'll bet that leads to some kind of water," said Birdy. He crunched an empty beer can in his fist and whipped it into the far grass for emphasis.

"What kind of water?" said Jean.

"Maybe a creek, maybe a pond. Hard to say." The car shuddered and grumbled beneath and around them. Jean smelled exhaust coming through the window, or perhaps through unseen holes in the floor. Birdy turned to Dorothy. "Whaddaya say, Roxanne . . . check it out?"

"Sure!"

"I don't know . . ." Jean began to say from the back seat. She wasn't quite sure how she intended to finish that thought. I don't know *if this is safe.* I don't know *if this is wise.* I don't know *what good anyone can expect to come of this but I guess it's not my call!* And it didn't matter because Birdy had already cranked the wheel and now they were bumping down, down the lane, crashing through weeds and grass that beat against the open window frames and filled the car with a swirl of dust and floaty particles that caught in Jean's nostrils. In the front seat, Dorothy held on to the boy's arm with one hand and pushed against the ceiling with the other, while Jean held on to the back of Birdy's seat and dipped her head the way she'd been told to do on airplanes during emergency landings.

They continued down like that for two or three minutes, Birdy swerving expertly to follow the twists in the lane. Jean thinking of

Milt comfy in front of the TV with Roy, and of what a good friend she was, really an exemplary friend. And then without warning they were level, and they were stopped. Birdy shut off the engine, and the stereo, so that all they could hear was the cloud of dust settling on the car, and the cicadas in the trees.

"What'd I tell you?"

"Wow," Dorothy whispered.

Jean raised her head and looked out. Beginning just a few yards away, a black pond stretched out in the moonlight, surrounded by the small, blue silhouettes of scrub trees. Birdy leaned out through his window, staring at the water. "Trout, I'm thinking." He lifted his cap and gave the top of his head a scratch. Then he turned back into the car. "So, who's swimming?"

For the next while, Jean sat on the fender of the Barracuda, beside a mound of clothing, listening to Dorothy and the Birdy boy splashing and hooting in the water, tormenting the trout, just like a couple of teenagers. When she put her hand back, the sheet metal above the engine felt warm, so she lay down with her head on the air scoop, which rose up in the middle of the hood like a big flat nose with enormous nostrils, and looked up at the stars. They were extravagantly bright, strewn like silvery jacks across the dark floor of the universe. What a pity people who lived in the city couldn't see stars like these, she thought. Adele couldn't see stars like these. She would have to show them to her, some night soon.

Jean had to admit to herself that she felt a little lonely lying there, without a hard young man grabbing at her goosebumpy behind and her cold-cinched breasts. But still she was coming to believe that everything was going to work out tonight, much better than she could have hoped. She knew that Birdy and Dorothy would soon be coming out of the water, and they were probably going to make love. Dorothy would want that, it would help make the evening complete and familiar for her, so Jean cast a silent wish on her behalf. Thinking about that likelihood, and hearing the two swimmers coming closer, Jean sat upright on the fender again and looked around for something to do with herself. There were probably some interesting plants around the edge of that pond, she considered. So she slipped down off the hood and fetched the little keychain flashlight out of her purse. And when Dorothy and Birdy emerged from the pond holding hands, naked and sparkly with water, she announced, "I'm going to go exploring for a little bit. Don't leave without me." Then she kicked off her pumps and trudged off into the weeds and sludge.

It felt well past midnight when things finally seemed to calm down in the Barracuda, so Jean was surprised when she examined her watch in the starlight and saw that it was only eleven-thirty. Time, she supposed, lost its shape when you were standing in your bare feet at the edge of a boggy pond, wondering if those were penny toads landing on your toes, having no way of knowing because your flashlight batteries ran out long ago, while you were swatting mosquitoes and your friend was being riotously screwed in the unsprung back seat of a muscle car by the son of the boy you once wanted to marry. But that was okay, thought Jean, as long as Dorothy was happy. This was her night.

Young Jeff Birdy had some work to do turning his car around and getting it back up the two-rut lane. At one point he got one of his fat rear wheels lodged in a patch of mud, and so with Dorothy steering, her hair all loose and wild, it was Birdy and Jean pushing together on the rear of the car, as the two-barrelled tailpipe pumped exhaust against her shin. But they shoved it free – Jean getting a firm handshake from Birdy for her effort – and the ride back into town went quietly after that.

Jean directed Birdy to where her car was parked on Main, all alone now save for a few pickup trucks in front of the Ol' Town Tavern at the far east end, and she waited with the key ready in the ignition while the boy and Dorothy made their goodbyes. Dorothy had not forgotten how to kiss, that was obvious. Jeff Birdy could count himself lucky for the lesson.

When the two of them were finally alone in Jean's car and Birdy had rumbled off, Dorothy melted with a sigh in her seat. "Oh, God," she said, with her eyes closed. "I'm a bad woman, Jean Horemarsh." She chuckled a little wickedly. "It's my fervent hope that I have corrupted that boy for life."

"I'm so glad for you," said Jean.

Dorothy opened one of her eyes. "Are you? It wasn't weird for you, considering Ash and everything?"

"You deserved every moment of happiness tonight. I believe that truly."

Dorothy let out a slow, deep breath. "Thank you," she whispered. "You're a good friend."

That was all that Jean had hoped to hear. She believed it to be true. She believed it. And to have Dorothy say so just confirmed for Jean, as she drove to Dorothy's house on the outskirts of town, that she approached with the purest of intentions what was now to come. There wasn't even a question about that, really, but it was comforting to have it reinforced. She was a good friend, just as she had been a good daughter. It was just that as a friend she was better prepared. She had the foresight of experience, which she had not had with her mother. Imagine, she thought, if her mother had been able to enjoy a night like this before she died, a night when the pain was carved right out of her, and the hole was packed full of laughter and bliss. What a blessing that would have been for her, what a blessing now for those who loved her. Jean brought a hand to her face and flicked away tears as she drove.

And the fact that Dorothy had spent her last night doing the thing she had done so often when they were girlfriends back in high school – swimming and screwing – wasn't that funny? It was funny how little people changed. Perhaps that wasn't true of everyone, perhaps it was only true for Dorothy. Maybe screwing herself silly was the only thing that had ever made her happy. If so, that was kind of sad. But what luck that everything had worked out the way it did. Jean thought now that, if she'd believed in God, she would have thought it was His hand guiding events. But no, there was no God, and there was no Afterlife. When people died they were gone. So what mattered was how they lived. And whether they were granted a last moment of beauty, which was rightfully theirs. A Last Poem. Or a last screw . . . Well, whatever the case may be, Dorothy had had hers.

So.

Dorothy was asleep in the seat beside her. Jean drove along the narrow roads leading to Dorothy's house, the occasional street lamp shining down on her friend's untroubled face, almost childlike but for the etchings of age, and the smears of makeup, and the small wound on her lip. It would be lovely to do it as she slept, Jean thought, but that was impossible because there would probably be a mess, and Milt was going to be getting back into the car, and he wouldn't understand. No, he would not. Just thinking about how much Milt would not understand made it all the clearer for Jean that she was right not to tell him about any of this, just as she never told him about her ceramics before they were made. Because until it was done, it was just an idea, and an idea was too easily dissipated. And somebody not understanding, in the panicky way that Milt would not understand, was a sure dissipater.

The closer Jean got to Dorothy's house, the slower she went, because she realized that she hadn't brought any of her tools, and she needed time to figure out what to do. Then she remembered: wasn't there a little fold-up shovel in the trunk? That could work nicely.

As she approached Dorothy's long country driveway Jean shut off the headlights. They were so late she worried that Milt would be checking out the window for them. For fifty yards or so she drove with only the moonlight to guide her. There were no street-lights, no houses in the distance. Then she turned into the lane and shut off the engine. Beside her, Dorothy began to wake up.

"You're home," said Jean.

Dorothy rubbed her face and looked out. "Why did you stop here?"

"Oh. Well, there's something in your lane, and I wasn't sure I should drive over it." Jean opened the door to get out and walked toward the back.

"What are you doing?"

"Just getting a shovel from the trunk."

"Strange," said Dorothy. "I don't see anything."

"It's up a ways," said Jean. She opened the trunk, rummaged around, and finally laid a hand on the shovel as Dorothy got out of the car.

"What time is it?" she said.

"A little after midnight, I think."

"Oh, God. Roy's going to be so upset."

"Don't even think about that," said Jean. She set the trunk closed without slamming it. "Remember, you deserved your fun tonight. You did have fun, didn't you?"

Dorothy sighed. "Jean, it was the most fun I've had in years."

"I'm so, so glad."

"So where is this thing in the driveway?"

"It's up ahead. You look for it."

Dorothy walked slowly forward as Jean struggled to unscrew the shovel's locking collar. She wondered why Milt had never oiled it. What good was a folding shovel if it couldn't be unfolded? "Don't go too far," she called. Finally it came loose, and as she walked up the lane toward Dorothy she was able to straighten the shovel to its three-foot length and lock it into place.

"I still don't see anything," said Dorothy.

Jean was right behind her. Her heart was thumping harder than she'd expected, but just because she wanted to do well. She didn't want to ruin anything.

Dorothy stopped in the lane and peered forward. "Was it an animal or what?"

"Just keep looking, you'll see."

Jean lifted the shovel over Dorothy's head, knowing that what she was doing she was doing because she loved her friend, because she had been taught by terrible experience that to leave old age to chance was to open your arms to the dragon's fire, to let the flames lick at will. And the flames were terrible, they were merciless, and they consumed life's beauty first. And when it came to her dear friends that was something Jean Vale Horemarsh could not allow. She gave the shovel a wave in the air, to get a feel for its heft and to line up her swing. But it was an old shovel, made of a kind of cast iron, and quite a bit heavier than she'd anticipated. So it travelled a few inches farther than she wanted and plunked Dorothy in the back of the head.

"Ow!" she said. "Jesus, Jean, what the hell?"

Jean's heart nearly stopped. "Sorry! I'm so sorry, Dorothy! That was an accident."

"Christ, that hurt," said Dorothy, rubbing the back of her head.

"But . . . you're still happy, aren't you?"

Dorothy wobbled her head as if to clear it, then she straightened her hair and put her hands on her hips. She sighed, looking off toward her house. "Yes, I am."

"Phew," said Jean. She raised the shovel again over Dorothy's head and brought it down like an axe.

Chapter 9

"Mrs. Yoon, I don't know."

They were alone in the tasting room, the heavy oak tables and chairs scattered around them mute and unmoving, like appalled grandmothers. Through the square-paned windows came self-righteous rays of sunlight. The beamed ceiling suspended above them made Cheryl think of the underside of a drawbridge about to drop on their heads. *Do it, God*, she thought. *Do it now.*

Sitting across from her, Mr. Binderman had his sleeves rolled up, his bare elbows on the table, his bristly cheek resting in his hand. On his face hung a look of bewildered disappointment. Except for his stringy white hair, his workman's overalls, and the purple stains on his hands, he had the appearance of an Austrian schoolteacher watching his student getting it all wrong at the blackboard.

Mr. Binderman was Cheryl Nunley's lone employee, the last of the Bier Ridge Vineyard staff. He had asked to meet her at noon, which meant he had something important to tell her. Among all the hours of the day, noon was about as good as it got for Cheryl. She was able to stand straight at noon, was able to see and hear and understand most of what was said to her if she concentrated very hard. And with her mental machinery running at nearly full strength, Cheryl knew what Mr. Binderman meant when he said *I don't know*. He meant that he didn't know whether he could keep working at the winery. Or whether he even wanted to. He didn't know if he could do the jobs of four or five men any more, men younger than him, men who had gotten fed up and quit. He didn't know if he could face, again, having to pick the owner of the winery off the parking lot pavement a few hours after dawn.

"Mrs. Yoon – "

"Mr. Binderman," said Cheryl, her head still, her eyes open only as wide as necessary, "please don't call me that. I asked you yesterday. I keep asking."

Mr. Binderman smushed a rough, stained hand noisily over his face and gripped his sturdy nose before releasing it. "In the parking lot, that is what you were trying to say?"

"Yes."

Mr. Binderman frowned. "It did not make so much sense to me." He compressed his lips in the prissy way he had, which made Cheryl feel like a six-year-old walking into church with a jam stain on her blouse. "You don't speak so clear sometimes."

"I'm speaking clearly now, Mr. Binderman. I want you to call me Miss Nunley. Cheryl Nunley. It's my maiden name."

Mr. Binderman shrugged and brought his hands down flat on the table. "So, okay. Miss Nunley, yes? We are here to talk now." He patted the table, taking his time, and Cheryl did not hurry him.

Any time spent not listening to or thinking about bad news was almost like being happy.

"Here is what I think now." Mr. Binderman stared at his hands. "I think I can't do for you any more what you need with this winery. I am just a single person, you know. This is not so easy for three or four men here, but for one man it is just too hard." He pronounced the last word like *heart*. It was too *heart* to work here. "So what I think, maybe you can sell this place. Okay? That is a good plan for you I think." He patted the table once more with his purple hands. "You sell this place soon, and make a good life now. Forget about everything, yes, and start from the new."

He looked up at her, finally.

"And for now I think you forget about Mr. Yoon."

Cheryl made a spitting noise. "Who?"

For a moment Mr. Binderman regarded Cheryl with grave concern. Then he brushed away the strands of white hair falling over his eyes and compressed his lips with finality.

"Listen now and I tell you all what needs doing. In the barn, you have in the red tank six hundred gallons of Cabernet Franc that needs soon to go to the barrels. That's a big job for two men. Also, in the white tank eight hundred gallons of semi-dry Riesling that is ready for the bottling. Another big job for that, and when it's done, where do we put the cases?"

Cheryl tried to comprehend. Even in her best hour, this fragile hour of noon, a fog sometimes engulfed her, making things grey and distant, pulling what passed for clear purpose and coherence out of her reach. Sometimes the fog comforted her. Sometimes she thought she might be smothered by it. Like so many of the things in her life, it seemed, the fog was not altogether reliable.

Opposite her, Mr. Binderman raised a stained digit for every task he named, and though Cheryl focused on the digits, they

weren't enough. The digits did not provide sufficient information. She tried focusing on Mr. Binderman's mouth.

"In the cold room is already four hundred fifty cases full. I
know you are drinking it, but even you, I'm sorry, can't drink that
fast. So that needs to be sold. Or we leave the cases and sell the
Riesling for bulk. Anyway, another man for that. Now think about
the vineyard. Yes? Miss Nunley?" He waved his hand in front of
her face. Silly to do that. Silly Mr. Binderman. "Miss Nunley, in
the vineyard is another big problem. Because the mildew comes
now and so it needs spraying. I can do that."

When he spoke, Mr. Binderman seemed to use many more *T*s
and *D*s than necessary and this made listening to him even more
complicated. Cheryl lurched forward out of her fog. "Can't?"

"No, *can*. Listen, *can*. It's very clear. But also now is the time to
rise the catch wires. You understand? The catch wires all over the
vineyard have to go up now. To rise up the vine shoots." He lifted
his arms like a gull. He appeared to be trying to make things as
easy to understand as possible, which was probably a strain on his
Austrian dignity, and Cheryl appreciated this effort and hated it.
"This is so the sun can come on the grapes to make them get ripe,
you see? Also a very big job. So there is many jobs to do right now.
And I can't do it all."

She tipped toward Mr. Binderman. "Can?"

"No, no. *Can't. Can't.* You have to listen please, it's very important." Mr. Binderman smushed his face and gripped his nose once
more. "Mrs. Yoon . . . Miss Nunley . . . I don't want to leave you in
a bad position, but one man here is not enough. A winery is a
living thing, you know. It's a . . . what you say . . . an organism. Yes?
Like a person. Everything must work together or it all stops. So if
one part is not working, like a leg" – trying hard, he extended a
leg and shook it for her to see – "then maybe it survives, but if the

other leg goes and then the one arm" – he made his second leg stiff and contorted an arm into a hook, he was a scarecrow – "soon you know the whole thing is gone kaput." He collapsed his limbs and let them lie limp, the arms of a rag doll, for a moment of Austrian chagrin. Then he gathered himself up, reached across the table to lay a rough purple hand on her wrist, and said, almost in a whisper, "Soon we go kaput I think." He patted her wrist in a way that Cheryl thought was probably meant to be comforting but wasn't at all.

"I am sure you know the truth," said Mr. Binderman. He sighed and stood. "And how is the bird?"

Cheryl stared from under her heavy lids at the space where Mr. Binderman had been. "The bird is an asshole."

"But a good friend to you I think."

A *gut frent*, Cheryl heard. And closed her eyes.

Chapter 10

Welland waved frantically at Jean, and his hands closed into tight, waggling fists at his sides, the way they would when he was a little boy excited about building a sand castle or finishing his model of a World War II Messerschmitt and afraid that no one would see it before Andrew Jr. stomped it into ruins.

"I found her!" he said.

Jean had come to the police station because she'd received a call around nine o'clock that morning from Suzy Felter, saying that Andrew Jr. wanted to see her down there right away. She'd gotten that call at home, while she and Milt were in the middle of being mad at each other. Milt was mad at Jean for the same reason he'd been mad the previous night. Because she had left him alone with Roy for more than four hours – "At the mercy of that idiot," was how Milt put it – and then rushed him out the door without a chance to say goodbye to Dorothy. And without answering any of his questions, such as what the heck took so long and why were her feet covered in mud and where *was* Dorothy, anyway? And Jean was mad at Milt for being generally unsupportive and prickly when it should have been obvious to him (they had only been married for twenty-nine years) that just now she needed calm and tempered interactions. Because she had a great deal on her mind.

Jean had questions of her own plaguing her. For one thing, she wondered whether it had been right to drag Dorothy's body into the ditch by the side of the lane. Half the night Jean had spent thinking about that. And should she have left her in a jumble in the weeds, her hair all tangled and limbs every which way, or should she have laid her out in a manner that might have been considered more traditionally respectful? Nothing with friends was ever easy, because no one wanted to hurt anybody's feelings. Jean remembered the time that she and Louise had gone to Niagara Falls for a weekend, and Natalie had found out and wanted to know why she hadn't been invited, and the whole thing had become very tricky. Jean had had to spend money she didn't really have so that she and Natalie could get hot rock massages together. And Natalie didn't even *like* Niagara Falls.

So questions such as whether Dorothy got or didn't get a certain kind of treatment that someone else might or might not want – Jean took those things seriously. On the other hand, she had to remind herself that sometimes practicalities dictated the course of events, and you couldn't always plan out every single detail. And surely friends could be forgiving about that sort of thing, just every once in a while.

But something else was weighing on Jean too. It was embarrassing to admit even to herself, and yet it was true – she was beginning to have doubts. Because here's what happened when she got home: After the petty fight with Milt that had begun in the car, which was really more a tense standoff than an argument, she'd escaped into the bathroom to have a soak in the tub, and when she was down there in the water, comfy, with suds around her knees and shoulders, she started to cry. Just like that. It hadn't even been two hours since she'd given Dorothy a last joyous experience and swifted her past all the pain and fear of old age. And already she was missing her. Suddenly every little thing they had ever done together, every insignificant chat on the phone or quick coffee or exchange of clever, inexpensive Christmas gifts rang as the most lovely experience never to be repeated. And never again would she be in the vicinity of Dorothy while she was having frantic sex with a young man, which in a certain way was the experience that had bookended their long friendship. Sitting in the tub, Jean seemed to miss and cherish Dorothy more than she ever had when Dorothy was alive, and she began to realize – it occurred to her for the first time – how hard it was going to be to carry out her plan to its completion. She saw, more plainly than she ever had before, what a sacrifice she was expecting herself to make. Giving up all her friendships as a good deed . . . she didn't know if she could do it. She wasn't sure she was selfless enough.

That's what was going on in Jean's head in the central corridor of the police station when she was going to meet Andrew Jr. And now Welland was waving and saying he'd found somebody, and Jean was at a momentary loss.

"You found who?"

"Cheryl Nunley!"

"Oh," said Jean. And then she remembered. "Oh! You found her! That's wonderful!"

"I know," said Welland, beaming.

It seemed that Ted Yongdale had gotten somebody onto training Welland on the CPIC data system almost as soon as he'd gotten off the phone with Jean (which Jean was not surprised to hear). And so Welland had been up to speed on the CPIC within a few hours. And he was given a couple of hours on the RMS and the NCIC and one or two other data systems for good measure. (Jean thought this smacked a bit of "Let's train him on every damn thing and be done with it." But she kept that thought to herself.)

At the end of all that training, said Welland, he was able to hunt around in the records of police departments from Baffin Island to Puerto Rico. It meant he could punch in the name Cheryl Nunley and see if it came up anywhere, for anything. A speeding ticket, say, or maybe a protest march for something.

"I can't imagine Cheryl Nunley ever protesting anything," said Jean.

"That's not the point," said Welland. "Are you letting me tell the story or – ?"

"Sorry!" Jean made a zipping motion across her lips.

When Welland did the search, he came up with about a dozen different Cheryl Nunleys. But most of them were women who were either too old or two young or too something else (there was a transsexual prostitute named Cheryl Nunley in Vancouver, Welland discovered). The one citation for a Cheryl Nunley that might have fit – she'd gotten a ticket for running a red light in Portland, Oregon – was about twenty-five years out of date. He looked for the name in the Portland phone book, just in case, but nothing. So Welland thought he was stumped.

"That's when I had my brainstorm," he told Jean with a grin. "I thought, what if she's not called Cheryl Nunley any more?"

It seemed that one of the databases connected to a huge regis-try of marriage licences. Welland looked in there to see if any Cheryl Nunleys had been married in the last twenty-five years, and sure enough some had. It took Welland all of the next day to work through the various Cheryls. Old and young, black and white, living and dead. "I didn't even break for lunch," said Welland. "Just worked straight through." And finally, Welland said, he found her.

"Guess what her name is," he told Jean.

"I couldn't possibly guess."

"Cheryl Yoon," said Welland, looking as proud as if he'd carved somebody's head on a mountain.

"Yoon?"

"She married a guy named Tam Yoon. Now she's living in Bier Ridge, New York. That's in the Finger Lakes. I only found her because she was arrested for driving under the influence and causing damage to municipal property in March."

"No." Jean had begun shaking her head at the word *arrested*. "That's not Cheryl."

"Oh, no?"

Welland took from his back pocket a folded sheet of paper and opened it with a snap in front of Jean's face. It was a laser-printed mug shot of a bleary-eyed woman with messy, piled hair and an expression of utter surrender. It was the picture of an aging woman who had fallen into the embrace of some incalculable despair. And it did not take much studying of this strange, frightening image for Jean to see, hidden somewhere within this tragic woman's features, the very same Cheryl Nunley she had known so long ago.

"Ha!" exclaimed Welland. "I guess I'm not bad at this police stuff."

When Jean entered the waiting area outside Andrew Jr.'s office there was nobody sitting at Suzy's tidy desk. Andrew Jr.'s door was closed and Jean could hear muffled giggling coming from the other side. She decided to wait. When the door finally opened, Suzy's hand was leaving Andrew Jr.'s arm and the two of them were all big-teeth smiles and laughter, as if policing were just the most uproarious work imaginable. Then Suzy saw Jean, and her face set into a wax slab of gravity. It was a look that came so sudden and sure, Jean wondered if she practised it.

"Jean, I didn't know you were here."

"Why would you?"

"Andrew Jr. wants to see you."

"I know."

Inside Andrew Jr.'s office, Jean watched her brother roll out his big leather chief's chair and waited for an invitation to seat herself. Andrew Jr. set his bulk into his chair and coughed into his fist.

"Jean, were you out with Dorothy Perks last night?"

"Yes, I was. Milt and I went out with Dorothy and Roy to Ted's Big Catch. Why do you want to know?"

"Did you go out with Dorothy by yourself after that?"

"I did, as a matter of fact. She and I went for a little ride."

"Who with?"

Jean gave up waiting to be asked and sat herself in the round-backed velour guest chair. She had vivid memories of this chair; it was the same one she would jump up on as a child, when she and her mother would come to visit her father in the days when Andrew Jr. was still being pushed around in a stroller. She'd perch on her knees on the chair's thick cushion and do drawings at the corner of Drew's desk. Crayoned pictures of places in her imagination, where camels and cats and puppies and fish and teddy bears all played together, far from scalpels and garbage bins and her mother. She would conjure them up with such creative fury that the crayons would sometimes slide right off the paper and leave waxy scars on the surface of the desk, so that her visits with her father invariably ended with a shooing motion.

"Who says we were with anyone?" said Jean.

Sitting across from her, Andrew Jr. made no sound but gave her a droopy-eyelid look that she recognized from years of her brother being unimpressed by anything but drinking and foot-ball. Throughout his teen years Andrew Jr.'s droopy-eyelid look had been a permanent fixture of his wide, fleshy face.

"Well, as a matter of fact," she said, "we went out with that Jeff Birdy. Ash's boy. He took us to a nice swimming pond out on some concession. I couldn't tell you which one; we drove around so long I lost track."

"How long were you with him?"

"Andrew Jr., I'm not answering any more questions until you tell me what this is about."

"Dorothy Perks is a friend of yours, correct?"

"You know that. She was at Mom's funeral."

Andrew Jr.'s expression became very solemn. Almost broth-erly, Jean thought. He coughed again into his fist. "I'm sorry to tell you this, Jean, but . . . Dorothy Perks has been murdered."

Jean knew that she was supposed to be shocked by this news. She had been anticipating it, of course, ever since Suzy's face went so very flat and waxy. And it has to be said that she didn't like hearing the word *murdered*. It was a grubby, commonplace word, making her think of gravel-voiced gangsters, or B-movies about conniving business partners, or slavering serial killers with pic-tures of their victims pinned to a dank basement wall. But she knew that something more than being grated by a word was expected of her in this moment, and if she didn't provide that something, then even more questions would be asked, and life might become much more complicated. Again, she saw that practicalities had a way of dictating their own terms. And right here, right now, practicality demanded a display of emotion. The trouble was that Jean had never been a particularly good actress.

School plays had been things she attended, not performed in. The only acting she'd ever done was smiling in the face of a friend's terrible choice of hairstyle, or pretending that she wasn't hurt when someone cancelled plans at the last minute. Masking she was good at. But big emotion on cue – it was out of her range.

In front of Andrew Jr. she did the only thing she could think of . . . she covered her face with her hands. "Oh my God," she said into her palms. It sounded wooden even to her.

But apparently for Andrew Jr. it was enough. For once, Jean was able to enjoy a benefit from her brother being such a big lummox around feminine feelings. She saw through her fingers that Andrew Jr. was becoming flushed and agitated. He coughed twice into his fist and tried to look anywhere but at Jean. It seemed that, for him, watching his sister being affected by terrible news was an excruciatingly uncomfortable ordeal.

"Oh my God," Jean repeated, just to stick the knife in a bit further.

After a second's hesitation, Andrew Jr. got up from his chair and hovered near his office door with his hands in his pockets. "Look, uh, Jean," he said, "I think we're getting a handle on what happened, so . . . maybe Suzy has a tissue or something."

He grabbed the knob of his door and wrenched it open. Before he was able to call Suzy for help, Jean rose from her seat and rushed out, past the danger zone of Suzy's desk (Suzy had always struck Jean as being one of those women with radar like a bat) and into the safety of the corridor beyond.

The next day, the Kotemee *Star-Lookout* reported that police were questioning witnesses at Ted's Big Catch about incidents leading up to Dorothy Perks's murder. Jeff Birdy was declared a "person of interest" and brought in for interrogation, then released without charges. It wasn't long after that that Roy "Big Boy" Lundquist was arrested for brutally slaying his wife in a fit of jealous rage. It was the first ever murder in Kotemee, so there were lots of reporters and TV cameras from the city as Roy was taken into custody. Jean felt a bit sorry for Roy, who looked sad and bewildered as he was led up the steps of Hern Regional Jail, but then, of course, as a violent man with a jumbled brain, he was probably much better off in an institution. Certainly Milt was keen to express his horror at these events and remind Jean repeatedly that she had left him alone "with that murderer" for what he now described as "half the night." She dearly wished that he would take a summer teaching position somewhere so that he would have a reason to leave the house and give her time and quiet to think.

Instead she had to escape to her shop, which meant exposing herself to the sympathies and commiserations of what felt like half the membership of the KBA.

"Isn't it horrible . . ." said Gail Greenhurst (The Lux Shoppe).

"What happened to Dorothy . . ." said Cynthia Mingle (Mingle's Hair Salon).

"That brute of a husband . . ." said Margaret Gwyn (Kotemee Jewellers).

"The man should be strung up and flayed . . ." said Jane Pettie-Wier (Jane's Panes).

When Natalie Skilbeck came in, she shut the door and stood wordlessly for a moment near the entrance, as the jangling from the overhead bell faded. From that distance she looked at Jean with an unreadable expression on her face, and the thought crossed Jean's mind that perhaps Natalie suspected something. But no, it seemed to be just a dramatic pause, as if she meant to give both herself and Jean a moment to reflect on the sudden and profound new truth, that there was one less of their small circle in the world. Then she rushed forward and engulfed Jean in an enormous hug and held her, weeping, until her tears began to spill onto Jean's shoulder and trickle down to the small of her back, and Jean cried a little more, too.

After that storm had passed and Natalie had brought out the cupcakes, Jean said, "You know, I never thought you liked Dorothy all that much. I guess I was wrong."

"Well, I liked her as your friend," said Natalie, peeling the paper cup off a lime-frosted angel cake. "As a person herself she was all right. Just not somebody I would have ever talked to. But as your friend, she was lovely."

"I see," said Jean. She watched Natalie sink her teeth into the frosting. "So when you were crying just now, it was –"

"Because I was sad for you." Natalie's eyes began to well up again, and the napkin she used at her mouth was put to work dabbing at her tears. "I guess I still am."

Natalie stayed to comfort Jean for about an hour, until Jean thought she might scream. When she finally left and the shop was quiet for a moment, when it looked to Jean as though there might be a vista of uninterrupted time in which to think about what, if anything, might come next – never mind resume her work on *Kudzu Attack!* which she hadn't touched in days – she glanced up and saw, through the front window, Fran Knubel standing on the opposite sidewalk, in front of The Pita Plate. She was dressed in a pastel-blue linen jacket over cream slacks, and in her hand she held a small white paper bag.

She appeared to be waiting for a car to pass, and when it did, Fran began to walk across the street toward Jean's shop entrance with a straight-backed stride that announced rectitude and purpose. She might have been a wartime nurse, delivering hope and comfort to a legless Marine, a missionary bringing the Light of God to the residents of a straw hut, a prospector marching toward her California claim. Fran was coming. And Jean realized she could not get to the door and lock it without being seen.

So she tore the lid off a bucket of clay in the corner, ripped through the plastic bag inside, and dug out a head-sized hunk of damp porcelain which she pounded onto her work table. And as Fran pushed open the door of the shop and jangled the bell, Jean sank the fingers of both hands into the clay until her knuckles disappeared.

"You poor thing!" exclaimed Fran, shutting the door.

"Fran, hi," said Jean. "Gee, you've caught me at a really bad time, as you can see." She blew a nonexistent strand of hair off her forehead.

"I can't believe you're working." Indeed, as Fran came forward, her face betrayed a mixture of horror and astonishment. Then suddenly it changed, as if she'd been struck by a great revelation. "Do you know what this is? This is the blessing of being an artist. Whatever material rewards you may lack, at least you have a way to channel your grief. I'm in awe of you."

"Oh." Jean forced a chuckle. "Don't be."

"So, tell me about what you're doing."

Jean looked from Fran to the formless grey mass into which her hands were shoved. "Actually," she said, "I'm just at that really crucial creative time right now? When the idea is really fragile? So if I don't just get on with it . . ." She left the thought unexpressed, in hopes that Fran would seize it as her own.

Instead, Fran held up the little white bag in her hand. "Guess what I've brought you."

"Hmm," said Jean. "Pita?"

Fran scrunched up her features in confusion. "Pita. Why would I bring pita? No, no, no. This is from Lundy's Chocolate Works in Hillmount. Look, see?" Fran turned the bag around and showed Jean the glossy black label sticker. "I wanted to bring you something special. I didn't even get any for myself because that would have sullied the gesture. I said, 'If anyone deserves a special treat it's Jean Horemarsh, after all she's been through. Her mother dies and right after that her close friend is murdered.' I mean . . . my God. Jim said, 'Just get her some cupcakes from Dilman's.' Can you believe it? Implying you couldn't appreciate anything better. Men are awful. Well, we have proof of that now, don't we? Not like we needed it." As Fran ripped open the bag she shook her head, perhaps at the awfulness of men.

Jean tried to disengage her hands from the clay, because the ruse was clearly not working. But she'd left them in too long and now they were gripped hard in the fine-grained porcelain and it was going to be difficult. Fran began to rhyme off the varieties of the truffles she'd brought, and before Jean had retrieved either hand Fran looked up.

"So, name your poison."

"Oh, uh, I don't know." She tried to lever her forearm up and over to expand the finger holes.

"Here, just open up and I'll surprise you." Fran reached into the bag and brought out a dusty chocolate ball and pushed it into Jean's half-open mouth. Then she moved her own mouth rapidly as if instructing Jean on how to chew. "Isn't that divine? That's mocha-almond. I love all the coffee flavours. Here, hurry up, now try this." She brought out a dark shiny cube. Jean hadn't yet finished the first and now the second was being forced through her lips. When she'd pressed it home, Fran's eyes went wide with vicarious delight. "Ginger-orange caramel! Isn't it exquisite? You just can't get anything like it here in this poopy little town."

In Jean's purse, on the floor beyond her reach, her phone began to ring. Fran, who'd been surveying the contents of her bag for the next flavour to inflict, looked up. "Don't worry, I'll get it." She set the open bag on top of Jean's mound of clay. "Just look in there and think about what you want next." And she crouched down to the purse on the floor and began to root around. It took her three rings and a lot of rooting before she took out the phone and opened it. "Jean's store – oh, *pfffft* – Expressions. Jean's Expressions. Hello?" She stood and listened for a moment then looked at Jean. "It's your husband . . . No, Milt, this is Fran Knubel. I've never been to your house but I'm sure we've met. I was at the funeral . . . That's right, and it looks like I'll be going to another one . . . No, Jean's here, she's just tied up. How can I help you? Well, as I say, she's working hard and can't come to the phone."

Jean was struggling fiercely to free a hand while with her tongue she tried to push the caramel clear of her teeth. It felt like a dream she'd once had in which she'd been bound and gagged and dragged naked through the condiments section at Costco. When finally she did wrench one hand loose and reached out with it, sloppy with clay, Fran shook her head with distaste.

"Just tell me what you need and I'll relay the message to Jean." She winked at Jean. "Well, hold on, don't anticipate a problem until there is one." She held the phone against her breast. "Milt says he needs the car and hopes you don't mind. He's going to get a lift in to pick it up."

Jean shook her head and grasped at the air with her messy free hand. The caramel in her mouth held her teeth like some kind of epoxy cement, but she managed movement enough to say, "O!"

"Why not?" said Fran. "I can drive you wherever you need to go." She held the phone to her ear. "Milt? I don't think it's a problem . . . No. Jean seems worried but I think we can work it out."

Milt was a little mysterious, for Jean's taste, about why he needed the car. He arrived at the shop in a Mazda driven by their neighbour, Rick Chaaraoui, who let him off at the curb out front before carrying on to a tennis game somewhere (at least if the short yellow shorts Rick was wearing were any indication). So not only did Milt need the car but he needed it in such a hurry that he couldn't spare the time to walk the seven blocks from the house. On top of that, Jean noticed, he needed it while wearing his favourite sweater vest. And yet the only thing he could say as he opened the car door, when Jean quite reasonably mentioned the sudden suddenness of it all, was, "It's not a problem. I'll be back before dinner." And then he was in the car and the car was starting and then he and the car were gone. And Jean was alone with Fran.

"Well," Fran said to Jean on the sidewalk, "I guess you'd better get back to work."

Inside the shop, it became clear that Fran had a particular notion as to how the rest of the day would proceed: that Jean would work on her "new art idea" while she, Fran, would wander around the shop, from shelf to shelf and display table to display table, shifting pieces, murmuring at prices, humming tunes from *Les Misérables* and intermittently asking Jean such questions as, "Why are none of your pieces ever glazed in purple? It's such a popular colour." And Jean, who'd been making a desultory attempt to appear engaged with her blob of clay in hopes that Fran would get bored and leave, finally gave up.

"Fran," she sighed, "I think I'm going to close up and go home."

"Oh, all right," said Fran, sounding a little disappointed. She shifted the piece she'd been looking at into something like its original position. "I guess that happens sometimes, with art." She hesitated in the middle of the shop, fiddling with the buttons of her linen jacket, not moving. "But, didn't you need to drive somewhere? I was going to give you a lift."

There was something both wretched and hopeful about the expression on Fran's face. It wasn't quite the expression of the last child at the ticket counter of a sold-out matinee, or of the husband asking permission to try something new and odd in bed, but it was close, and worse in its own way, and it made Jean feel very mean all of a sudden.

"I can just walk," she said. But she didn't say it with any conviction, and she didn't back it up with any movement. In fact the two women stood in the middle of the shop, facing each other without a word, until Jean noticed again the bag of chocolates. Fran had neatly closed the bag and set it by Jean's purse, so that she wouldn't forget to take it with her. And Jean, regretting what she was about to do but not being able to stop herself, shrugged. "You could give me a lift to the bookstore, I guess."

At this, Fran's face lit up like a traffic flare. "Let's go!"

Jean had only one reason to go to the bookstore in the mall out on Highway 18, and that was to get a detailed map of the Finger Lakes district. She'd planned to drive there after Dorothy's funeral, but Dorothy's sister in Halifax had made it known that the family was having the body cremated and that a church service would be held in that city for family members only, so there was no reason to wait. Part of Jean was very sad about that, and a little annoyed at the sister for being so selfish, but she knew that was only out of habit. She reminded herself that the ritual of saying goodbye to the bodies of dead friends and relatives didn't mean anything to the dead bodies. All that mattered was what happened before the bodies became dead. Was the store of beauty filled to the brim? Were the reserves of wonderful experience topped up? Or had it all been allowed to drain dry?

They drove to the mall in Fran's Cadillac SUV with the air conditioning turned up high, Fran explaining that she knew Jean's Hyundai wasn't equipped and thought she'd enjoy the treat. As they went, Jean tried to find the quiet space in her head that would let her think. She needed to know whether the qualms she was feeling were temporary qualms. Whether they were similar to the insecure feelings she might have before giving a presentation to the KBA about some new suggestion for Main

Street, when it was inevitable that she would have to listen to Tina Dooley give her budgetary counter-arguments despite her not even being a vice-president. If so, those were qualms she knew she could handle, it was just a matter of staring hard at those qualms as if they were just little Tina Dooleys with nothing constructive to contribute. But if they were real qualms – if her fear of living without her remaining friends couldn't be stared down – then she might have to give up the whole plan. And then what would she do with her convictions?

That's what Jean tried to think about during the drive to the mall. But Fran wanted to talk about whether air conditioning was unhealthy, so she couldn't.

The bookstore displayed its maps in a tall metal carousel at the back, and it took Jean no time to find a map of the Finger Lakes district. As she unfolded it to see if it was detailed enough, Fran skimmed the titles on alphabetical display and rhymed off the places she and Jim had been. Bali. Jamaica. Jerusalem. Monaco. Paris. Prague. The Pyrenees. Scotland. South Beach. Vietnam. It was too bad, said Fran, that this bookstore had such a terrible selection, because she and Jim had been to so many other wonderful places in their lives, which was one of the benefits of having a husband who'd made such a great deal of money in corporate law before his early retirement.

"Fran," exclaimed Jean, "why are you here?"

"Because I'm giving you a lift," said Fran. She looked confused, and a little bit worried, as if she thought Jean had forgotten how she had arrived at the bookstore, as if she thought perhaps Jean had a *memory* problem. "We drove here from your shop." She touched Jean's arm. "You came in my car."

"I know that. I'm asking you why you're taking such an interest in me that you bring me chocolates and talk to my husband and then you drive me here." Jean knew that her manner was

133

bordering on harsh, and she tried to down-shift into a less aggrieved mode. "I mean, I'm sure you have other important things you'd rather be doing."

"I just thought you might need a friend right now, that's all."

"But you're *not* my friend." That was unfortunate. She had realized the road she was on and tried to veer off it. But something had pulled her back at the last second and she'd gone smack into the thing she was trying to avoid. "I'm sorry," she said, "but, I mean, we haven't really done the sorts of things friends do. You've never even been to my house. I've never been to yours . . ."

Beside her, Fran was looking at the maps on the stand, touching the edges of the "P" maps and the "T" ones. She blinked once or twice, and her mouth was working, moving, as if she might be trying to stop her lower lip from trembling.

"Yes, that's right," she finally said, in a voice softer than usual. She fleeted a glance at Jean and tried to smile, though her eyes looked moist. "So, maybe I'll just wait for you in the car."

Fran's SUV was sitting out front and running when Jean emerged with her map in a little paper bag and her souring guilt sitting as a great big ball on her neck. She got in the front seat and shut the door, and without a word Fran immediately put the car in gear and started off. The first minute or so, when they seemed trapped by the circuitous exit lanes of the mall parking lot, were the most excruciating. Once they were out on Highway 18, they sped along silently for several minutes, past the trailer campground and the Marble Monuments store and the Pioneer gas station advertising firewood, ice, and marshmallows. Fran still had the air conditioning on, but set to low.

The whole time she sat in silence in the passenger seat, Jean tried to unravel her dislike for the woman next to her. She wondered if it was based mostly or even entirely on money. She thought it was possible. She had a suspicion that Fran wanted to be her friend because of the flattering contrast between their household incomes. Perhaps that was unfair, but in her view of Fran that idea was too big to avoid. There were also Fran's constant putdowns of the town Jean had grown up in, which was the next thing to insulting Jean herself, and the way in which Fran seemed to regard Jean's ceramics as the peculiar, amusing product of a slightly addled mind. And something even less definable, something about Fran's apparent insistence on being her friend, as if it were already a *fait accompli* and Jean had no say in the matter. Individually these were really no more irritating than the habits of other people she genuinely liked. But somehow they added up to something overpowering, an aversion that had an almost physical dimension, the way allergens could confuse the natural defences and make your whole body itch. That's how Jean felt just now. Fran's personality was an irritation that had entered her cells and made her inflamed.

She sighed. "Have you ever been to the Finger Lakes District, Fran?"

"You don't have to make conversation with me," said Fran. Her two hands gripped the wheel and she stared bolt-straight toward the road in front. "I'm nobody. Just consider me your chauffeur."

"No, Fran. If it's all right, I'll consider you someone who was very thoughtful and helpful to me today. And someone I was probably not very fair to. And I apologize."

Beside her, Fran stared hard at the road, her hands pale with pressure on the wheel. Then she took in a breath and lifted her chin.

"We have, actually, Jim and I," she said. "We went about five summers ago, to visit his sister before she had her surgery. Parts of it are pretty."

Jean wished she could take a pill to suppress her Fran reaction. But there was no such thing.

Chapter 11

Milt was such a . . . well, Jean didn't want to even think the word, because it was childish and spiteful. But he *was* what he *was*, and that was why she could not drive to the Finger Lakes District the way she had planned. The path from cause to effect was clearly marked, it seemed to Jean, carved out with a machete from A to B, and about this she was not in a mood to be "understanding," as Milt had so hopefully put it.

It all came down to laziness and procrastination. When the garage had told Milt, weeks before, that the brakes on the Hyundai needed to be replaced, he had mentioned it to Jean on the phone. She'd still been at her mother's at the time, her attention entirely consumed by matters of pain and loss and impending death, which effectively obliterated any other small concern. So there was nothing she could do but assume that Milt was seeing to the tiny, minuscule brakes problem. If the garage said that your brakes needed to be replaced, you went about having them replaced; there didn't seem to be a terrific variety of options available to a person of common sense. But Milt had chosen the option of not feeling any urgency about the problem, the option of taking no action. And then, after he'd rushed off yesterday in the car and while he was driving to wherever it was that he was driving, the brakes had failed, and Milt had smashed into the back of Harv Clute's Dodge pickup.

"You should be happy I'm alive," said Milt, pouting, as he washed egg yolk and marmalade residue from the morning dishes. "It was lucky I was wearing my seatbelt."

It was luckier that Harv Clute was not of a mind to send the claim to insurance because he was planning to ditch the old Dodge anyway. And luck wouldn't even have been a factor if Milt had been a person of normal inclination and fixed the brakes when he was supposed to. These were Jean's thoughts as she sat at the dining room table reading the entertainment page of the *Star-Lookout*. She just didn't say them out loud because she was still observing an angry silence over the Finger Lakes, which she couldn't drive to now because the car was well and truly in the shop, and was probably going to be there for *weeks*.

"Why do you even want to go to that Finger Lakes place anyway?" asked Milt from the kitchen, where he seemed to be doing an unusually thorough job on the egg yolk.

"Why did you need the car all of a sudden?" she piped from the dining room. "That question has yet to be answered."

Milt stopped washing and sighed. "I wanted to go pick strawberries. As a surprise for dinner. So, too bad, now it's not a surprise any more."

"Strawberries? Since when have you ever wanted to pick strawberries?"

"I just got the idea."

"Out of the blue."

"Yes."

"Interesting."

"What?"

"I said that's interesting."

"Not really."

"Not really, no. More like extremely odd."

Considering everything, as she read the paper in the light from the window and tried to ignore Milt, Jean decided it was probably just as well that she hadn't driven off to the Finger Lakes and presented herself on Cheryl Nunley's doorstep without any warning. She'd been caught up with the excitement of Welland locating her long-lost friend, and her mind had conjured up all sorts of wonderful scenarios. Emotional, storybook scenes of meeting and reacquaintance and apology. But, thinking practically, who knew what sort of state Cheryl might be in? She had looked miserable and lost in the picture Welland showed her, a woman without hope, and if that was any indication of Cheryl's current condition, then someone showing up out of nowhere, someone from the past who dredged up difficult memories, might make things even worse. So in a way it was a blessing that Milt had made all that trouble with the car; he had saved her from what her mother had frequently called her "reckless enthusiasm." Although the fact that he had saved her from anything was something Milt would breathe his last without ever knowing.

Instead, she decided that some time within the next couple of days, when she had a quiet moment to herself, she would call Cheryl on the telephone, and take things from there. It wasn't as picture-perfect, but it was more prudent.

And yet, Jean was unsatisfied. All those thoughts of the past and of reuniting with Cheryl, all that joyful anticipation, not to mention the lingering sorrow of knowing Dorothy was gone and being shipped to Halifax in a jar, had left her yearning to spend time with someone with whom she had a real history. Someone who went back. And the best she could do for now was Adele.

It was a long shot, because Adele was by far the busiest person she knew, but Jean got out her cellphone and started dialing. Washing dishes in the kitchen, Milt would have heard this:

"Adele? . . . It's Jean . . . Sorry to bother you at work . . . I'm sitting here looking at the entertainment section in the paper, and there's a little review here for that new musical *Hold Everything* at the McArthur Theatre . . . Yes, sometimes the *Star-Lookout* does reviews for the big shows. We're not total hicks here, you know! Anyway, they say it's really good. If I got some last-minute tickets, is that something you'd like to see with me tonight? . . . Oh, that's wonderful. I'll call you right back."

When Jean closed up her phone, Milt appeared at the door from the kitchen with a dishrag in his hand.

"You're going into the city?"

"Yes, Adele and I are going to the theatre." Jean found the box office number at the bottom of the review and circled it with a pencil.

"How are you getting there?"

"Well, I guess I'll have to take the bus, won't I?"

"Why didn't you ask me to come along?"

"I didn't think you'd be interested."

Milt made a little coughy sound of incredulity. "I teach English," he said. "I love the theatre. Why don't you know that about me?"

Jean recognized this as the start of a spiralling conversation, like one of those pinwheel galaxies out in the universe that keep spinning and spinning without end for all eternity, and long ago she had learned that the best way to squelch a discussion like this with Milt was to leave the room completely. She got up from the table and patted him on the arm.

"Why don't you help me," she said, "by calling the bus station and finding out the schedule for buses to the city?" Then she took her cellphone and the entertainment page from the paper and locked herself in the bathroom.

There were buses at four and six and eight p.m., Milt discovered, and because the ride from Kotemee to the city took an hour and a half, Jean decided she would board the early one. Before that, she told Milt, she wanted to check on her mother's house.

She walked over to Blanchard Avenue, up past the elm and beech trees that alternated along the south side of the street, thanks to a town initiative decades before, to the large olive-green house at the top of the hill. When she unlocked the front door, she walked through the foyer and up the stairs, directly to her mother's bedroom.

Inside Marjorie's closet, on the top shelf, sat a large, circular hatbox decorated in peach and cream stripes. Jean took it down.

All her life, the hatbox had contained a wide-brimmed raffia sunhat that had been an object of Jean's fantasies as a child because it had seemed to her the sort of hat that Queen Elizabeth II would wear. Her mother had bought it one Fifties summer during a visit to Martha's Vineyard, before Jean was born, and had worn it nearly every summer since – but only at the lake, and only during the two weeks of vacation she allowed herself annually. The rest of the time the hat had stayed in the box, Marjorie refusing to take it out even when Jean, at age eight or nine, had pleaded tearfully to be allowed to try it on in front of a mirror. There had been something satisfied, even proud, about Marjorie's refusal. The hat was for holidays, and other than that she would never take it out of the box, never. "That's how things last," she had told Jean.

In the days after Marjorie died, before the funeral, Jean had begun the task of sorting through her mother's things. She hadn't given a thought to the hat in years, but when she'd opened the closet her eyes had drifted up almost involuntarily to the striped box on the shelf. She'd taken it down, of course – there'd been no one to stop her – and when she'd opened it and pushed aside the tissue, she'd had to admit that in one sense her mother had been right. The hat showed none of its decades of age. Even the band of pale pink ribbon inside seemed nearly new.

There was a moment when Jean, holding the hat in her hands, could easily have set it on her head and glanced up: the mirror was just there, on the vanity at the end of the bed. But although she had realized her opportunity, she'd chosen to ignore it. There were no fantasies attached to the hat now, and wearing it – being allowed to wear it – conferred no special status. Instead, Jean had simply stuffed the hat into one of the several heavy-duty garbage bags to be filled with dresses, blouses, and nightgowns that she pulled from her mother's closet. All of these she'd planned to send to the Goodwill, where she knew the hat would be touched and tried on by the multitudes.

Now, in her mother's bedroom, Jean set the hatbox on the bed and lifted off the lid. Inside were all of Marjorie's unused jars and bottles of prescription drugs. It had seemed a kind of sin to throw out such expensive medicines and, emptied of hat and tissue, the box had been the perfect container.

Among the drugs were a package of disposable latex gloves and a month's supply of Fentanyl patches. Each of these patches consisted of a wide, squishy pouch, like an individual serving of strawberry jam. But instead of jam it was filled with clear Fentanyl gel, a painkiller a hundred times more powerful than morphine, which passed through an adhesive membrane into the skin. Jean had learned to don the protective gloves and strip and adhere one of these patches to her mother's upper arm whenever the pain became too great. It occurred to her now that all she would have had to do for her mother was attach a second and a third patch to her arm, and her torment would have been over. Nothing could have been easier. But those days had been quite turbulent and confusing, and with her mother writhing in the jaws of her agony, Jean hadn't been thinking properly. Instructions on a package had been a kind of anchor for her, keeping her steady.

Now everything was calm. Her thinking was altogether clearer and her duty to her friends was plain. The only question left for Jean was whether she was strong enough to follow through, or whether her emotions would get in the way and ruin everything.

She sat for a moment on the edge of the bed and, as she did, she noticed the oddest thing. The bed was made. The pink marseille bedspread had been carefully smoothed and draped. And Jean realized that of course it was she herself who had dressed the bed with fresh sheets and pillow cases, and taken pains to pull and tuck everything tight, the way her mother liked, and she had done all of this an hour or perhaps two after Marjorie's corpse had been wheeled away. A thing her mother would often say came back to her: *Jean Vale Horemarsh, what could possibly have been going through your mind?* She had heard that question on so many occasions. The time she'd stayed up till four in the morning listening to Beach Boys albums the night before her Grade 11 exams. The time she'd cut a big hole into the middle pages of her copy of *Pride and Prejudice*. The time when she was thirteen and she'd painted a big blue star on her cheek for school photo day. And the time she was six and Marjorie had lifted the lid of the garbage can to find all of Jean's stuffies mouldy and wet at the bottom, and then a week after that when she'd caught Jean walking home with soaked shoes.

Each time, in the hot light of her mother's glare, Jean had struggled to answer that question, even though she had always had reasons for doing the things she'd done. She'd listened to the Beach Boys all night because she'd been nervous about her exams and Brian Wilson's candy floss voice was the only thing that soothed the worry out of her mind. She'd carved a secret well into her *Pride and Prejudice* because Andrew Jr. was stealing her baby-sitting money and she needed a place to hide it, and she knew he'd never in a million years think of opening a book. She'd painted a star on her right cheek because on the left side of her face was a super-big pimple and she was trying to use distraction. The sopping stuffies in the garbage can were something she could never talk about to her mother, and so neither could she talk about the shoes. Because they were soaking wet for the reason that she had been sitting with her feet in the Mott Park fountain. You had to have *something* in the water when you made a wish, or the wishes couldn't ride to Heaven on the water jets. And it was important that her wishes get there, because she was asking the puppies to forgive her mother, and the stuffies to forgive her, for what had been done to them.

It sometimes occurred to Jean that her mother's view of her as frivolous and impractical might have been different if only she'd been able to answer the question of what had been going through her mind. But then again, here in her mother's bedroom, she had to admit to herself that she had no idea why she had made the bed like that. Not the faintest clue.

She opened a plastic shopping bag, dumped in the packages of Fentanyl, and grabbed the disposable gloves while she was at it. She slid the striped hat box onto the top shelf of the closet, and she left.

Milt stood with his hands in his pockets in the hallway of their house on Edgeworth, staring into their bedroom watching Jean as she rolled on antiperspirant. She had told him not to expect her back that evening; it would be late when she and Adele got out of the theatre and so she'd catch a bus in the morning instead.

"I guess that makes sense," he said.

"What are you going to do with yourself?" she asked, stepping into her sleeveless emerald rayon dress.

Milt shrugged. "I guess I can do anything I want. Bachelor's night out."

It was the sort of thing Milt said when he was being pouty, so Jean chose to ignore it. "I wish you could make some friends," she said, "so that you're not lonely on nights when I'm away."

"I'm not lonely."

Jean knew that was just defensiveness talking, because it was a simple fact that men just didn't make strong, lasting friendships the way women did. They had no awareness of themselves as part of a community, of being woven into something greater than themselves. Compared to women, men just floated unconnected through life like helium balloons lost on the wind.

Feeling sad for Milt for being like a balloon, Jean turned around and let him zip up her dress. After that she put on her black-and-gold bolero jacket and checked it all out in the mirror.

"Nice," said Milt.

It was an ensemble better suited to cooler weather, but Jean was feeling lately that her arms were getting flabby and the jacket hid those well, and the only other theatre-appropriate thing she owned that fit her just now was the black jacquard dress she had worn to the funeral, and she thought she would leave that in her closet for a while. As for shoes, she pulled out a pair of black open-toed pumps and a pair of gold sandals and asked Milt for his opinion.

"Black ones," he said. But she chose the sandals instead, because they looked that little bit snazzier. Milt muttered something about not being needed and wandered away, probably to get himself a snack.

Jean touched up her lipstick in the mirror – a rich cinnamon red that just jumped from her fair skin and perfectly complemented her orangey-blond hair. When she was done she popped the lipstick into her boxy overnight case. The plastic bag from her mother's house was tucked away in a drawer nearby, and she reached for it and took out some disposable gloves and four Fentanyl patches. There was momentum in all of these movements and she carried them out without thinking, but now with the patches in her hand the momentum stopped. The truth of it was that Jean wasn't quite sure what she expected of herself in taking the patches to Adele's. She knew what she *hoped* of herself, and it was in the spirit of this hope that she had brought the patches home from her mother's. But now, in the act of packing, the patches in her hand seemed to suggest something more certain than hope. They traced a route on a map in pen, with a big black *X* at the destination. Since her wave of missing Dorothy, Jean wasn't yet convinced she could go all the way to that *X*.

Milt was oddly distant when she went to kiss him goodbye. He sat on the end of the couch by the living room window, his grey eyes focusing into the distance as if his mind were consumed by something complicated and serious. It might have been a posture for her benefit, Jean considered, or it might have meant that he was quietly condemning himself for something . . . perhaps a lack of friends. It was all right for a husband to quietly condemn himself once in a while; it helped to maintain a certain equilibrium in the house. But Jean thought there was a chance that she'd been too quarrelsome with Milt over the last few days. She dropped her bag and her little black evening purse and sat on the arm of the couch. In both hands she took the heavy cheeks of his face, felt the smooth, shaved skin against her palms, and steered his head toward her the way she might move a roast of beef, looking for the best place to carve.

For a moment he resisted meeting her eyes, like a child, and then she said, "Milt!" and he relented. "I don't want you being sad that I'm going out tonight with Adele," she said. "I'm sorry if I've been . . ." She stopped and wondered what she had been.

"Kind of mean?" Milt offered.

"Or not as nice as I usually am." She stared into his eyes, looking for a twinkle. "It's just us going through a transition, getting back to normal. We'll be fine."

"I dunno . . . you've seemed a bit . . ." Milt hesitated, and Jean joggled his face so that he would complete his thought. "I guess a bit hard or something," he continued, "since you got back from your mom's."

"Hard," she said. She let go of his face.

"Or something."

Jean tried not to bristle too obviously, because she'd been hoping to leave with both of them in a pleasant frame of mind. But the word grated on her. It seemed to be the view of men that whenever a woman wasn't nurturing, the way a fantasy mother might be, or pliant like a prostitute, she was automatically hard. There was no middle ground for a woman; in the eyes of men she was like a dial with three positions: nurturing, pliant . . . or hard. So if she was determined, she was hard. If she was tired, she was hard. If she failed to suffer fools. If she made snap judgments. If she held others to a high standard. If she was practical . . . then she was hard. This was as good a reason as any why women needed women friends – so there would be someone around to see them as they really were.

Jean cleared her throat, looked down at Milt, and forced herself to smile. "I apologize," she said.

Milt nodded, and his face softened a little. "I'm sorry too," he said. "I guess you've had a pretty shitty time with your mom and then Dorothy." He shook his head. "Dorothy. Wow."

Jean leaned over and kissed Milt on the forehead. "Don't worry about Dorothy," she said. "She did all right."

She boarded the bus ten minutes before it was to leave and found a seat next to a girl of about fifteen, with lanky blond hair, green eye shadow that glistened like algae in a pool, and dark-green polish on her nails.

"I sometimes use a glaze that colour," Jean said to the girl, smiling. "In the ceramics that I do." But the girl was piping music into her ears and didn't seem to hear, and appeared to have no interest in a middle-aged woman sitting next to her. Jean imagined that the girl's mother, whoever she was, would be hoping for and expecting more pleasant and engaging behaviour from her daughter in such a situation. But . . . no. She supposed it was impossible for a parent to know how much of the training and effort devoted to a child really soaked in and presented itself to the world as evidence of proper upbringing, or how much of it glanced off like so much light rain against a windowpane, or how much sat just below the surface of a daughter's consciousness, like mould beneath a tile, waiting for the right conditions to bloom.

The drive to the city went as it usually did, the route graduating from two-lane to six-lane highways, and clear sailing most of the way. All the traffic was coming from the other direction, cars filled with city workers headed home. Jean watched out the window and grieved again at how far the new housing developments stretched. Block after treeless block, houses hammered together without any sense of history or place. None of the people Jean knew lived out here. These people hardly ever came into the centre of town. Did they even know where they lived? More and more, Kotemee was becoming a bedroom community, tied irrevocably to the city. To a future that had nothing to do with its past. Soon it would feel pressures it had never felt before, and it would be forced to change in ways no one could ever have imagined. And with change came death – the death of whatever had been, to be replaced by something that was no better or worse, just different. Just unrecognizable.

Beside her the teenaged girl took a green-skinned apple out of a bag, and a paper towel. As the bus hummed along the highway, Jean sat with her hands in her lap. And though she'd had no intention of watching the girl eat, she soon found herself fascinated.

Beside her, the girl took a bite of the apple, and chewed for a while, and then she held up the paper towel like a plate under her chin and spat out the rumpled skin. Again and again the girl took a bite and chewed, carefully ingesting the flesh but eschewing the peel, until after ten or fifteen minutes a mound of green, translucent remains, like the desiccated husks of a dozen praying mantises, sat in the paper towel in her hand. Jean had never seen anything like it. And while a part of her felt a middle-aged urge to explain to this child that she was rejecting the most nutritious part of the apple, another part thought she saw in this girl's actions the way of life itself. How it consumed, scraped clean, all that was sweet and good in a person, until nothing remained but the bitter, chewed-up shell.

So that they would have time to eat before heading to the theatre, the plan was for Jean to meet Adele at six o'clock at a new restaurant that she'd raved about over the phone. It seemed that Adele was always raving about something or other – a new restaurant, an artisanal tart bakery, a German Expressionist movie, a Korean plum – and whatever it was was available only in the city, and neither Jean nor anyone she knew had ever driven there to find out whether it or anything was nearly as nice as Adele claimed it was. So Jean was eager to see what the fuss was all about regarding the restaurant called Vedøy, named after the owner, Gudrun Vedøy, who was a Norwegian former model whom Adele had met at an Endicker Trust shareholders meeting.

"She's connected to the Norwegian mafia," Adele had murmured into the phone. "But you cannot tell that to anyone."

"I didn't even know there was a Norwegian mafia," said Jean.

"Oh, there is," replied Adele, "and they'll carve out your heart and serve it on a Triscuit. But that's the last you'll hear of it from me."

The bus pulled into the midtown station at half-past five and Jean got off, saying a cheery goodbye to her young seatmate who ignored her completely, which was only as Jean had expected. Being pleasant to a rude teenager was her way of girding herself for the ordeal of venturing into the teeming city, and indeed, once she was out onto the sidewalk she was immediately engulfed in what seemed like the whole of humanity rushing to catch the subway, and she gripped her overnight bag tightly and bent into the oncoming squall of flesh and fashion.

She had to go five blocks north on Sander Street, and then east on Esais Road for three, and at first Jean was torn about whether to take a cab. But walking a block in her gold sandals, in the heat of the day, through crowds of attractive young working women, past all of the mirrored glass buildings whose reflections could not have been less flattering if they had been designed for a carnival funhouse, made the decision for her. She hailed a taxi and asked the driver to turn up the air conditioning as high as it would go.

Taking the cab allowed Jean to get to the restaurant twenty minutes early, so she had a chance to tug open Vedøy's heavy, hammered-steel door and become thoroughly uncomfortable before Adele arrived. Greeting her was a severely cheekboned hostess who stood about six-foot five on her wedgy heels and wore a flowing sage ensemble that wafted against her protruding bones without her having to move, so that she seemed as slender and cool as a river reed and as likely to strike up a conversation, and made Jean, in her dark green rayon dress and her stiff, arm-hiding bolero jacket, feel like a bloated Spanish toad.

The restaurant's interior rose to a height above her and seemed constructed mostly of metal, like a sea-going destroyer, the furnishings and walls accented here and there with a brass stud or a bit of wood, like shards from some pitiful vessel smashed against the ship's hull. With a smile that was merely a straight line stretched, the hostess plucked up two menus and wafted Jean past empty table after empty table toward a far corner banquette and sat her, as if deliberately, so that she was forced to stare at her reflection in a pillar clad with shiny hammered tin. But *reflections* was a more appropriate word because each of the hammered divots shone back at Jean a small, distorted image of her face, so that for what was probably fifteen minutes but seemed like an hour she had dozens of short-browed, wide-cheeked Jean heads gaping and blinking and gradually reddening before her eyes.

And that was why, when Adele arrived in her fabulous cocktail attire and exclaimed, "Darling, don't you look lovely!" Jean finally burst into tears.

Adele flung herself down onto the banquette and wrapped Jean in her arms and listened as Jean explained about trying to look her best and feeling as though the city was pitted against her. And Adele offered the sort of comforting advice that reminded Jean why she'd been so fond of this woman for so long.

"Screw the city!" Adele said. "Let's have some aquavit!"

They ordered two small glasses of ice-cold aquavit from the waitress and then two more, and though Jean had never had it before, and had never been terribly fond of the taste of caraway, she found herself lapping it up. And when it was time to order food Adele said to ignore the menu because she had been told personally by Gudrun Vedøy what to order, and Jean just let it come.

They had little *lutefisk* cubes on tiny mounds of *surkat*. Adele said something to Jean about lye in the fish, that's what made *lutefisk lutefisk*, and Jean just laughed because that was absurd and the sound of *lutefisk* was funny and what were all these little bugs in the cabbage? Those were caraway seeds, Adele explained, and Jean realized she was already rather drunk. They had *sursild* with pickled onions and *sursild* with pickled beets, all served on crunchy little bread wafers that fell apart when Jean bit into them and tumbled down her chin, which shouldn't have happened but just seemed to anyway. They *sure slid*, giggled Jean. And she kept drinking the aquavit because Adele kept ordering it, which was surprising to Jean because she had never thought of Adele as being much of a drinker. Although she did remember one time when the two of them had been in a college dorm room together. And they'd been drinking something, or smoking something. Maybe it was both! And they'd had a lot of fun until Jean had decided she had to go home, and pretty soon after Adele had left for Cornell.

There were more plates of pickled this and fishy that. *Fishy, fishy*. There may have been some cured moose as well. *Moooose* meat – was that even legal? And Jean just marvelled at how well aquavit seemed to complement every kind of Norwegian food, making everything so much tastier than it had any right to be. And Adele was so sweet, thought Jean, for making her feel better after falling into the dumps the way she had. The city wasn't so bad, now that Adele was here. Adele. Adele. She wasn't stuck up at all. Natalie could not have been more wrong. Adele. Was. So. Sweet. Jean put her head back on Adele's arm, and watched her as she ate little creamy pastries one-handed. She admired her straight,

straight hair and her porcelain ear and the corner of her fine-drawn mouth. Adele was so . . . something.

"You're so *something*," Jean said, and giggled.

She wasn't pretty. Not really. But she was good-looking. She looked good, the way her jaw moved as she ate, the way her lips moved as she sipped. *Handsome* was the word. Would Adele like to be called handsome? Would anyone? Jean didn't know. It seemed like a dangerous word, and she giggled just thinking it. *Handsome.* But that's what Adele was.

"You're so handsome, Adele," said Jean. And Adele looked at Jean and smiled. She didn't seem to mind at all.

Pretty soon they were out on the street, walking in the summer night air. Cars somewhere were honking. Because it was the city. Jean seemed to remember having tickets to the theatre. That was why she was all dressed up! She twirled on the sidewalk to let Adele see her outfit, and then she had to rest against the side of a big building. Adele said it was too late for the theatre and too dark to see and they should just go back to her condominium, have some more to drink, and relax. Jean had never seen Adele's condominium, which she'd bought a few years before, and she thought that was a very good idea. Then she stopped.

"My bag!"

"Your bag?" said Adele.

"My overnight bag! I can't leave it!"

"Is that it in your hand?"

Jean looked at her hand and there it was. Just like magic.

They climbed into a taxi and Jean lay her head on Adele's shoulder as they drove along the city streets with lights flashing past and people out having a good time. Young people and people walking their dogs and nice older couples and crazy loud people on the sidewalk, everyone had a good time in the city, thought Jean.

"Are we having a good time?" she asked Adele.

"Yes," Adele said.

"Good," said Jean. And she held Adele's hand and closed her eyes.

When they got to Adele's building the lobby was marbled and empty, and they took the elevator up to the twenty-third floor. Jean leaned against Adele and kept her eyes closed because the elevator light was so bright. She felt a little wobbly but Adele held her so she wouldn't fall, and Jean was so thankful that they hadn't gone to the theatre because . . . well . . . it just wouldn't have been good.

The elevator door opened and Adele steered Jean down the corridor to her apartment, and when she opened it and they walked in, Jean just went . . .

"Wow."

It was a great big amazing apartment with an amazing view of the big black sky and the sparkling city below, and amazing big jumbly art on the walls, wow, and an amazing big wide couch constructed of blocks of cushions that Jean decided she had to flop down on that instant.

"Wow," she said, looking up at the ceiling. "This is an amazing couch."

"Wine?" said Adele.

"Do you have any more aquavit? I think I love aquavit."

"No, I'm afraid not." She took off her earrings. "But I have a lovely Muscadet."

"Are you going to rave about the Muscadet?" Jean giggled. "Because if it's here in the city, in Adele Farbridge's apartment, it must be the most amazing Muscadet anybody has ever tasted."

"It's very good."

Jean thrust a hand toward the ceiling. "Then I will drink it!"

In a moment, Adele brought a tray with two glasses of wine

and some cheese and crackers. Jean was staring at the buttons of her bolero jacket as Adele set the tray on a low coffee table and sat down beside her. Jean would have looked up, but the buttons commanded her attention.

"I hate these buttons," said Jean, taking hold of the glass of wine Adele placed in her hand. "I hate this jacket."

"It looks quite nice on you."

"I only wore it because my arms are fat."

"No they're not."

Jean sat up suddenly, spilling some of the wine on her hand before she could set it down, and wrestled with the jacket to get it off her. It might have been alive it was so hard to get off! But she did finally manage it, flinging it across the room, and then she showed Adele the arm that was closest. "See?" she said, squinting. "Fat, flabby, middle-aged arm, that's what that is."

Adele reached out and drew her fingertips down Jean's skin from her shoulder to her elbow. "I think it's a lovely arm," she said.

Jean giggled. She felt goosebumps rising on all her limbs and a shiver going right down to her toes. And then another shiver, because Adele leaned over and kissed her on the cheek. Suddenly Jean's throat felt parched and she reached out to grab her wine glass.

"You relax," said Adele, rising to her feet. "I'll be back in a minute."

While Adele was gone, Jean lounged on the couch and drank most of the wine in her glass. She wasn't sure it was the best thing to be doing, because she was very obviously drunk. But she didn't see what actual harm it could do, and anyway, she felt safe in the big wide apartment with the whole dark world outside.

She called out, "Why have I never been here before?"

"I didn't think you were interested," came Adele's reply from another room.

Jean swivelled her head against the couch cushions and looked around her. There were plants in pots, she noticed, flanking the wide view of the city, and she lurched to her feet to examine them. It took her no time at all to realize they were Virginia chain ferns. The spores on the underside of each delicate leaflet were gathered in what looked for all the world like a series of tiny chain links. This was the very plant that had first got Jean interested in greenery; she'd seen one in a professor's solarium and couldn't get over how something as ordinary as a leaf, the leaf of a plain old fern, could reveal itself to be so fascinating. And when she was young and investigating the possibilities of her life, this discovery seemed to tell her something about the world. There were flowers that got all the attention, and leaves that did all the work, and lots of those leaves were dull and boring. But if that's all you thought about leaves, you missed something. Because if you looked closely, if you didn't get fooled into thinking one leaf was like any other, you found out that some of them were truly bizarre.

Jean was holding one of the leaflets in her hand when Adele came up behind her and stood very close.

"Adele, these are my favourite ferns in the whole world. I can't believe you have them. They're Virginia –"

"Virginia chain ferns," said Adele. "You told me about them."

"I did? When was that?"

"When we were in college. We used to talk a lot back then, late into the night, remember?"

"I remember we got drunk." Jean giggled.

"Do you remember I used to give you back rubs?" Standing behind her, Adele laid her hands lightly on Jean's shoulders and began to rub and squeeze.

"Mmm," said Jean, closing her eyes. "That feels nice."

Jean tipped her head forward a little, let Adele's fingers slide over the straps of her dress and scale the tense incline from her shoulders to her neck. She hadn't realized how stressful the last weeks had been, and how all of the tension had migrated to those particular muscles, and now here was Adele doing just the right thing to make it all go away. She was like a kind of angel, and such a good friend. Her hands were so strong, and yet so soft, and they seemed to know just where to go and what to do. When Jean was thinking the word "wine," or maybe she said it out loud, Adele's hands brought more wine. When she felt very sleepy, they led her to a soft place to lie down. To Jean, with her eyes closed, anything Adele's hands did seemed to be right. So when they slipped down over her arms, and her hips, and then her breasts, that felt nice too, and right in a way, if a little unexpected. Jean was feeling quite hazy, and just then what was right and what was unexpected were blending and floating together in a very interesting way, becoming part of the same misty cloud of experience. And when Jean felt the tickle of hair on her face as Adele bent over her, and the warmth of her breath, and the pressure on her mouth from Adele's lips and her tongue, that was also unexpected. That was quite unexpected, actually. Jean thought the word, "Oh," or maybe she said it out loud. And then she opened her eyes and saw that Adele had no clothes on, and they were in her bed, and she said it again.

"Oh."

Adele lay down on the bed with a lazy smile and drew a finger across Jean's cheek to brush away a hair.

"Adele," said Jean. Her head was clearing rather quickly. "What's happening?"

"We're just enjoying ourselves."

Adele seemed to enjoy sliding the straps of her rayon dress off her shoulders, Jean noticed, and reaching around and pulling down her zipper. Being naked and having other people be naked seemed to be something she enjoyed very much.

"I'm just a bit confused," said Jean.

Adele kissed her shoulder. "Why are you confused?"

"Well," Jean put her hands over her eyes and tried to focus, "I know we're very good friends. Because we've known each other for so long. But now I think you're taking off my dress."

"I am."

"Right. So . . ." She watched as Adele pulled down the top of her dress to reveal first her left breast, and then her right one. "It's just unexpected, that's all."

Adele began to explain to Jean, and as she explained, she rhythmically kissed Jean's breasts, first the left and then the right, so that Jean found it very hard to concentrate on exactly what Adele was saying. But it seemed that Adele had felt this way for a very long time, since she and Jean had roomed together in college. And it had always been Adele's hope that one day she would be able to make love to Jean. In fact, she explained that one night she had gotten Jean very drunk and she had tried her best to seduce her. But before it could happen, Jean had sat up and announced that she had to go home. And because at the time Jean was living with Adele in the residence, "home" meant Kotemee. Jean had just packed a bag that night and left. She was gone for three days, and during that time Adele realized that she was in love with Jean, and she could never have her. That was quite clear. So she decided to do what her parents had always wanted her to do, which was to study economics at Cornell.

"You left art college because of me?" said Jean.

"I just thought it was easier that way. I never brought it up because I was happy just to be your friend, and I didn't want to risk losing you again."

Jean thought that might have been the sweetest thing she had ever heard. It was certainly nicer than anything Milt had ever said. So as she lay on Adele's bed, with the top of her green rayon dress bunched around her rib cage, exposing her breasts to this woman she had known, but not really known, for so long, Jean collected her courage like someone gathering tomatoes after a frost. Carefully, uncertainly, hoping to make the best of what was there.

"Adele," she said, "is this very important to you?"

Adele was blowing a tickling stream of air down her neck from her ear to the ridge of her collarbone. She stopped and said, "Yes."

"If this happens, will it make you very happy?"

"It will make me wonderfully happy."

"Then . . . we should probably get this dress all the way off."

There was no bluff or bluster to Adele Farbridge now, no city airs, and Jean wondered if that rarefied manner of hers, which so grated on Natalie and others, had for all these years been a kind of shield. Well, at least now she saw her the way she really was: worn by years, more brunette than Jean had realized, and needing love like any poor soul.

When Adele lay back on the sheets, Jean was able to see for the first time the long white scar and puckered skin where her friend's left breast had been. In the bell of light from the bedside table, it had its own kind of beauty, and Adele seemed not to mind when she drew her finger along that sinister line, and over the small drumlins of flesh, from the place her nipple had been to the hollow beneath her arm. Lying against Adele's small, marked frame, feeling the velveteen brush of her tight skin, Jean was aware of her own body's fluid expanse, its carnal heft, like the weight of her responsibility. And so, still just a bit light-headed, she embarked on her quest to make Adele happy, to receive the pleasure Adele seemed determined to provide, and to give the same in return.

The receiving, it turned out, was . . . oh . . . remarkably easy. It was tender and deep, felt both sisterly and sinful, and Jean was quick to compliment Adele again and again and again. The giving, she quickly found, was the more stressful part of the exchange. Not that she didn't know what she was doing. She'd spent so many years willing Milt's appendages into various movements and places she had a ready catalogue of what worked and didn't. But Jean knew what was coming, there was no doubt about that now. Adele had sacrificed the happiness of being with her (in that way) for the sake of their friendship, and Jean could not let her down. And if she'd needed one last sign of the rightness of her course, it came in the form of Adele's scar. The moment she saw that she knew she could never abandon her friend to the lottery of malignancy. So as Jean made her way down the slippery paths, she felt the force of her obligations. The pleasure she gave couldn't be just any pleasure. It had to be the greatest gratification Adele had ever known. A part of Jean was glad to be able to give Adele that gift, but as she worked away, measuring the increments of her success in moans, she felt sympathy for men she had known who had crumbled under similar pressure.

But after a while, and another glass of wine, Jean felt that she had done her very best. Adele lay dreamy and languorous on the pillow beside her, and the air they breathed seemed to glow.

"Are you happy?" Jean asked.

"Oh, yes," Adele groaned.

"Good. Do you know what I'd like to do now?"

"What?"

"I'd like to give you a back rub."

"Really? On top of everything else? You don't have to do that."

"I want to," said Jean. "You just get comfortable on your stomach and I'll do the rest."

She slid out of bed and padded naked to the living room where her overnight bag lay. On her feet, moving amid the apartment's hard edges and monochrome palette, Jean felt a little fatter, less in proportion, than she had in bed, more awkwardly aware of her townish self. But as she took up the hard, leather handle of her overnight bag she saw again the Virginia chain ferns. She knew now that Adele had bought them as a way of keeping her close, and she felt surer than ever that she was doing the right thing. To Jean, the affection she felt for Adele in that moment, a deeper bond than she had ever thought possible, would be rendered sham and disgraceful, a contemptible hoax, if she walked away now. If she condemned her elegant friend to the crass blatancies of a painful, unlovely end.

In the bedroom, she caressed Adele's legs, eliciting a quiet purr, then climbed onto her back, straddling her like a palomino, and opened her bag beside her. She rooted around for her nail file and laid it on the bed beside her. She plucked out the vinyl gloves, thin as plastic wrap, and pulled them on.

"What are those for?" said Adele, watching with one eye.

"Oh, I'm going to use something on your back and it's gooey," said Jean. "But anyway you shouldn't be peeking. Turn your head." She made a twirling motion with her gloved finger and waited until Adele obeyed. Then she pulled out the first Fentanyl patch.

"What are you doing back there?" said Adele.

"You're supposed to be relaxing. Clear your mind."

Jean used the nail file to poke a hole right through the seal of the patch and the membrane underneath. She squeezed out the drug into a glassy blob in her hand and held it out over Adele's shoulder blades.

"This might be cold," said Jean. "Or hot. I'm not sure."

"You haven't used it before?"

"Just shush." She smeared it on quickly as Adele shivered, then she poked through the second and third patches, squeezed out the contents, and spread the gel with both hands over the whole of Adele's back.

"That stuff smells weird," said Adele. "But it feels warm already."

"You're enjoying it?"

"Mmmm. Why don't you lie on top of me? Squish around."

"No, I don't think so."

"Is that menthol or something? It's really going to my head." She paused as if to catch her breath. "Come on, lie down."

"Just relax." Jean tried to make the strokes of her back rub more forceful.

"Please?" Adele reached back and grabbed Jean's wrist, trying to pull her down onto her glistening skin.

"Stop it, silly!" Jean resisted for a moment and then didn't so much pull her forearm out of Adele's grip as find it released, and Adele's arm settled down at her side. In the bedside lamp's soft light Jean could see that the skin of her back no longer shone; the gel was soaking in quickly. She drew her gloved hands once more down Adele's back and rested them lightly on her shoulder blades, feeling the ebb of their rise and fall. Then she leaned down close to Adele's cheek, kissed her, and whispered into her ear, "Are you still happy?"

In reply, Adele gave a distant, ethereal whimper.

"I'm so glad."

Then Jean opened and smeared on the gel from the fourth patch, just to make sure.

Chapter 12

It was early Saturday morning, and so the bus that took Jean back to Kotemee was only a third full, a ragged crop of heads, mostly middle-aged tourists, day-trippers, a few mothers with toddlers half-crazed for a splash in a lake. Her overnight bag on the seat beside her, Jean sat looking out an east-facing window, letting the city outskirts, the scrublands, the farmers' fields earmarked for development all blur past her eyes, and the memories of her times with Adele run together like watercolours. She had tidied the apartment, washed and put away the wine glasses, pulled a duvet over Adele's clay-cool back. More than once, when they'd lived together during that year of art college, she'd done precisely the same thing after a late, wine-soaked night.

Milt, annoyingly, wasn't answering when she called at eight-thirty, so, slipping her phone back into her purse, she abandoned the idea of having him pick her up at the station. Then she had to give herself a little mental kick because, of course, the car wasn't available at all. It was sitting in a garage waiting for parts.

Hardly a cloud. And not too hot. Today would be a good day to be in the studio; the sidewalks would be filled with strollers from the city looking for ways to commemorate their trek into the hinterlands, something to show off to their friends, an artifact from that quaint little town. They'd rattle the bell of Jean's Expressions, look around with their noses up, and conduct their interrogations. *How long have you lived here? How do you pronounce it? Do you ever wish you were closer to the city? Is there any place to get a decent sandwich? Why just leaves? Don't you have anything with animals?*

Jean decided she could do without that today. She was, admittedly, a little hungover. And she was wistful about Adele. About leaving her there in the city, that place of noise and smoke and garbage and gangs. Living her whole life in the quiet of Kotemee, the city had always seemed to Jean to be a place where death – startling, violent, inexplicable death – happened every day, just one of the common transactions of a tumultuous urban existence. She wondered whether, in that savage swirl of mayhem, anyone would really notice that Adele Farbridge had ceased to be. There was a part of Jean that couldn't bear that thought. Another part was fine with it, admittedly, because the longer Adele went undiscovered the better it would be for Jean, and for the rest of her friends. But overall, she was wistful. Adele had shown her what true sacrifice for a friend looked like, and Jean knew that she had so much work to do to match her example. For Natalie and Louise and Cheryl . . . especially Cheryl. She had an awful lot to make up for there.

At a quarter to ten, with the sun in her eyes, Jean was carrying her overnight bag up the hill of Conmore Avenue from the bus station, crunching along the gritty shoulder in her gold sandals, wondering what she'd been thinking not to pack a proper pair of shoes. Three cars drove past her the wrong way carrying people she knew. They all waved a friendly hello and looked perplexed as to why she was walking. *My husband* . . . she wanted to tell them . . . *crashed our car.*

As she was coming to the brow of the hill she heard the sound of a vehicle slowing behind her and turned to see – what else? – Fran Knubel's Cadillac SUV. It had obviously just been washed, was still dripping sequins from the wheel wells, and it came to a stop right beside her. Fran, in the driver's seat, remotely lowered the passenger-side window.

"Need a lift, there?" said Fran from the cool, dark hollows of her monstrosity. "I wasn't going this way, but when I was coming out of the car wash I saw you getting off the bus and I figured you'd be getting tired."

Getting tired. In other words, thought Jean, Fran had waited until she'd covered four blocks in her sandals before offering her a ride, and also – and *worse* – Fran was of the opinion that four blocks was just about all the walking Jean could handle. Getting tired. As if Fran Knubel herself was an Olympian with an opal brooch. Jean regretted ever having apologized for what she'd said in the bookstore.

"No thanks!" She showed her a big wide smile. "I'm doing great!"

"Suit yourself," said Fran. A hidden motor whined as the passenger window climbed and then she started off up the road, the fat tires kicking up fans of roadside grit.

Within ten minutes Jean was home and launching her sandals across the foyer. She ripped the bolero jacket off her sweaty back and sent it halfway to the dining room, and for a moment she just stood in the front hall letting her chest heave and her temperature cool. Then she called out for Milt, and got no response. She limped a bit to the foot of the stairs.

"Milt!"

In the kitchen, she found unwashed dishes from what looked like the night before, including a pot with the remnants of chili caked into a hard tomato glaze. Upstairs, the bedroom looked tidy, except for a pair of Milt's beige socks on the floor. The flowered curtains were drawn and the bed made.

Jean let her green rayon dress fall around her feet, stripped off her underwear and unhooked her bra, and then stepped into the tub for the hottest, longest shower she could remember having in years. She leaned against the tiles with her eyes closed and let the spray do its worst, until she was pummelled numb on one side and turned around to let it have at the other.

Milt was still not home and Jean's skin was still sore as she propped a foot on the edge of the tub and dried off. Buffing her back and her legs with a fluffy cream towel, she decided to take advantage of the uncommon luxury of an empty house to call Cheryl. She dressed, and from her everyday purse she pulled out the sheet Welland had given her, with Cheryl's address in Bier Ridge and her phone number.

She lifted the receiver from the kitchen wall phone and punched the number in.

It rang once, twice . . . it rang five times as Jean's anxiety and anticipation steadily mounted. Then the rings stopped and she heard the click of the receiver being lifted and she was ready to burst. *Cheryl!* she opened her mouth to say. *Cheryl, it's me, Jean!* But there came a hollow clunk on the end of the line, the sound of the receiver being dropped, and after that a repeating percussive thud as she imagined it being dragged over a series of obstacles, or being used as a weapon to fend off an attacker, though she could hear no voices, no cries of anguish, just the dull *cunk, cunk* of the receiver meeting one hard surface after another, and in the background a strange whistling noise.

And then one word. It came out muddy and distant, low and

dark enough to have been the voice of a man, but Jean was sure it had come from a woman. She was sure that it was Cheryl. "Busy," said the voice. Except that it didn't sound like that. It sounded drawn out, angry, forced through clenched teeth. It sounded like *Buuusssssyyy*. And then the person on the end of the line hung up.

Jean didn't know what to think. She didn't know what to do. Cheryl had been right there, within reach of her voice. She dialled the number again and let the phone ring eight times. But this time no one answered.

The day was thickening with the sort of heat and humidity that foretold a thunderstorm. Jean sat for a long time at the dining room table in her empty house, sipping iced tea and thinking about Cheryl, wondering if she should call her again. She hated to be a pest with the telephone, but if the situation required she could punch numbers as relentlessly as any machine. The one thing she could not do, which she wanted to do desperately, was get into her car that instant and drive the seven hours to Bier Ridge. And she could not do that because of Milt.

She ruled out renting a car because there was no way of knowing how long she would be in Bier Ridge. It might be a day, a week, or a month, depending on ... well, Jean didn't know what it depended on. There was nothing yet to know. All Jean had to hold on to were her unshakeable beliefs. That everyone, especially her dear friends, deserved a moment of transcendent joy in life before that life ended. That after all these years she yearned for the chance to prove to Cheryl that she was one of those friends. And that not being able to go to Cheryl right now, this minute, was Milt's fault.

Jean leafed through a copy of *Martha Stewart Living*, getting angrier at Milt with each recipe and clever decorating tip. The morning became noon and Jean suffered her fury at Milt and the rising heat of the day in equal measure. When Milt finally walked in the front door at nearly one o'clock, it was sweltering and Jean stood perspiring at the sink, soaping his unwashed dishes. As her husband wandered into the kitchen she gave him a look over her shoulder.

"Milt," she said, her voice quavering, "I'm so mad at you right now I could spit."

"Oh?" said Milt. Something about what Jean had said, or the way she'd said it, pressed him half a step backward, as if her voice had delivered the force of a small, contained gale. "Well . . . is it the dishes? I'm sorry. That was a mistake."

"It's not the dishes I'm mad about."

"Okay," said Milt. "All right, then . . ." His voice took on a measured calm. He set every word down gently as if it were made of ash. "I know I should have been home earlier –"

"And I'm not just mad," said Jean, cutting him off, "I'm *furious*." She was speaking now to the dish suds. "And you know very well why."

For a moment, silence filled the space behind Jean. "How . . . ?" started Milt. "How did you . . . ?"

As Jean took a scrub brush to the chili pot she looked around. "How did I what?" she said. But she'd barely gotten the words out when she knew something was wrong. Standing in the doorway between the kitchen and the hall, Milt looked stricken. He looked crushed. His face slack, his eyes full of torment and wonder, he looked like a condemned man. It was not the visage of a husband whose wife was furious with him over a mishap with the car.

"Milt?" said Jean. She let the chili pot slide from her hands into the suds. It hit the sink bottom with a sonorous thud.

"Nothing happened," said Milt. "I mean, not really."

Jean took up a dishtowel to dry her hands. As she did that, and with her heart hammering, she turned fully around so she could look square at Milt, so that she could really see him, because now the infuriating business with the car was gone and forgotten, it was nothing, and what was important was standing right there in front of her. Still wearing the same checkered shirt he'd worn the day before. In front of her eyes Milt's shoulders sagged and his head tipped forward and he started to trudge out of the kitchen.

"Where are you going?"

At first all Milt did was sigh. Halfway across the living room carpet and almost out of earshot, he finally said, "To sit down."

Outside the window, in the middle of the street, the Craiglees' eleven-year-old and his friends practised on their skateboards, making those terrible banging and cracking noises that to Jean sounded like gunshots as their jumps and twirls and spills caused the boards to strike against the asphalt. Sitting on the sofa, she had to listen past all this noise in order to concentrate on Milt's slow, sigh-filled confession. He had spent the night at Louise Draper's house, he explained. It wasn't the first time. While Jean was away taking care of her mother, Milt said, he had spent a few nights at Louise's. More than a few, actually. Probably about . . . fifteen. But no matter how many times it had been, he said, no sex had yet occurred, out of respect for Jean and Louise's own shy uncertainty. Still, there was obviously something "brewing" that couldn't be ignored, despite what he'd always claimed. And he knew, Milt said, that he was a bastard.

It was just about then, as Milt was proclaiming himself a bastard, that Jean suddenly fastened onto the image of a strawberry. She made a fist and bashed the arm of the sofa.

"Louise is the only person I know who drives out to a strawberry farm every summer," she said. "We've got jars of her freezer jam down in the Frigidaire."

"So?" said Milt.

"So I *knew* you would never think of picking strawberries on your own. Not in a million years."

Looking at Milt, slumped at the other end of the sofa, Jean waited for a wave of outrage and betrayal to overwhelm her. She knew that outrage and betrayal were rightfully hers as a cheated-on spouse, that she could expect them to crash down upon her and wash her into an acid sea of despair. She waited for the wave and it didn't come.

What she felt instead was a greater sense of understanding. In a funny way, she thought, there was something inevitable about what was happening. It was as if years ago the two of them, she and Milt, had contracted an illness that had gone into remission, and then, in the course of things, it had come back.

And she saw, more clearly than before, that some people placed a greater value than others on the concept of friendship. And marital fidelity. And *forgiveness*. Because some people viewed forgiveness, being forgiven, as the gift of a second chance, a fresh opportunity for the transgressor to prove himself, or herself, worthy of trust. And other people, apparently, viewed forgiveness as a licence to transgress again, to recommit whatever detestable act – *infidelity*, it was such a satisfyingly Edwardian word – had required the forgiveness in the first place. And it seemed that people who so easily dismissed forgiveness were willing to sacrifice a friendship in the process. Clearly friendship and fidelity and forgiveness were all woven together; they were of the same fragile thread. To damage one was to damage all. Some people understood that, and some people didn't. Those people could not be counted as friends.

After a long while of sitting on opposite ends of the sofa, with the skateboard racket from the street unrelenting, Jean asked Milt what his plans were. When he said he hadn't thought about it she told him he'd better; they weren't getting any younger and there was no sense in putting off important decisions. She decided not to tell him that his whole confession had been prompted by a misunderstanding. Milt was looking woeful, and she thought telling him about the misunderstanding would just make him more so. For the same reason, she decided not to tell him that she hadn't really been attracted to him for many years. Not since they'd attended the high school graduation of Andrew Jr.'s daughter, Marlee, as proud aunt and uncle. Milt had worn the nice grey suit that he'd bought when she'd encouraged him to get a full-time teaching position, and a blue-and-gold-striped tie, and his hair had been freshly cut, and Jean could still remember how much like a banker he'd looked that day. She didn't know why his looking like a banker had been such an attraction, but she could clearly recall coming home and stopping him in the act of loosening his tie, and how eager she'd been to have him push her down onto any handy horizontal surface. As a banker.

But that was the last time, as far as she could remember, that she had really wanted Milt. And she didn't think she would tell him that, in spite of what he'd confessed to her (that was nice of her, she thought). Instead she focused on his plans.

"I thought you'd be upset," said Milt. "I didn't expect you to be so . . ."

"Practical?" said Jean.

"I was thinking 'hard.'"

Jean nodded. "Of course you were."

From the street came a particularly complicated crash, a sound built of sequential stages – bang, smack, clatter, smack, thud – following in rapid succession, and Jean looked with a certain detachment out the window. Two of the Craiglee boy's friends were down on the pavement and one was clutching his shin. It seemed they had come together in some unfortunate way; one of them, or both, had made a mistake. A friend was to blame, and a friend was hurt. But after a minute the boy with the injured shin rolled over onto his knees, got up, and carried on with his play. And everyone was still friends. Maybe that sort of easy recovery from disaster had to do with childhood, Jean thought. Or maybe that was how boys were different. As she imagined the equivalent happening to two women – a collision real or metaphoric – she knew that no matter what smiles were flashed in the immediate aftermath, some sort of bitterness would linger.

Jean wanted to get out of the house but couldn't bear to be alone, so she called Natalie and arranged to come and stay with her for a little while. Upstairs in the bedroom she packed a proper suitcase. Her lipstick was lying on the top of the dresser and she swept it up in her hand, glancing only briefly at the wedding picture of her and Milt set in a folding silver picture frame. Milt hovered in the doorway the whole time, his mood a mix of misery and resentment, like a child who'd admitted to stealing candy from the corner store and now watched as all his favourite toys were taken away from him as punishment. Nothing for him to do but accept the consequences of his actions. Jean couldn't help but feel a little sympathy for him; she knew that she was tougher, emotionally, than he was. She had been through more. His own parents were still alive, summering in the Gatineau Hills of Quebec, wintering in one of the Carolinas. To him the concept of loss was still a theoretical one. Soon, perhaps within the hour, he would find out how it really felt.

When she had filled her suitcase until it was almost too heavy to lift, she lowered it down the stairs one step at a time, resisting the urge to just let it go, let it tumble head over tail and land with a crash at the bottom as a kind of parting metaphor for their lives together that Milt might appreciate.

At the foot of the stairs Jean glanced around. "Well, I guess that's everything for now." She was conscious of holding her breath, and keeping her face very still, giving Milt nothing to read. He was standing stiff near the banister post with his arms straight at his sides and his head hung low. She put a hand on his shoulder, leaned in, and laid a light kiss on his cheek, then thumbed away the lipstick mark. He hardly reacted to that and she knew he was lost in thought; after all these years she knew him quite well, and what affected him. Regret was headed his way, she was sure of it.

Out in the heat and humidity, Jean dragged her Sears suitcase along on its plastic-and-rubber wheels, west on Edgeworth, back down Conmore, bearing the indignity of leaving a man you'd been married to for decades and having to do it slowly, with no great flourish, just a ponderous, heat-soaked trudge. After Conmore she plotted her course to Natalie's grooming shop via the streets with the most shade trees, even if it took her slightly out of her way. For that reason she ended up walking along Mercer Avenue where the Holy Trinity Presbyterian Church still loomed on the north side. She remembered the Saturday night when Milt had parked his clunker of a Ford Torino in the gravel lot and he and Jean had necked for the first time, from eleven until one in the morning with the crickets singing around them. The Torino was metallic blue with a blue vinyl roof, and in every way utterly disgraceful. Jean shuddered to think of it. The fabric seat inserts were tearing away, it had rust pits on the runner panels, and some sort of engine leak meant that it burned oil terribly and left a cornucopia horn of black smoke behind them wherever they went.

The Torino had been Milt's first car. Then had come an old yellow Pinto, an older, seaweed-green Chevy Vega, a scrap-heap Audi that he was so proud of until the clutch and the radiator went in the space of two weeks, then a white Volkswagen Rabbit that ran forever but with a heater that never, ever worked, and the Hyundai. Milt had never had any luck with cars, thought Jean. He made terrible choices. She was long past the church, slowing with her suitcase under the shade of a red-leaf maple, when she stopped and sighed over the choices Milt had made. Alone on the street, she closed her eyes and bowed her head for the terrible, idiotic choices.

Chapter 13

Mr. Binderman was right, thought Cheryl. It was all going down.

In the western half of the vineyard, she stood between rows of Riesling that reached almost head-high and breathed in the sharp, green fragrance of dusty grapes still three months shy of harvest. It was noon, and so her mind was clearish. There was some fog, but much of that came from the fungicide carried on the breeze from the eastern acres where Mr. Binderman, with a tank strapped on his back and a wand in his hand, was spraying the Cabernet Franc, having sacrificed his day off to the greater need.

She asked herself a question: What was she good at? And the answer was she was good at making a decision. Taking all the available facts and acting on them. It was her one thing, and it had served her in school and in the claims department where she had worked, and it had helped her seize her opportunity with Tam. So with her feet set in the sandy grass between the rows and the sun high above her, with nothing in her stomach clamouring to come out and no urgent need to lie down, she looked out over the small bench of land toward Owasco Lake, a pool of Curaçao in the distance, and took stock of her life.

A meaningless career, discarded. *Puh!*

No children, no attempts, after her great loss (equipped with a "weak cervix," so she'd been told).

No friends left. None.

Two squandered husbands. The first, a dentist named Harold Shiner, whose image Cheryl could visualize now only in the most approximate sense, a vague impression made hazier by time, like a chalk drawing trampled by many feet. (She remembered most vividly the way he tucked in his shirts: incrementally with his jabbing thumbs, the way her mother had pinched pie crusts, which was an image so greatly irritating it almost seemed unfair to Harold to recall it.) The second, Tam Yoon, whose face as wide as a melon, whose deep-dimpled cheeks and short-lived cheer haunted Cheryl's every unfoggy moment.

A crummy little winery on the tiniest Finger Lake, which, because it was shallow and couldn't moderate the local climate like the other Fingers, was a really stupid lake on which to set a winery.

A collection, left by Tam, of antique corkscrews, including an eighteenth-century Florentine one with a handle carved from a boar's tusk. (By leaving her the winery and the corkscrews, it was almost as if he'd given her the gun, and the bullets, and left the rest up to her.)

A single, remaining employee – dear, old, prissy-lipped, Austrian-not-German Mr. Binderman – whose reason for staying was hazy to

Cheryl, like so many things were hazy, but seemed to hinge on a quaint, Old World sense of honour.

A warehouse with hundreds of cases of bottled wine.

Two two-thousand-gallon stainless-steel tanks filled with fermenting juice.

A dented, four-seater Chevy truck she was not allowed to drive.

A three-bedroom house, empty of all life with the exception of . . .

A cockatiel with a death wish.

Cheryl was able to tally all this, the fruits of her existence, and see what she was: a woman descending the far slope of her days, not strolling downward gracefully at her leisure, not marching down with purpose, but stumbling, rolling, careering down like a barrel bounced off the back of a truck. She had nothing behind her but disaster, and nothing in front of her but a glass.

She had no reason to be.

Chapter 14

A friend you could count on – that was like a bit of found treasure. A blessing. Something you could never take for granted. Jean knew that and gave thanks. What would she ever do, she wondered, without Natalie Skilbeck?

When Jean had called to ask if she could stay over, Natalie had said, "Of course," without any hesitation. She had also said, "Don't expect me to clean up," which was just so *her*. It was one of Natalie's most wonderful and reliable qualities that she never hid whatever furry thought was scampering through her mind. In fact, it was the thing that had made the biggest impression on Jean at their first meeting twenty-three years before.

It has to be said, that first impression had not been a happy one. Jean had thought that Milkweed, her Bichon Frise, was looking scraggly and decided to try the new grooming shop,

Skilbeck Pet Stylings, that had just opened around the corner from her studio. When Jean went in for her appointment, Natalie was there with her blazing dark eyes and her blood-dipped lipstick behind a little wooden gate that separated the grooming area from the front counter, shaving down the hind end of a grey standard poodle. Jean picked up Milkweed so that Natalie could see her, and Natalie took one look and announced, over the barking of several caged animals, "That dog is fat!"

"Excuse me?"

"Fat!" repeated Natalie. "What are you feeding it?" She waved her shears dismissively. "Never mind, whatever it is, you'd better reduce it by half, or cut out the bacon treats, otherwise that dog's gonna be dead in about two years."

Jean thought this was an outrageous way for the owner of a new business to behave. She briefly considered the possibility that Natalie was just a hired hand, and that she should immediately report her rudeness to the owner. But when she asked Natalie's name and discovered she was the very Skilbeck advertised on the painted sign out front, Jean confronted her head on. Told her that Milkweed was not fat, just scraggly. Suggested a pet groomer should be able to tell the difference. Further, explained that she, Jean Horemarsh, was the daughter of a highly regarded local veterinarian, and if there was even a chance Milkweed was gaining weight, her mother would certainly have said something to her about it.

"Or not," Natalie said.

"What does that mean?"

The barking from the cages was incessant. "Shaddup!" Natalie yelled. She put down the shears, clapped her hands to knock off the poodle hair, and came closer. "Most vets I know are money-grubbing dickwads, and that includes the women. I'm not getting into your relationship with your mother, that's your business." She picked up the bottle of cola that was sitting on a nearby shelf, took a quick swig, and made a satisfied smacking sound. "Let's just say that your mom's one of the good vets, okay? Of which there are maybe . . ." She held up five fingers, then pulled down two. "If she's seen Milkweed here recently, and she hasn't hit the fatty alarm bell, she either doesn't care, or she's got some other reason."

Something about that assessment rang true enough for Jean that she thought she wouldn't, just then, storm out of Skilbeck Pet Stylings never to return. She allowed Natalie to shave Milkweed down to a nub, and then to show her where the dog's hips were supposed to be but, Jean had to admit, weren't.

The next day, Jean went to the house on Blanchard Avenue, thinking on the way over about all those times her mother had fawned over her brothers' pets; how she had whisked Bogart, Andrew Jr.'s hideous bulldog, into the office for X-rays at the first sign of a wobbly hind leg, and how she'd given Welland a special spray to take care of his yellow Lab's scabby ear. When her mother opened the door, Jean showed her Milkweed's missing hips and demanded to know why Marjorie hadn't warned her that her pup was grossly overweight. At first, Marjorie's face darkened as if she were offended by the question, or by Jean's effrontery in asking it. Then she simply shrugged a shrug that seemed to Jean an echo of so many similar gestures through the years, a shrug that distilled a lifetime's indifference. And she said, "If you weren't so focused on your leaves, my dear, you might notice a thing or two."

From that point on, Jean had looked to Natalie as her truth-teller, the one who would tell her when a colour or a cut was wrong for her, or would give her honest opinion about a new ceramic. Even if the opinion was a trifle blunt, and even if Jean disagreed, she knew that Natalie wasn't hiding anything. And at Kotemee Business Association meetings, she loved the way Natalie stood up to people like Tina Dooley, who seemed to think she had the only ideas worth listening to on a plethora of subjects. Tina, for instance, liked to issue memos to all association members in advance of important meetings, laying out what she saw as the vital issues – Main Street Christmas decorations, the placement of garbage receptacles, a man who shouted too loudly and seemed disturbed. Natalie called these memos "Dooley's Doodles" and "Dooley's Dispatches from the Front" and occasionally used phrases even less charitable, not only in private but at the meetings themselves. Invariably she said something to Tina that had Jean spitting into a coffee napkin.

When Jean arrived at the door of the shop, having slogged through the heat with her suitcase, Natalie seemed to know immediately that she was in a dismal state. She made Jean comfortable (as comfortable as it was possible to be surrounded by half a dozen caged cats and barking dogs) and went for two teas and some Dilman's cupcakes. Then for the next couple of hours she entertained Jean with a running commentary on the animals she was grooming.

A hissy white Himalayan cat was a Taliban operative who wanted to stone her to death. "A mullah mullet, that's what you're getting, Mister," Natalie said. When the cat bared its teeth, she scoffed. "Oh, big talk. Show me the rock you can throw that's gonna hurt me."

A taffy-coloured Goldendoodle mistakenly thought he was there for a sex-change operation. "Your owner says your name is Marvin," Natalie told him. "But you'd prefer Mavis, wouldn't you?" The dog licked her chin. "I know, Marv, but you're still going home with your willie."

A sad-eyed Gordon Setter was Bing Crosby reincarnated. "Sing!" cried Natalie. She took hold of one of the dog's long ears. "Damn it, Bing, I know you're in there. Sing for us!" And as she clipped the setter's tail she sang, "Mele Kalikimaka is the thing to say / On a bright Hawaiian Christmas Day" in a jaunty, Bing-like croon.

Once her customers had retrieved their pets, Natalie locked up the shop and drove Jean to her little ivy-covered cottage-style house on Andover Lane. Natalie seemed to make a point of not asking Jean any questions about what had happened with Milt, for which Jean was thankful because she wasn't really in the mood to hear blunt assessments of her marriage or her husband. There were times when blunt was precisely the wrong note for a given circumstance, like vinegar in a cream sauce, and this was one of them. She thought Natalie's unusual tact probably had to do with the fact that she had been divorced by her own husband, Sandeep Jaffir, some six years before. Sandeep was handsome and broad-shouldered, and quite a lovely man, employed to travel the world seeking out sources for the manufacture of alternative medicines. He'd become not-lovely the day he called from Jakarta and informed Natalie that he had met someone else and would not ever be coming home. Natalie closed the doors of Skilbeck Pet Stylings for a month, and a more despondent, inert woman the world has seldom seen. Everyone who knew and loved Natalie was relieved the day she came to a meeting of the KBA and told Tina Dooley to shove her latest Dispatch up her ass.

After Natalie showed Jean where she would be sleeping – the small loveseat in the living room pulled out into a bed – she went to work making a delectable dinner of baked salmon and fingerling potatoes with a big green salad. While the salmon was in the oven she opened a bottle of South African Chenin Blanc. But when she went to pour her a glass, Jean, who was seated on a stool at the kitchen island, held up a hand and shook her head.

Natalie raised an eyebrow. "That's not like you."

"Well, I was out with Adele last night and I'm still . . ." Jean made a fluttery gesture near her tummy.

"Oh, I see. Carousing in the big city."

"We were going to see a play and then we just . . . didn't."

Natalie began pouring herself a healthy glass of wine, which Jean was glad to see because she had never agreed with the habit some women had of tailoring their own drinking to match whichever relative or friend happened to be over. It put so much pressure on the guest, especially if you knew someone liked a glass of wine and then just because you weren't feeling up to it, suddenly they weren't either. Count on Natalie, thought Jean, to toss such silly "niceties" out the window where they belonged.

"So, how is Queen Adele?"

For Jean, the small glass salt shaker on the marble counter became an object of immediate interest. She picked it up, studied it, and gave it a waggle before setting it down. The edge of the counter required a rub with her thumb. "You know," she said, "you haven't really asked me about what happened with Milt. Aren't you curious?"

"Uh, let me guess." Natalie made a show of formulating a theory, pursing her lips and looking off. Suddenly she appeared struck by inspiration. "Milt's been having an affair with Louise."

For a moment Jean was silent. "I don't understand," she said. "Does that not come as a shock to you?"

Natalie tucked the wine bottle inside the door of the fridge and seemed, in Jean's view, to take quite a while coming up with an answer to that question. "Well, I know they had that thing once before. You told me about that."

"Yes," said Jean, waiting for more.

"So, just that." Natalie opened a cupboard and pulled out two white china plates. "Also, I saw them having lunch a couple of times while you were at your mom's."

"Lunch," said Jean. "Lunch . . . where was this?"

"That Chinese place I go for takeout sometimes, on Sterling."

"And you never *told* me?"

"Well, I thought everybody was friends now."

Everybody was *not* friends now, thought Jean. Everybody was anything *but* friends. She reached for Natalie's glass of wine and took a nice big gulp, and she didn't care that Natalie had to pour herself another glass. Oh, the salmon was going to taste just wonderful now that she knew it was being cooked and served by someone who knew her husband had been cheating on her and had said nothing about it. Yes, that was a nice bit of seasoning, wasn't it? Some truth-teller, thought Jean. Some blunt talker. Some friend.

The stove was making ticking noises from the heat, and Natalie was looking mightily chagrined standing over by the far counter. As well she should, Jean thought. She wondered now whether she would have to rethink her whole plan regarding Natalie, because it seemed that she could no longer trust her, and why should an untrustworthy friend be the recipient of her gift? Natalie took a long German knife out of a drawer, and a white plastic cutting board from below, and Jean watched her begin slicing tomatoes and a big pale onion for the salad. As she followed the blade's motion she thought about all the times she had been shocked or offended by the things Natalie had said but then, with determined and deliberate fairness, had reminded herself that such was the price to pay for frank and honest assessments when you really needed them. You couldn't have things both ways, Jean had insisted to herself, you couldn't have delicacy and truth, or delightfulness and truth. Because truth did not come bundled with anything but brutality. Cold, ugly brutality – and truth. That was the package, and if you wanted one, you had to buy them both. Unless somebody in the back of the shop decided to slip in some *lying by omission* and some *what she doesn't know won't hurt her.*

Jean took another big sip of the South African Chenin Blanc, which was clean and crisp and not butterscotchy like so many hot-country wines. She watched Natalie slicing the onion paper-thin, the way she liked it. It was a Walla Walla Sweet onion, which you could only get from the little "fine foods" shop on Main, which catered mostly to the tourists, and Jean considered the possibility that after her forlorn call from the house, Natalie had gone to the shop thinking, *I'll get a Walla Walla Sweet onion and make Jean a nice salad to make her feel better.* She decided against asking Natalie about it, because that might make it appear as though she regarded her statements of fact as truth and had already forgotten what a terribly dishonest friend she'd been. It seemed right to let Natalie stew in that unflattering self-awareness a while longer.

She sniffed at her glass. About Natalie, Jean was now of two minds, and she realized it was possible to have good and not-so-good thoughts about the same person or thing all at once. Like South Africa. It had been a bad place, and it was still very troubled, but it made nice wine. Perhaps a nasty country like North Korea also made nice wine, or some pleasant drink made with rice. To be fair to North Korea you really had to factor that in.

Not that you had to completely forgive them.

"This is nice wine," said Jean, without saying anything more.

"It's from South Africa," said Natalie, sounding very hopeful.

"Mm-hmm," said Jean.

Louise, on the other hand, would get no due consideration. Her betrayal was too clear, her transgression too great . . . worse even than Milt's. It seemed odd not to condemn your own husband for cheating on you, but it was simply true that Jean was far more hurt by Louise's duplicity. Perhaps it was because her friendship with Louise had felt so full of potential. It had begun in fire, in the searing, hostile heat of that first attempt at an affair with Milt. Pain and recovery had connected her to Louise like the scar tissue that formed between burned fingers and toes. With that kind of start there'd been no telling what shared pleasures the two of them might one day discover. Jean had felt they were approaching that time in their friendship when they would begin, not just to tell each other things, but to confide in each other. To let their insecurities show. To be in each other's company the women they truly were, not just the women they wanted to be or the women they allowed the world to see. And now all that was gone. The scar tissue was severed. They could never be friends.

Lifting her glass, Jean said, "The person I'm most upset with is Louise." As a hint at possible future forgiveness, it was all Natalie was getting; she would have to make do.

"Of course you are," said Natalie, gathering all the chopped salad ingredients into a glass bowl. "What a total bitch."

Natalie's words could be such a splash of ice water. But the more Jean thought about it, the more she examined Louise's actions, the more they seemed to fit. Imagine someone pretending to be her friend while sharing a bed, or a room, or . . . whatever they were sharing, with her friend's husband. Imagine betraying her friend while that friend was distracted by the unbearable burdens of family. Imagine doing that to a friend while that friend's *mother lay dying*. What a total, what an absolute *bitch*.

"I'm so angry with her, Natalie." Jean's voice trembled. Maybe it was the wine, or a sudden realization of what it all meant, the loss of her husband, the loss of her friend . . . she felt a surge of emotions, a welter of primitive, conflicting feelings, pouring into her. It was like she was a lake, a vast reservoir, and from every direction rivers of instinct and energy and heat were emptying into her, filling her up.

"Why shouldn't you be angry?" said Natalie.

"I'm just furious."

"You have a right to be furious." Natalie took up a spatula and half turned as if she were going to check the salmon in the oven. But then she seemed to reconsider, set down the spatula, and focused all of her attention on Jean.

"But maybe it's my fault."

"It's not your fault," said Natalie.

"It feels like it could be."

"It's absolutely not your fault. It's hers."

"It's hers." Jean took a shaky sip of wine. "I have been wronged."

"You've been very wronged."

"Louise was deceitful."

"You bet she was."

"She was *evil*."

"That's a strong word but, okay."

Jean clenched the fist that gripped the wine. "It makes me want to do something."

"Of course it does."

"I want to tell her what I think."

"You've got to let it out."

"I have a right to be heard."

"You have every right," Natalie said.

"I think I'm going to call her."

"Let's have dinner first."

"I'm going to call her *right now*!"

Jean reached into her purse for her phone at the same time Natalie swung around, turned off the oven, and yanked open the door. Jean's hands were trembling so that she found it hard to punch in Louise's number, but she managed it one shaky digit at a time as Natalie donned oven mitts, reached in, and brought out the salmon, the juices sizzling in the baking pan. Jean waited through the first ring, a second, and then a third, while Natalie used the spatula to transfer a salmon fillet and a portion of fingerling potatoes to each plate. And finally, as Natalie lifted the plates and began to carry them from the cramped kitchen toward the dining area, Louise's answering machine voice came on the line, asking Jean to leave a message, the message of her *anger*.

"Louise . . ." began Jean. "It's Jean. Your former friend. I wish you were there right now so I could tell you how angry and betrayed I feel." She looked toward Natalie for encouragement. Natalie was bringing the plates back to the kitchen. "Do you know what I've come to believe about my friends? I love them, and I would do anything for them. Anything. And because you are no longer my friend, that doesn't apply to you any more." Jean looked at Natalie by the oven. Natalie gave a tight nod and Jean nodded back. "Do you know what that means, Louise Draper? It means you should be very afraid. Because you know what's going to happen? You're going to grow *old*." Natalie was narrowing her eyes in that way she did when she was puzzled by something. Jean knew her friend so well. She thought maybe Louise would be puzzled too, so she went on. "That's right, you're going to grow old, and tired. Your feet are going to swell, and your breasts are going to wither up until they're like two little empty hot water bottles. And your back and neck are going to ache as your vertebrae crumble, and your joints are going to bite you like sharks under your skin." She was rolling now, she felt unleashed. Natalie was squinting at her as if she were confused, or maybe she was thinking about something else entirely, something to do with work. Dogs. It didn't matter! Jean felt herself flowing, she shone like sunlight, she held The Truth in her hands – the brutal, ugly Truth – and she was delivering it to Louise.

"I know all this, Louise. I'm not making it up. I've seen it, I've *seen* it, and it's going to happen to you. Because I'm not going to save you. You said that you wanted a Last Poem, and I was going to give you one, but I'm not now. I'm not going to make it nice for you, Louise. I'm not going to do anything to help you. And so you're going to get old, and your organs are going to betray you, just like you betrayed me. They're going to turn their backs on you. They're going to go on strike. And when they get tired of that, Louise, your organs are going to mutiny! Your own precious liver, your stomach, your intestines, every wet, wiggly thing inside you that you need to survive is going to turn on you." Jean wasn't thinking of Louise any more, she was thinking of her mother. She was looking into Marjorie's pain-dimmed eyes. Here was Natalie handing her a clean dishcloth and Jean didn't know why until she looked down at wet spots on her thighs and touched her cheek and realized her face was streaming with tears. "They're going to break out the swords, Louise. The muskets and the spears! Your organs are coming for you, Louise! They're coming for you! They're coming for you! And I'm not going to do *anything*!"

Sobbing, Jean snapped her phone shut and buried her face in the towel Natalie had given her. She wept into the towel until the fury, the hurt, the whole wide lake of emotions drained away. It took a long time. And when she was done, she inhaled deeply and looked up at Natalie, who was backed against the oven. The expression on her face looked like concern to Jean.

"Natalie," she said, "don't worry about what I said to Louise, all right? It doesn't necessarily apply to you." She folded the towel in her lap and noticed the plates set on the oven. "Your salmon is getting cold, and I'm so hungry. Let's eat!"

After dinner, Jean insisted on doing the dishes so that Natalie could relax, since she had already done so much. And later they watched some television, which seemed to be all that Natalie was up to. Jean felt euphoric after her message to Louise, and her mind swirled with images, faces, ideas, so that she hardly even knew what was happening on the screen. She thought of work – two or three exciting new ceramics possibilities that weren't yet fully formed – but mostly she thought of the people she loved, or had loved. Something about denying Louise her help, in a way that was final and absolute, underlined for Jean the importance of what she was doing for her true friends. It defined the boundaries of her actions and her reasons for them. It created within her a sense of right and wrong, of exclusion and belonging. She suddenly had a clear and thrilling insight into the roots of politics and religion, of how whole movements began. There were believers and non-believers. There were people who were meant to be held close, and others who deserved to be pushed away. Before, what she had been doing for her friends had felt right. Now, and this seemed glorious to Jean, it felt righteous.

And where did Natalie fit? Was she going to get a Last Poem? Jean wasn't altogether sure any more – trust being such a precious, delicate thing, so easily broken and so hard to repair. But that didn't mean she wasn't concerned for Natalie when eleven o'clock came and Natalie announced that she was tired and ready for bed. Jean wondered out loud whether she was coming down with something, because her mood and energy had changed so quickly around dinner, and sometimes when people were getting ill that's how it happened. But Natalie said no, she felt all right.

Just tired. As she ascended the stairs to her cute attic bedroom she said she hoped Jean would be comfortable on the pull-out love-seat, and Jean assured her that she would be. Even if she wasn't sure Natalie deserved her great gift, the last thing Jean wanted her to do was worry.

Chapter 15

Jean lay awake on Natalie's hideously uncomfortable loveseat. There had been times during her marriage when Milt's snoring had kept her from sleeping, and Natalie's fold-out bed, with its dense-as-soapsuds mattress, was like the torture of Milt's snoring made physical.

As she lay with her eyes open in the darkness, her mind drifted to Cheryl Nunley. She pictured Cheryl's face – the miserable one in Welland's printout – and imagined the first words they would say to each other, after all the hugging and tears.

Cheryl would want to know what Jean had been doing all her life. And Jean would insist that no, the first thing she needed to do was apologize. She needed to say what a bad friend she had been. How she had abandoned Cheryl for the worst, most immature reasons. She would say this even as Cheryl shook her head, telling her it was all forgotten, all in the past. *No!* Jean would say. *Yes!* Cheryl would insist. And Jean would repeat the words as often as she needed to, as loudly as required, that she was deeply sorry and hoped Cheryl could forgive her. And there would be more tears, and maybe some justified anger from Cheryl, sprung loose after all those years. And once all that had passed, Cheryl *would* forgive her.

Because she was like that, as far as Jean could remember.

And maybe that's all Cheryl would need to start feeling less miserable. Knowing she had a friend who had gone to all that trouble to find her and ask for absolution. That would perk someone up, wouldn't it? And then Jean could tell Cheryl that she was going to make it up to her, and that it would be a surprise and not something to worry about. *Don't even think about it,* Jean would say, when Cheryl tried to object. *Just know that I am here for you, and it's going to be all right now.* And Cheryl would smile a little. She would relax. And if the mood was just right, Jean might even tell Cheryl, *Guess what? Ash Birdy married Ruth Donoghue, and she ballooned right up!* They could chuckle about that together; they could bond a little over stupid Ash Birdy. And wouldn't that be a lovely irony?

With all that out of the way, the two of them would get down to the joyful business of sharing their histories, reliving all those missed moments, good and bad, and all the decisions that had shaped their lives. Cheryl would want to know if Jean had had any children, and Jean would tell her no. She would say that it was a choice she had made years ago, not to bring something so helpless into the world, something so dependent on her. That every so often, when she had a yearning she couldn't otherwise explain, she would wonder if she had made the right choice. But that she no longer had any regrets.

And you, Cheryl? Jean would ask immediately. *Did you have children?* It would be safe to ask then, because the subject would have been broached. She tried to picture Cheryl's face brightening as she began to answer. Because that would mean good news.

Just before she was finally able to fall asleep, Jean spent a moment or two thinking of the more distant future, the one that came after seeing Cheryl. How life would unfold for her, without Milt, and without her friends.

The picture there wasn't nearly as clear. And she thought she wouldn't dwell on it. Not right now.

Chapter 16

When Jean raised herself on an elbow and peered out Natalie's front window, she saw what she'd feared in the sky: an endless mass of vellum-grey clouds, the kind that came like drums and flutes before the marching storm. She worried not for her own sake but for Welland's. Today was the annual Police-Fire-Library Picnic in Corkin Park, and every year, for months before the date, he worked so hard on his part: arranging entertainment, such as it was, helping to round up sponsors for the picnic baskets and the petting zoo and the pony rides, setting up his lonely little booth in the Activity Zone. Jean went to the picnic every year, just to show her support, even though she didn't much care for what went on there. Mothers let their children run around with hands and mouths sticky from ice cream until it seemed half the picnic grounds were caked to them. Teenagers leered at each other or snuck off into the scrub brush. The dunk tank water quickly became so dingy she feared for the health of any town official or local radio "personality" who had to sit on the wobbly wooden seat. The Wheel of Fortune was all right; she'd won twenty-two dollars one year. But then she'd lost it all on the silly carny games. Why the balloon shoot and the basketball toss and the pickle pitch and all the rest were run by the husbands of librarians was something Jean could never fathom. But they did seem to enjoy barking at people.

It was almost eight o'clock before Natalie came downstairs, and when she did she was wrapped in a blue housecoat that, to Jean's eye, seemed at odds with her mood. The fabric of the housecoat had a fuzzy nap and was edged with a shiny satin ribbon. On the chest, over the heart, was a yellow Tweetie Bird. The housecoat, in other words, was entirely light-hearted. Natalie, however, appeared to be quite the opposite. *Pensive* was the word, and if she'd been asked about this, and if she chose to be honest, Jean would have said she was a little annoyed. If you were going to invite someone to be a guest in your house when their marriage was ending, the least you could do was be in a good mood around them. The least you could do was smile and offer breakfast and ask how they slept. Natalie didn't do any of these things. It was probably just as well, because then Jean would have had to decide whether to mention what a terrible bed her loveseat made. But, of course, she *wouldn't* have mentioned it. You simply didn't complain when your friend was offering her hospitality, however faulty. What you did was show a similar generosity of spirit. But Natalie didn't ask, and so Jean wasn't able to express her generosity in that way. Her friend just spooned coffee grounds silently into the machine in her tiny kitchen. She obviously had something on her mind.

"Is everything all right, Natalie?"

"Hmmm?"

"You're very quiet this morning." Jean perched on a seat at the kitchen island. "You were quiet last night, as well. And we both know that's not like you."

"I was just thinking about what you said on the phone to Louise. I've kind of been thinking about it for hours."

"Oh, that seems a shame," said Jean. She looked down and adjusted the way her pyjamas draped over her breasts. "I hardly remember what I said."

"It was all about growing old."

"Well, I guess I was upset," said Jean. "I don't know why you would lose sleep over it."

"It kind of bummed me out."

Natalie had stopped spooning coffee, and Jean could see the apprehension in her face. Apprehension had an unfortunate effect on Natalie; she lost all the vivacity in her dark eyes, and of course her sense of humour. She was obviously a woman who struggled with things that were uncertain, like the future. Under the circumstances, Jean thought it best to say something cheering.

"Oh, Natalie," she said, "I really don't think you need to worry about getting old just yet."

"Why not?" Natalie dropped the coffee spoon and folded her fuzzy blue arms. "I'm an overweight, middle-aged, single woman. I'm exactly the person who *should* be worried about growing old. And frankly –" she looked at Jean "– so are you."

What were the chances, Jean wondered, of Natalie ever *not* saying the blunt thing if she had a choice? If it was between bluntness and graciousness – or even something complimentary! – bluntness cut down all other options like a knight in the Crusades.

But never mind. Natalie was clearly anxious, and Jean realized how she could be generous with her this morning: she could put aside her own feelings and do her best to distract Natalie from her niggling fears.

Corkin Park, roughly triangular and set against the lake, was named after Oswald J. Corkin, one of Kotemee's original favourite sons. He had enlisted in the Anglo-Egyptian Nile Expeditionary Force in 1896 and fought in the Sudanese War under Lord Kitchener at Dunqulah and Omdurman. It was at Omdurman, on the western bank of the Nile – where in five hours Kitchener's men killed eleven thousand of the enemy and sustained only forty-eight losses and not quite four hundred wounded – that Corkin's name had become enshrined in lore. He'd got his toe shot off, the second on the left foot. But as the bullets flew he'd managed to find the piece of toe. He later brought it home in a handkerchief.

Just before ten in the morning, under a cloud-socked sky the colour of wasps' nests, Jean and Natalie arrived at the Police-Fire-Library Picnic banner and saw Oswald Corkin's namesake filling up with Kotemeeans. From the waterfront that defined the diagonal northeastern edge, to the southern line of scrub brush that acted as a buffer between the park and the old Pleasant Lane Cemetery (where nine-toed Oswald J. Corkin lay at rest), to the baseball diamond next to Howell Road, which eventually became Highway 18, along the western side, Jean could see as many as three hundred picnickers, a legion of sticky, feral children and their irresponsible parents, a multitude of leering, slouching, snack-devouring teenagers, and some older people who seemed to be hurrying through the questionable pleasures of pickle-pitching and picnic-basket bidding in advance of the coming storm. She was pleased about the turnout, for Welland's sake, but she was sad, too. With no sun to sparkle the water, the lake in the distance looked cold, and the dunk tank had about it a miserable, condemned air. In the petting zoo, the borrowed farm animals hunkered down in their stalls. In the baseball outfield, the Ferris wheel the Fire Department had rented stood blackly forbidding against the sky's unremitting grey. And no one was making use of the Fire-hose Cool-off Zone.

Natalie was standing off to Jean's left when a sudden burst of loud, crackling noise attracted her attention. "Is that thunder?" she said.

"No," said Jean. "It's just Welland's band plugging their speakers into the generator."

There was no missing the hopeful note in Natalie's question. In fact it had taken a fair bit of convincing by Jean to get her to come to this picnic at all. Natalie, in typical fashion, had said it was the sort of thing that made her wish for a crampy period: "It'd give me something better to do with my time." But Jean was shameless and insisted that this was the only thing that would keep her mind off Milt, and that she really wanted company. So Natalie had sighed herself into some Levi's and a pair of sneakers and come along.

The revelation she had provoked that morning, that Natalie was anxious about growing old, had burrowed away like an earthworm in Jean's mind all through the bagels and blueberry cream cheese Natalie had served for breakfast. She thought about all the years she had known Natalie, and how her friend had always presented a combative, ironic, foul-mouthed front. She wondered now, for the first time, if perhaps that public Natalie wasn't the true one, but simply a protective shell. All the snippy comments and brutal truths and epic rolls of the eye – maybe these were Natalie's way of hiding the fact that, inside, she was really quite fragile. How heartbreaking, thought Jean, if that were true.

Ever more it seemed as if the people she loved and thought she knew had been visible to her only through veils, like a play watched from behind a screen you didn't even know was there. What a disappointment to see the screen rise just before the story's end and discover . . . oh! . . . how things really looked. Perhaps it was true that you never really knew anyone until it was too late. Or maybe really knowing someone wasn't possible. Maybe all you had were theories, and one theory lasted until it was replaced by another. The way she had assumed Natalie was always honest until she'd learned it was only sometimes. Or the way she'd had one theory about her mother and her mother's opinion of her, which had informed her whole life until her mother's last breath, only to go to the funeral and have Welland tell her something quite different.

"Mom told me something about you, Jeanie," Welland had said. "When she first got sick."

They were sitting beside each other in the front pew of the church, before Andrew Jr. and his brood arrived.

"About me?" Jean had replied.

"She thought you were a strong woman. Stronger than her even. She said you never took the easy way. 'Impressive,' Mom said. She probably never told you that."

"No," Jean had said, staring into Millicent Keeping's hydrangeas by the altar. "She never told me."

"It's true, though. I'm not making it up."

"I didn't think you were."

Once those words had been spoken, Welland sat a bit awkwardly beside Jean, as if he wasn't sure what more was expected in the moment. He was likely confused, because he must have thought what he'd said was a good thing, not that it wasn't. And he'd probably expected Jean to react more happily, not realizing how hard it is to react happily to something that rearranges your whole emotional framework in one big swoop and you have to sit with it dumbly because the person you wish you could talk to about it is lying dead in a box.

Luckily for Welland and Jean, Andrew Jr. pressed in just then with his family and there wasn't any room for thinking.

Welland coming to mind gave Jean a reason to look around the park, and after a short wander through the Activity Zone with Natalie in tow she found him, Constable Welland Horemarsh, sitting on a stool in his Kotemee Police Department booth. He was accompanied by Billy Walker, his foam child, placed on a box with his legs out straight in front of him, and a thousand traffic safety pamphlets arrayed along a folding table in stacks of varying height, like a ruined brick wall. Welland made sure he and Billy were sitting off to the side, so as not to block the large black-and-yellow sign cut in the inverted triangle of a Yield symbol that announced, "Billy Walker says: Play Safe around Cars!" Jean had always wondered if that sign wasn't sending a mixed message, but she'd never had the heart to mention that to Welland.

In front of the booth, two boys whom Jean judged to be about nine or ten were grabbing pamphlets from the stacks and swatting each other with them, and each grab of a pamphlet sent two more fluttering to the ground. Another boy about the same age was lunging across the folding table in an effort to grab Billy Walker's foam foot. Welland was doing his best to shoo all three of them away while maintaining his "friendly cop" manner. He had his stiff smile on and kept leaning over and waving at them as though they were yellow jackets hovering around a bowl of fruit. It was having no effect.

"Boys," Jean said, striding over to the booth. "Boys! Where are your parents?"

The boys continued to swat and lunge. "Jean!" called Natalie, coming up behind. "Did you hear? There are girls showing off their underpants over by the Ferris wheel."

"Underpants?" said Jean.

"Pink ones!" said Natalie.

With a shout, the boys tore off.

A sheepish look passed over Welland's face. "I can't be associated with that," he said. "But thank you."

For a few years it had been Jean's hope that Welland and Natalie might see something in one another, but it had never happened. Welland had probably been too nice for Natalie's taste, or Natalie too sharp-edged for his. Now, of course, given the gaps in Natalie's honesty, it was just as well.

"Natalie let me sleep at her place last night," said Jean, "while I recovered from Milt leaving me for another woman."

"Milt left you?" Welland, bless his heart, appeared both shocked and terribly concerned. It looked rather handsome, that concern, against his dark-blue policeman's uniform. Jean hoped Natalie wouldn't notice.

"He's having an affair with Louise Draper," she said. "So that's as good as left me."

"Your friend Louise?"

"My former friend."

"Holy cow." There was something odd about the way Welland was looking at her, Jean thought. He appeared caught, somehow. Torn between one thing and another.

"Welland?" was all she said.

"Well," her brother pointed vaguely south, "I thought I saw Milt a little while ago, over by the pickle pitch."

"No." Jean shook her head. "That doesn't sound like Milt." The pickle pitch involved trying to toss dill pickles into the mouths of large pickle jars. You got three pickles for a dollar, and to win a prize you had to get one whole pickle into a jar; half a pickle cut in two by the jar's glass rim, or any amputated piece of one, didn't count. Milt had no hand-eye coordination at all, and vinegar made his nose itchy.

"And," Welland adjusted the back of his cap, "um . . ."

At that moment an enormous boom sounded across the park, followed by an ear-ripping electronic crackle and a piercing wail of amplified feedback. Not far from Jean a terrified toddler clutched her mother's knees, her lower lip trembling.

"I think it's time for the entertainment," said Natalie.

On a flatbed trailer set up on Corkin Park's southern edge, against a backdrop of scrub brush, three bedraggled and sleepy-looking young men took up positions with their instruments and stared with apparently limitless fascination at their own feet. Closer to the front of the stage a skeletal girl with lank, dirty-blond hair, wearing purple tights and a jean jacket covered in what appeared to be beer labels, grabbed the microphone stand in front of her with a sudden, jealous vehemence.

"*Hello, Kotemee!*" she shouted, emphasizing the *meee*. There was a speckling of applause from the thirty or so people, most of them elderly or mothers with infants who happened to be sitting at the picnic tables arranged haphazardly between the Activity Zone and the stage. The girl wrenched the microphone toward her mouth once more, as if furious with it for trying to escape. "*We are . . .*" She leaned back and let a dramatic pause swell, or, perhaps, given the way her mouth hung slack, she had forgotten what she was going to say. No, here it came. ". . . *Swamp Fire!*" At this, the bedraggled boys began to flail and shrug, and the amplifiers unleashed a sound like something forged hammer upon anvil. In front of them, the girl convulsed in rhythm.

Jean looked up at Welland, whose expression was apologetic. "Well, it's sort of countryish," she yelled above the music.

"They had their own generator," Welland yelled back. Then he added, with something like optimism, "A John Deere."

Natalie held out her hand and looked toward the clouds.

Whatever else it was that Welland wanted to tell Jean, he seemed reluctant to express it at a shout. So Jean and Natalie made their way toward the other side of the Activity Zone, where a parked snack truck gave off smells of popcorn and fried dough, and where the music was no more oppressive than that sound produced by the teams of weed-whackers deployed semi-annually by Kotemee Council on all town-owned lands. As they went, the two women were forced to wade through children like Mennonites through fields of flax. But Jean was determined to make good on her private pledge to lift Natalie's spirits, so she tried to draw Natalie into the sorts of Activity Zone diversions she herself would normally have avoided. The petting zoo and the pony rides, for instance. In all their cow, goat, pig, rabbit, and saddled-pony glory, they seemed a bit pathetic, even cruel, to Jean. But she figured they'd be naturals for Natalie. She was an animal person, after all.

But as they approached the perimeter fence of the Animal Zone, Natalie would have nothing to do with either the petting or the ponies.

"I don't want fleas," she said, shuddering.

"But you love animals," said Jean.

"What makes you think that?"

"You're a *pet groomer*!"

Natalie shook her head. "That's faulty logic. Maybe I'm a pet groomer not because I like animals, but because I hate messy ones."

They went next to the Ferris wheel, because Jean thought it would offer a nice view, and because for a little while it would place Natalie above just about everyone in Kotemee, which Jean thought would probably appeal to her in some deeply psychological way. But Natalie wasn't interested in the Ferris wheel.

"Have you seen the delinquent who's running the thing?" she said, jabbing her thumb toward a boy of about sixteen whose shirt was smeared with grease and also what looked like some mustard. "I wouldn't trust him to run his own mouth."

Jean laughed and gave Natalie's shoulder a light, joshing swat. But really it seemed that she was just being difficult, and Jean thought there was a good chance her own patience was going to run out, and soon. She decided the best thing was to steer them toward the one annual picnic activity she herself actually enjoyed, which was the Wheel of Fortune.

As usual the Wheel was set up on the theme of playing cards, with suits and card values crudely painted on the plywood wheel and matched by betting spaces on the worn, painted-vinyl sheet laid lengthwise along a narrow table. A crowd of people was gathered around the betting table but Jean saw an empty space and squeezed in, and laid two dollars on the Jack of Clubs. Natalie could just mind herself for a while.

Pete Besseler, one of the librarian husbands, ran the Wheel. Pete was one of those men with a big Adam's apple and a wiry, ageless body so unlike Milt's. He had on the same dirty canvas apron that he wore every year, with big bulgy money pouches and a spray of card suits printed on the front. Jean suspected that some librarian with an eye to raising money had bought the apron and the wheel and the betting sheet all together in one big package ten or fifteen years before. Maybe the same librarian knew she had a ready Wheel runner in the family. Pete certainly acted as if he was born to the job.

"No more bets, no more bets!" he said, waving his big hands as though he were fending off autograph seekers. Without taking his eye off the betting board, as if he could trust no one, Pete reached up with his long, crane-like arm. He gave the wheel a tug, and it began to turn, the sprung metal tab at the top chattering against the nails. Jean loved that sound. Except it always seemed to her that when she had money down on the table, Pete never really gave the wheel a proper spin. She felt as though she had to beg the wheel to go around more than one full turn. Possibly it was a matter of perception, and possibly not.

After a moment the wheel came to a stop on the five of hearts. "We have a winner!" called Pete. The winner was a little dark-haired girl betting her mother's money. *Isn't that cute*, thought Jean, as Pete swept her coins off the jack of clubs into his pouch.

She put another two dollars on the jack of clubs. To her there was something boyish and fun about the jack, something ready for action. Other people around Jean placed money on various spaces, inexplicably choosing fives and threes and eights, numbers with no personality. They seemed to be betting indiscriminately, as if they were trying to get their money in before the storm came. Pete stretched out his hands in anticipation of the horde of auto-graph seekers. Beside Jean someone placed another two dollars on the jack of clubs.

"Oh," said Jean, half turning. "No, I think he's already waved off the bets."

"No he hasn't," said the bettor.

"No more bets, no more bets," waved Pete.

"*Now* he's waving them off."

Jean suddenly realized the bettor standing beside her, standing firm and still with a pale-yellow sweater draped around her shoulders and her hands clasped in an attitude of confident repose, was Fran Knubel.

"Oh, Fran," said Jean, feeling her face pinch. "Hi there."

"Jean," said Fran. It was more an acknowledgment – *I see that you exist* – than a greeting.

Pete was reaching up to hook his long, grappling fingers over one of the nails.

"Pete!" called Jean. She pointed down at her jack of clubs space. "I had my money in here first."

Fran made a huffy sound. "Two people can have their money in the same space," she said. Jean noticed that for once Fran wasn't wearing any attention-grabbing jewellery. Perhaps she thought it would be at risk among the common crush of Kotemeeans.

Pete shoved his hands in his money apron and came over wearing an official-looking scowl. "What's the problem?"

Jean leaned toward him in a way that he might have thought was friendly, or even flirty, and if he did then so be it. "It's just I had my money in here first." She tapped Fran's coin. "This one's Fran's."

"There's no problem," said Fran, her hands unfolding in the manner of an open book. "Two people can bet in the same space."

Around Jean, people who'd put their money down were getting restless. Someone grumbled, "Come on," and a child echoed it more plaintively, "Yeah, come *on!*" There were spreading murmurs of agreement. It seemed to Jean that Kotemeeans these days were more impatient than ever. Was the world pressing down on them so relentlessly?

Pete wrapped his hand around the back of his long neck and looked down at the jack of clubs space. He swallowed and his Adam's apple slid up and down like a little elevator.

"I don't see the problem, Jean. Five people could put their money in there if they wanted."

"Oh," said Jean. "Really?" She sensed Fran nodding fiercely beside her. "Well, all right. I just wanted to make sure."

A few of the other bettors cheered with ironic verve as Pete reached up and finger-hooked a nail. "No more bets! No more bets!" he repeated, and gave the wheel a nice tug for once, perhaps out of frustration.

"People do it all the time at the roulette tables in Las Vegas," said Fran, as the metal tab chattered against the nails. Her voice sounded small and tight, as though she were wearing some sort of corrective collar. "Whenever Jim and I go, the chips are just piled on."

"I am sure you're an expert on betting at Las Vegas, Fran," said Jean, watching the wheel spin. "But this is Kotemee, and I thought the rules here might be different."

"You just didn't want me in your space."

"Well there are *lots of spaces*," said Jean, spreading her hands. "I don't know why you have to copy me."

That was when Fran turned to Jean. She turned with a full-body jerk, and Jean could tell that something big was coming, and that it was unavoidable. Fran turned, her mouth pursed tight but her eyes wide and wet as brimming soup spoons. She turned and said, "And I don't know why you have to be so hateful. *How's that?*" Fran stared wetly at Jean, not blinking. "I try so hard to be friendly and yet you push me away. You just push and push and I don't understand!"

It felt to Jean as if Fran was not actually expecting a response but just setting out her anger and frustration and dismay like a centrepiece on a dining room table. *Look at my bright dismay*, Fran was saying. Her big, wet eyes, her turbulent mouth, her aspect of injury; altogether it was something quite impressive, almost something to be admired.

"We have a winner!" called Pete at the wheel.

"So fine," said Fran, her voice gone faint. "You don't like me. That's really the only thing that matters. And I don't need any more humiliation."

Watching Fran turn into the crowd, Jean had the strange and empowering sense that she was becoming almost a student of human nature. Something about striving so hard to find the roots of her friends' happiness was making her more attuned and observant. She turned back to the Wheel, ready to train her new powers of perception onto Pete Besseler, and noticed that Pete was sliding eight dollars toward her across the vinyl betting sheet.

"What's that?" said Jean.

"Your winnings!" said Pete. "Yours and the other lady's. Where did she go?"

Jean felt her shoulders sag. "I'll take it to her."

"No," said Pete, giving his head an official shake. "Can't let you do that. Half that money's not yours."

"Don't be ridiculous," said Jean, grabbing the money out of Pete's hands. "If you feel the need you can call the police. My brother has a booth."

The air felt weighted and damp against her cheeks and the dark clouds bulged oppressively low, like the underside of a vast, mouldy bunk bed. Jean wandered around the perimeter of the Activity Zone looking for where Fran might have gone and came to the sudden realization that she had completely lost track of Natalie, too.

"Natalie?" she called. She turned in a complete circle, search-ing, searching, aware that she must look like a grandmother who'd lost a five-year-old child. *Incompetent woman*, people would be thinking. *I'd never trust her with mine.* As she peered out over the dozens of heads she caught on one that looked famil-iar. But it wasn't Natalie's, or Fran's. It was grey and combed and bobbing pertly in the direction of the Picnic Basket Zone. It was . . . Milt. Seeing his head so far away, so disconnected from her, gave Jean a queer sensation. It was as though she were lost at sea, her body tossed between the waves, and Milt's head were a buoy. She was in the grip of the tides, the cruel, unthinking hand of nature, and Milt's head was the only sign of civilization, her only connection to humanity. She stood on her toes and stared at Milt's head as it receded, as the currents took it farther from her, and the urge to cry out to him was so strong . . .

But then she noticed another head. It was near Milt's, it was also familiar, and it seemed to be moving in the same direction, at the same pace. Jean felt her stomach twist and she lost the ability to breathe. Her face went tingly and cold. She turned away, made her feet carry her in the opposite direction. She pushed past two young men gnawing like jackals on buns stuffed with sausage and sauerkraut, past a little girl holding a puff of blue candy floss, past a busty T-shirted woman with a swoop of black hair down her back, past an old man bending down for a quarter. They were in her way! She would push through! She would keep going in this new, better, happier direction even if it took her back to the Fiery Swamp!

In the midst of her flight over the trampled grass and dirt and food wrappers of Corkin Park, through the flaxen fields of children, away from the spectre of those two heads . . . she nearly collided with Fran, who was turning away from the Kotemee Garden Club booth with something cupped in her hands.

"Oh, Fran!" blurted Jean.

Obviously startled, at a loss for words, even embarrassed, Fran glanced down at what she was carrying – a small, pressed-paper pot of soil that sprouted a slender green shoot – then looked up and around as if for a path of escape.

"Fran," said Jean. "We won!" She showed Fran the money in her hand.

Fran frowned as if she were confused. She reached up to adjust the sweater around her shoulders, and her gaze flitted between Jean's face and the coins in her hand. "We won?"

"On the jack of clubs! Here." Jean pushed the money into Fran's palm.

"How much?"

"I guess eight dollars."

Like a prairie morning, Fran's face filled with a sudden light. "Well isn't that . . ." She held out the little pot. "This Blood Lily was seven dollars and eighty-five cents. And now . . . it's like it's free. Oh!" She looked mortified. "Is this *our* money?"

"Um, no," said Jean, swallowing. "No, that's yours. That's yours to keep."

"Well," said Fran, relaxing, "I mean that's just . . ." She seemed not to know what to feel, what emotion to display for Jean's benefit. She opted for a small, relieved smile. "What a nice surprise."

For a moment the two women stood at the fringe of the Activity Zone with a darkening sky overhead and the air around them thick and alive and close to trembling.

"I should say . . ." began Fran. "Before, that wasn't very . . ." She stopped when Jean glanced around behind her. "I guess I'm boring you."

"Oh, no, Fran. That's not it." Jean touched the woman's wrist. "I'm sorry, it's just . . . Milt, my husband. He's . . . he's here, somewhere, and I don't want to see him. Or him to see me.'"

"Is that why you were rushing?"

"Yes."

Fran became alert. Her eyes sharpened, her features firmed, her whole bearing shifted, as if somewhere inside her a hidden switch had been flicked from *standby* to *on*. "Is something wrong? Has something happened?"

Jean hesitated. The problem was she was made a particular way, with a fundamental makeup – the way wood has a grain, with all its fibres laid and arranged in a certain direction – and that makeup insisted that only friends were told personal details about one's life. And friends were not acquaintances or people you met at a gathering, and they were not someone who came into your shop on a regular basis and seemed to want to intrude into your existence, they were not a woman who drove a Cadillac SUV and travelled frequently to Las Vegas, or who wore brooches to the supermarket and disparaged the town that had always been your home. They were not Fran. But just now it seemed too difficult, too much work, to resist Fran's desire to be involved. Jean had other needs for her energy, other purposes for her time. So she found herself nodding.

"Recently Milt told me that he was having an affair."

Fran recoiled. "No!"

"Yes."

"I can't believe it. He seems like the *last* person, other than my Jim. I mean, the two of them, I would have put them in the same pea pod."

"I didn't know you knew Milt."

"Well, people have pointed him out to me," said Fran. "And we chatted that one time, remember?" Fran gave a tug to her sweater and shook her head at the unfathomability of Milt, who had been pointed out to her, having an affair. "It's so sad. I always imagined you two having great conversations."

Jean made an effort to keep her gaze steady and her expression neutral. She admired newscasters for their ability not to look horrified at the crimes they reported.

"So, Fran, I think it's going to rain. You should probably get that lily home."

"Who was it with? This affair."

"Oh, I don't think that's important." She began to back away as Fran shook her head in apparent agreement; *no, it wasn't important*. "Have fun with that lily. And I'm sorry about the jack of clubs before."

Fran held up her coin-stuffed fist and gave it a triumphant waggle. "We're winners!"

"Yay," said Jean.

A sudden seriousness overtook Fran's face as the ground spread between her and Jean. "Do you want me to say anything to him? If I see him?"

Jean tried to gather this in. "Do I want you to say anything to . . . my husband?"

"Yes, the bastard."

"No." Jean shook her head. "Thank you."

She heard thunder, or sensed it, as she wandered past the petting zoo toward the picnic tables looking for Natalie. The skinny girl and bedraggled boys of Swamp Fire made it difficult to hear anything but the screech of children (evolution clearly intending for that sound to pierce any other). But the air itself was a warm body embracing her, and she felt it shudder. She had an image in her mind of Milt and Louise running through the coming downpour, laughing, getting soaked, pulling off their wet clothes in the shelter of the living room she had decorated, standing naked on the carpet she had vacuumed, drying themselves with the towels she had bought on sale at Sears.

Her mother had always made her believe that in choosing Milt she had failed. Marjorie's measure of a man, a husband, stood the height and width of Drew, tackled tasks in the same direct, unimaginative fashion, charted his course by the same unblinking stars. And perhaps that had contributed to Jean's choice not to take Milt's name, which lingered for years as a small hurt for him. But in the face of what she'd believed to be her mother's disappointment and disdain, she had always held to the certainty that Milt was a man she could grow old with. Their experiences together had been investments in the memories of their infirmity. *Some day we'll laugh at this* – that had been their motto. Twenty-two years ago, when Milt's stuffy Aunt Agnes was visiting and

Milkweed showed her his pink, pencil-thin erection . . . sixteen years ago, when Jean had done a terrible job tying Milt's father's canoe to the roof of the car and it went flying into a roadside cucumber stand . . . eleven years ago, when they were eating marinated octopus on a bench in Athens and someone snatched Jean's purse with all their credit cards . . . six years ago, when Jean collapsed from low blood pressure and awoke to Milt giving panicky directions for the ambulance and heard in his voice how much he loved her . . . two years ago, when Milt put Styrofoam Chinese food containers in the hot oven . . . every one of these experiences and dozens more were securities meant to bring returns later, a kind of pension of reminiscence. But the investments had turned out to be worthless.

Where was Natalie? Natalie would understand, thought Jean. Natalie was divorced. Natalie had her own failed portfolio of recollection. She too faced the prospect of a desolate old age.

Standing in the middle of Corkin Park, Jean realized that she and Natalie were closer to kindred spirits now than they had ever been. And she saw, with a fresh slap of horror, how she had wronged Natalie. How she had abandoned her own duty by not thinking the best of her friend, by not forgiving her immediately for her lie of omission, by which she had probably only meant to protect her, and even if not, no one was perfect! There were degrees of betrayal, shadings from light to dark, and compared to the hard, black mark against Louise, Natalie's was barely a smudge! And Jean knew with a ferocious clarity, the conviction of someone reborn into her beliefs, that Natalie deserved her gift. Of course she did. If anyone was worthy of the sacrifice, it was her.

"Jean!"

It was Welland, running up behind her. As she waited for him she felt the first drop of rain on her cheek and held her hand out for more.

"Welland, I have to find Natalie before it opens up on us."

Her brother was red in the face from running and couldn't speak just yet. He put a hand on his chest and bent over as he pointed to another part of the park. "I saw her," he wheezed. "When I was looking for you."

It was a good thing Welland was in Community Services and not doing actual police work, Jean thought; imagine if he ever had to run to catch a jewellery thief, or a murderer. But of course, as a sister, she would never actually say that. She loved Welland. It was crazy to her that he had never found a woman to really appreciate him and care for him. Because he was handsome and big, and wore a uniform, there was never any shortage of floozies at bars who wanted to drape themselves on him like a Roman toga. But he was too nice for that type, too gentle-souled. As she watched Welland trying to catch his breath she had an image of him becoming like their father before he died, silent and isolated, sunk into a chair in the basement, waiting for the inevitable. That was no way for someone to live.

"Welland," she said, "are you getting enough exercise?"

Her brother nodded and heaved with his hands on his knees, and he made a little racquet motion with his arm.

"Well, if you can walk I'd like to go find Natalie."

"Sure," he breathed, "no problem."

They made it past the Animal Zone and the Ferris wheel and approached the chip wagon selling cardboard containers of greasy French fries – there was still no sign of Natalie, and Jean had felt half a dozen more drops – before Welland seemed able to string a sentence together. When he did he became a very sombre presence beside her. Jean thought perhaps he had some advice regarding Milt, but that wasn't it.

"Adele Farbridge," said Welland. "She's your friend, right?"

Jean stumbled slightly at hearing Adele's name and she had to reach to catch Welland's elbow. She looked back at the ground they'd just passed as if she'd been tripped up by some unevenness. "Yes," she said, finally. "I saw her just the other day."

"I have something bad to tell you."

Could it have made the news already? Jean didn't see how that was possible. She walked along with Welland, through air that carried the scent of malt vinegar from the chip wagon, trying to fathom the logistics of how the information about Adele could already have been discovered and reported – it was only yesterday morning that she had left her. Had the news simply wafted out on a breeze? Beside her Welland was slowing, stopping, his hand on her arm, as if he needed to tell her face to face. A boy passed with a pile of salty, golden fries heaped like kindling on his plate. She heard a man sneeze and looked around.

"Maybe we should sit down," Welland was saying.

It was Milt. He was twenty feet away, wearing his green-checked shirt and his khaki shorts and his brown shoes with brown socks pulled high on his calves, something Jean had never been able to get him to stop doing. "Wear your sandals with shorts, Milt," she would say. But no, he wouldn't. He had no regard for her opinions. Her feelings. He did what he wanted, no matter who he hurt. For years she had asked him to apply for a full-time teaching position and he wouldn't. He *wouldn't*. He liked his freedom, he said. She understood that now. As he walked from the chip wagon toward the Picnic Basket Zone with his own plate of French fries, he stopped and sneezed again, burying his face in the crook of his arm while holding the plate high above his head.

"Milt?" she called out, embarrassing herself with the febrility in her voice.

He continued on, apparently unable to hear her over the squeals and laughter of roaming children, the distant frenetic clamour of Swamp Fire, and, wafting toward them from the Activity Zone, the bossy, blaring voices of the librarians' husbands.

"Jean," said Welland, laying his hand on her shoulder. "We really need to talk."

Kotemeeans, at least the ones who came to the annual picnic, were very messy eaters, it seemed to Jean. They produced a lot of garbage – paper cups and cardboard plates and plastic straws and tissuey napkins and waxed paper wrappers and bags of every known material. And suddenly the garbage wasn't confined to waste receptacles or corralled on top of picnic tables or even dropped discreetly underneath, it was everywhere. Because as the thunder and darkness of a rolling deluge advanced over Corkin Park the Kotemeeans began to scatter, and they left their garbage behind. And when the rain truly came, it came in thick, heavy dollops that thumped the ground and the picnic tables and the awnings of the Activity Zone and the roofs of the snack trucks like falling bits of flesh. And soon it was sluicing the garbage off the picnic tables and out of its hiding spaces and lodging it in the mud underfoot. And Jean ran through it. She ran to find Natalie. After her talk with Welland, she ran as fast as she could.

Her brother knew that something had happened to Adele, but not because it had been reported in the news. He was checking the police systems regularly now: the CPIC, the RMS, the PIP, and the NCIC. It was all part of his daily routine, thanks to Jean. It seemed to Welland that he was finally doing real police work. He expressed that to Jean with a combination of relief, and pride, and nervous elation. Without any orders to go by, or any real purpose, he roamed the networks and the databases looking for names he recognized, crimes he found intriguing. He had slipped into the station early that morning, he told Jean, before coming to the park. And as he'd scrolled through the identities of victims, he'd seen one he thought he knew. He'd clicked on it, and learned that Adele Farbridge, the finance executive, had been found in her apartment by her cleaning lady, discovered face down on the bed. There was a picture included, a driver's licence photo, and when he studied the face he knew this was someone he had met . . . this was Jean's friend.

Telling her all of this, Welland seemed the image of torment. Oh, he was such a sweet man, Jean thought. Such a good brother. It broke her heart to think that Welland would be distraught at having to deliver this news about Adele. *The last thing my poor sister needs . . .* that's what he'd be thinking.

To the south, a pulse of lightning flashed and lit the sky beyond the scrub brush, and a count of two later the thunder barrelled over them. Perched on the bench of a picnic table, Jean tipped back her head as Welland spoke and stared up at the blackening sky. She caught a few lucky raindrops on her cheeks, breathed with a hoarseness she hoped would signal distress, and asked the questions she thought someone hearing this news would ask.

"How did she die, Welland?" Jean asked. "Do they know who killed her?"

Welland's face bloomed with horror. "Oh, no, she didn't die."

Jean blinked at her brother as another drop glanced off her cheekbone. She was quite sure she hadn't heard that correctly.

"But –"

"Oh, gosh. I'm sorry, Jean. I didn't mean to –"

"Welland, what are you talking about?" Jean swiped the rain from her lashes. "Didn't you say her body had been discovered?"

"She *was* discovered, thank goodness. Before it was too late. She's in a coma," said Welland. "They found some heavy drugs in her system." He touched Jean's arm in a way that she knew was meant to be encouraging. "There's still a chance she'll come around."

This news so widely missed the mark of *encouraging* that Jean pulled her arm back.

"It's upsetting, I know."

"Yes," she said. What could have gone wrong? She retraced in her mind those crucial moments with Adele, when she had spread glob after glistening glob of narcotic into her skin. How could someone so skinny have survived? Part of Jean thought she should admire Adele for that, but she couldn't because it was so disappointing. She had worked so hard to make those final moments beautiful . . . and final . . . and now there was a chance it would all be shattered. There was a chance that at any second Adele would wake up and demand to know what Jean had been thinking. And undoubtedly other people would want to know as well. *Jean Vale Horemarsh, what could possibly have been going through your mind?* And then it would all get so complicated, and she might not be able to give Natalie or Cheryl their Last Poems . . .

"I wish I hadn't had to be the one to tell you," said Welland. "It's just so rotten. Because you've already lost Mom, and your friend Dorothy. And now you might lose another."

Jean leaned forward. "She might still die?"

"Well, maybe." Welland pressed his wide thumbnail into the soft, damp wood of the picnic table, and Jean could tell, as his sister, that he had something else to say. She waited. Welland wasn't very good at handling being rushed. She waited as he lifted off his cap and used the bill to scratch his scalp through his sweat-damp hair. And she waited as he watched a father run by the picnic table in pursuit of his little tomboy daughter. She could just wait and wait if necessary, without ever letting Welland know how urgent her situation was . . .

"The thing is," Welland finally continued, "the circumstances are suspicious. There were drugs in her system, but no sign of her taking anything. So, according to the report, they suspect foul play."

Welland kept talking and Jean tried to listen, even though she found the phrase *foul play* distracting in its implications of fedoras and whisky and snub-nosed .45s, and even though her imperatives pressed down harder with each passing minute. Welland mentioned that Jean's name had been listed in the report as one of Adele's contacts – probably it had been lifted from her address book – and so, just as a routine matter, she was probably going to get a visit from some city detectives. It was no fun talking to city detectives, Welland told her, his face full of concern.

"Welland," she said, stretching her arm across the rain-spotted picnic table, "I don't want you to be too upset about Adele." She laid her hand on his wrist. "If she *does* die – and what are the chances of that, by the way?"

Welland made a helpless flaily-arm gesture. "It didn't say in the report."

"Well, assuming she does, we can just think of her as being lucky. She's already had a mastectomy. There's no telling what awaits her. If she dies this way then at least she won't have to die like Mom did. She'll have been spared all that pain. And that's good, don't you think?"

Welland looked at Jean and squinted with one whole side of his face. It was similar to what would happen to Drew's face when he was trying to noodle a thing out, and Jean was sad for her brother that it was just about the only part of their father that he had gotten.

"She's young, though," he said.

"Not so young, really," said Jean. "My age."

"But you're young, Jeanie!"

She shook her head. It was obvious to anyone who looked, without the veils of affection, that she was getting on. When she focused a clear eye on the mirror she saw nothing of the girl she'd been, only the wearing, dragging, unforgiving work of age. Just as when she looked at her friends, the ones she had known the longest, she saw not just who they were but how much they had changed. Their faces and bodies were billboard advertisements for the passage of time, explicit proof of how old she was getting, and therefore how close to her mother's fate. She was never going to convince Welland of this, though; he was too big-hearted, which made his judgment unreliable.

But she couldn't waste any more time. She patted Welland's hand and stood.

It must have been that abrupt motion that attracted the attention of Fran Knubel because, from the other side of the Picnic Basket Zone, separated by perhaps twelve or thirteen tables, she could be heard calling out, "Jean!" The sound of her voice reached Jean at roughly the same moment the clouds above gave way and the chubby drops began to fall, hitting the ground with their fleshy thuds and knocking the paper cups and bags and wrappers off the picnic tables into the mud and under Jean's feet as she began to run.

And as Jean ran to find Natalie, ran to her responsibility, ran through the Kotemeean refuse as fast as she possibly could, it would have looked to Fran as though she were merely dashing to get out of the rain.

It was a desperate sound, a frantic yelling, that finally drew Jean to Natalie. She found her, to Jean's great surprise, at the dunk tank.

The Activity Zone was mostly deserted. Rain pooled in the awnings, slammed down on the lids of coolers and the game tables being folded and packed away by librarians' husbands slopping through the mud. Natalie stood in front of the dunk tank, hair smeared to her forehead and neck, a spout of water running from her nose, her white blouse showing pink where it stuck to her skin. She had three baseballs clutched to her chest, and one more in her hand, which was raised to fire.

"Stop! I'm *begging* you, Natalie!"

The yelling came from Tina Dooley, who was in the dunk tank. It was an old and very poorly designed dunk tank. There seemed to be only one way out of the Plexiglas surround filled rib-high with grey, sloshing water; that was to stand on the triggered platform on which the dunkee sat, and step from there to a wooden ledge, which led to a set of descending stairs. Natalie seemed to have discovered this design flaw, and every time poor Tina Dooley tried to step on the platform to get out of the tank, Natalie hurled a ball with the accuracy of a sniper toward the padded target, triggering the platform to swing away and dropping Tina into the drink.

"Natalie!" cried Tina as she was knocked sideways by the wave she had created. "For God's sake! What's the *matter* with you?"

Natalie seemed not to hear, or perhaps the sound of Tina's pleading only fed whatever revenge-lust gripped her. In her blue-and-lime one-piece bathing suit with ill-advised frills around the hips, Tina struggled once more onto the platform on her knees. Natalie waited for the precise moment and whipped another ball, sending her tumbling backward into the rolling water with an enormous glunking splash that climbed the sides of the tank and sloshed over the top. There were no organizers to intervene; all of them were scrambling through the rain to dismantle and pack away other displays and pieces of equipment. Tina, her coppery hair clinging to her skull like seaweed, her eye makeup trailing down her cheeks like squid's ink, clutched herself as she rose to her feet. Hands trembling, teeth chattering, she leaned back, exhausted, against the Plexiglas wall as the water lapped at her.

"I *hate* you!" she wailed. "I hate you, you *cow*!"

Jean tugged on Natalie's sleeve. "Natalie," she said, "let's go."

"One more!" Natalie shouted. She was as wet as Tina, but something inside her cooked with a kiln-like heat. She spun the ball in her hand like a pitcher as she watched Tina struggle onto the platform. "It's her own fault. I told her last month if she sent one more of her goddamn memos I'd get her."

Jean heard sloshing behind her and turned to see Fran charging through the slop, her prim tennis-shod feet launching little tsunamis of murky rainwater with every step.

"*There* you are! Oh, thank God!"

One whole hemisphere of Fran – from the left isthmus of her designer jeans straight up to the tectonic plate of her jaw and cheek – was slathered in a layer of mud, and she followed Jean's gaze to the disaster zone of her own body.

"I took a spill by the pony rides," she explained. "But it doesn't matter because I found you!" She squelched up to where the two women were standing and reached to clutch Jean's dripping elbow. "Jean, I feel terrible," she said, blinking against the rain. "I should have asked you before and I hope it's not too late. Would you come for dinner tonight at our place? I just think you shouldn't be alone right now, and I know Jim has been dying to meet you."

"Oh," said Jean. She looked at the splendid mess of Fran – her hair, half her blouse, most of the yellow sweater around her shoulders iced a rich mocha – and tried not to imagine what Fran could have said to make Jim so desperate for an introduction.

"Actually," she said, "I think Natalie's already made plans for us this evening."

She turned toward Natalie for confirmation, but Natalie's attention was all on Tina Dooley as the woman hauled herself from the water onto the shaky platform like an air crash survivor mounting a fragment of fuselage.

"Natalie," piped Fran over Jean's shoulder, "would you like to come over to our place for dinner tonight?"

"Nope," said Natalie, lining up her target.

"Do you mind if Jean does?"

"Nope," said Natalie, cocking her arm for a throw.

"See?" said Fran. "It's all set." The teeth of her smile gleamed bright against the mud mask sliding down her cheek. She thumbed muck off the crystal of her watch. "Try and come for seven, okay?"

With a great woof of exertion, Natalie threw her last ball. It sailed a foot above the target and bounced off the trunk lid of a departing Fire Department cruiser.

"Ha!" yelled Tina Dooley as she climbed to safety on the wooden ledge. She thrust a middle finger in Natalie's direction. "Eat it, Skilbeck."

"Damn," Natalie muttered, shaking her head. "Wanted it too much."

Chapter 17

Cheryl came to her decision in the western end of the vineyard. Then she made her way back to the house. Before she arrived in the large, mahogany-cabinetted kitchen of her house, a bottle of Riesling disappeared. In the kitchen, she took a twelve-inch carving knife from a woodblock, waved it like a flag as she got its heft, and used it to cut up an apple for Buzzy, largely but not entirely avoiding her fingers. As she pushed the bloodied apple slices one by one through the bars of the cage, Buzzy made his whistling kettle noise, and each slice as it landed sent up a cloud of seed husks and feathers from the disarray on the cage floor.

She wandered through the empty house for a while, through echoey hallways that no longer featured artistic travel photographs on the walls, past rooms that no longer contained exercise and computer equipment, Chinese heirlooms, and the smell of

Partagas cigars. She was lost between the soothing idea of her end and the inspiration for how to achieve it, until she remembered the knife and went looking for it.

The knife was . . . there, on the counter where she'd left it. She picked up the knife and considered it for a moment, considered the knife and its function as an idea . . . could not quite get the whole, messy picture of the idea in her head all at once, to see what she would do, how it would happen, what it would mean. If she couldn't think it, she couldn't make it occur. No knives.

Between the kitchen and the basement, a second bottle of Riesling disappeared. In the basement, Cheryl considered electrical cords. There were short white ones and long orange ones, swaying from nails on the wall. The long orange ones with ribbed sheathing seemed promising. She could tie one end of an orange electrical cord to something high, tie the other part around her neck, and then fall. That might work, she thought. Okay, she thought, she would try that.

There was nothing high in the basement, so she dragged the coil of orange electrical cord up the stairs. A tree maybe, Cheryl thought. Between the thought of the tree and the discovery of a suitable oak at the edge of her yard, most of a bottle of Cabernet Franc disappeared. The remainder was lost when the bottle slipped out of her hand and the wine dribbled out and seeped into the earth.

The large oak tree at the edge of her yard had many branches, and looking up at them to try and choose one made Cheryl woozy. So she spent some amount of time attempting to fling the plug end of the electrical cord over one of the branches above her without actually looking up. She made more than a dozen attempts and, each time, the cord fell uselessly to the ground. For some further amount of time, Cheryl stood beneath the oak tree and wept until her shoulders shook over her inability to get an electrical cord over a branch.

When she was done weeping, Cheryl heard the sound of a car with a blaring radio and lifted her head. From where she swayed, she could see the paved two-lane road that passed in front of her property. The car roared past, right to left, and she thought about that for a while. Then Cheryl looked into the distance, where the road narrowed to a point. There was some kind of truck approaching. She watched this truck, saw that it was a pickup, and followed it with her eyes as best she could, until it too sped past, the tires howling over the pavement.

Then Cheryl started walking toward the road.

Chapter 18

The storm drummed on Corkin Park, and the lakeshore, and the pretty avenues of Kotemee for another half an hour or so. While it did the gutters coursed and the sidewalks danced, and hissing cars along Howell Road carved plumes through puddles big as lawns. One of those cars, Jean saw as she walked toward home with Natalie, was Jeff Birdy's orange Barracuda, and the sight of it disappearing into the downpour was almost nostalgic for her, although she gave the boy inside little thought. She concentrated instead on the problem ahead of her. Because the terrible news of Adele's survival brought with it the prospect of detectives at her door at any moment, and the chance that she might never be able to give another friend her beautiful, practical gift. If that happened, she didn't see how she could live with herself. So she walked through the rain, hardly saying a word to

Natalie, hardly lifting her gaze from the grass encroaching the limits of the sidewalk, and felt the pressures of her obligation building with each soggy step.

Natalie wasn't like her other friends. Jean couldn't help but dwell on that fact. The whole foundation of her gift was a last moment of joy, and yet Natalie was someone who seemed to *reject* joy, to refuse it and its consolations on principle. How could such a person ever be fulfilled?

As she walked, Jean riffled through the easy options like someone thumbing through paint chips. Sex? No, that one was easily dismissed. Unlike for Dorothy and Adele, sex didn't appear to be a priority for Natalie. She snickered with contempt whenever other women ogled a handsome man, or leaned in during pairs figure skating as the male skater lifted his partner and clenched. Perhaps that was a camouflage, a way of protecting herself from disappointment. But even so, it seemed clear to Jean that sex was not the thing Natalie needed. For the same reason she rejected any ideas relating to food that wanted to push into her brain. The notion of some kind of grand last supper for a woman who occasionally liked to indulge; it was just too cheap.

A spa treatment, glorious and relaxing? Hot stones? Pedicure? Mud bath? No, no, no, thought Jean. These were paltry, make-do ideas. They showed no imagination, no specificity, no truth. The beauty of the moments she'd made for Dorothy and Adele was that they had just happened. They were real, and so the joys were authentic.

She sensed she was searching in the wrong place, for the wrong thing. For this friend, Jean reasoned, the experience of complete, immersive happiness took an entirely different form. To anyone else, it wouldn't even *look* like happiness; that's how different Natalie was. If she needed a reminder of that, she got it on the walk home. By the time the two women had reached the north end of Calendar Street the storm had largely abated, the grand elms and beech trees were shaking off more rain than the clouds, and light filtered into the sky like an afternoon dawn. Jean's feet were squishing in her running shoes and she stopped to take them off so that she might pour the excess water out. As she stood barefoot on the cold, wet sidewalk, she looked back where the sky was brightest and saw an immense rainbow arching over the outskirts of Kotemee.

"Look, Natalie!" she said, pointing. "Isn't it exquisite?"

Natalie squinted up at the arc of colour. "Sandeep used to go gaga over rainbows. Something about Allah and His Holy Last Messengers." Her upper lip kinked into a sneer. "He kind of ruined them for me."

Who on earth didn't like rainbows? What kind of person sneered cynically at something so magical? She almost chided Natalie until she seized on the answer. Someone who pushed against the world. Someone for whom everything was fraught and complicated and sharp-edged. Someone who called timid old ladies terrible names and stood in the teeming rain firing baseballs to feed a lust for revenge. Someone who relished conflict.

In that moment, Jean realized what she needed to do. She needed to give Natalie something to struggle against, something to fight. And for it to be worthy of Jean's goal, and of Natalie, it couldn't be just anything . . . it had to be the ultimate thing.

The rest of the walk toward Natalie's house felt much lighter to Jean. There was a moment when she saw a police car coming along Calendar and froze. But then she saw it was Bill Courtly behind the wheel; Bill was just an ordinary constable and sort of dopy, and Jean thought if they were going to send somebody to arrest her it wouldn't be him. But she didn't wave or attract any attention to herself just in case.

With not far to go, she announced to Natalie that she needed to make a quick stop at her shop. So they turned at the corner of Main, passed under the ornamental street lamp, its wrought-iron curlicue still dripping, and walked up the street past the pots of flattened geraniums. When they arrived at the shop, Jean paused as she put the key in the front door, and wondered out loud whether Dilman's was open.

"I'd say they'd better be," said Natalie. And off she went to buy an assortment of cupcakes, which gave Jean time to stand before her wall of tools, consider the array of options, and make the very best choice.

At Natalie's, each of the women spent a while under the spray in her tiny shower, where turning around meant being careful not to hit your head on the little metal shelf of shampoos, and Jean no longer wondered why her friend had chosen such a small house to live in after her divorce. It was the sort of house that made everything – bathing, cooking, entertaining guests – much more difficult than it needed to be, and it was clear now that was just how Natalie liked it.

When they were done it was about three in the afternoon, and bundled warm in their terry-cloth robes they met downstairs in the little kitchen. Natalie had already set out the cupcakes on a plate and was in the middle of making coffee when Jean joined her. For a brief moment Natalie struggled sliding in the basket that held the grounds, and when she swore at the coffee maker and gave it a whack with her hand, Jean smiled to herself.

As she sat at the kitchen island, she set a small paper bag by the foot of her stool.

"What's that?" asked Natalie.

"It's what I wanted to get at the shop," said Jean. "A little surprise for you."

"A ceramic?"

Jean shook her head and gave Natalie an admonishing look. "No guessing." She passed her gaze over the assorted cupcakes. Was there chocolate? Yes, but only one, and she knew that was Natalie's favourite. On another day, she might have invoked guest's privilege and taken it, but not today. Instead, she took a lemon with white icing and sprinkles, which she didn't mind.

"Natalie, I want to thank you again for being there for me and letting me sleep here during this whole stupid Milt thing."

Natalie was reaching up to grab two mugs from the cupboard. "That's what friends are for, kiddo." She set the cups on the counter and tugged open the fridge. As she brought out a carton of milk, she giggled.

"What's so funny?"

"I just think it's pretty hilarious you're going to dinner at Fran Knubel's."

"Yes, and thank you so much for your support," said Jean. "That's one instance where you were *not* there for me."

"You could have just said no, like I did."

Jean tore off a piece of cupcake with her fingers and held it like a cotton ball ready to dab a puncture wound. "But that's your way. I'm not like you. I accept invitations that I don't particularly want, because I can't bear to hurt someone's feelings, even someone like Fran. You're different. You do things and say things that most people would never do or say."

Natalie batted her eyes. "Does that make me a bad person?"

"It makes you a challenge." Jean popped the pinch of cupcake in her mouth. She pointed down at the plate and joggled her eyebrows expectantly. "I left the chocolate one for you."

Natalie made the face of someone quite unimpressed. "You can have it. I'm off chocolate."

Jean just looked at her friend, saying nothing but invisibly shaking her head. Because wasn't that typical? That was *so* typical. Really, Natalie Skilbeck was the most difficult, most challenging person Jean had ever known. She thought to herself that it was amazing they had remained friends for so long, because, looked at objectively, Natalie's personality could be very off-putting.

"Well, which one do you want?" said Jean. "Which one are you craving?"

Natalie sighed. "I dunno, maybe the carrot."

"Then have the carrot. Have the one you want. This is your chance."

"I'm not sure I even want it."

"Then why did you buy it?"

"Why are you pushing me?"

"I'm *not*."

Jean held up her hands and let out a big breath, because suddenly they were both in a bad mood and this was not how she wanted things to go. Natalie turned to face the counter and began pouring coffee into the mugs, and Jean adjusted her robe and cinched the belt. It was, perhaps, a subconscious action but she caught herself doing it, and that focused her mind.

"Natalie," said Jean, "do you have any gloves?"

"What kind of gloves?"

"Any kind, it doesn't matter. But probably not little knit ones."

Natalie handed Jean her coffee. "What do you want gloves for?"

"They're for you, to put on."

Natalie brought her coffee mug to her mouth and took a careful sip, looking the whole time at Jean with a furrow across her forehead.

"Why, though?"

Jean made a sound of mock exasperation, which really wasn't so mock. "It's for the surprise!"

The crease in Natalie's forehead eased a little. "So you *are* giving me a ceramic. It's one of those prickly ones with the thorns."

Natalie meant the *Bramble Berry* series of ceramics Jean had done a few years before: one each of *Raspberry, Dewberry, Blackberry, Loganberry,* and *Tayberry,* in which a single bright berry glazed in purple or red or blue was surrounded by a thatch of spiny branches and leaves. Even though Jean had used these dabs of vivid colour, which was rare for her, the series had not sold well. One visitor to the shop had actually called them "wicked," and not as a compliment.

Jean looked off noncommittally and smiled.

"I probably have some leather ones somewhere," said Natalie. "I usually pack all my winter stuff away." She set down her coffee and left to go rummaging in her front closet. Within a few minutes she came back flapping a pair of brown lambskin gloves.

"Good," said Jean. "Now put them on."

"Is it really necessary?"

"Yes, I think it is."

Natalie sighed and pulled on first the left glove and then the right. Standing in her bathrobe, she held up her hands to show that she was ready. "You know, Jean," she said, "you don't have to give me something just because I'm giving you a place to stay. I'm your friend. That's what friends do."

"I *know*," said Jean. She found her voice going strangely hoarse and had to clear her throat. "I *know* you're my friend. It's not a thank-you present." She felt flushed. She looked at Natalie holding up her gloved hands and a wave of emotion that was quite unexpected washed through her. For twenty-three years she had known this woman, and she could see all of that time, all those shared memories, all those spent days spread through every inch of Natalie's face, every slight discoloration, every crease and fold of skin and every coarse grey hair sneaking past the battlements of tint and curl. For Jean, looking at dear Natalie was like seeing her own hand clutching the ledge that kept her from falling into the abyss, and watching it lose its grip, finger by finger.

She patted the stool next to her. "Sit here," she said. And when Natalie sat, facing her, Jean made a twirling motion. "The other way."

"Do you want me to close my eyes?"

"Good idea."

Natalie repositioned herself with her hands in her lap. "This is actually kind of exciting."

"I know. Now the next part is going to seem odd, but no arguing. I want you to hold your hands a little higher, and together, kind of like you're praying. Even though neither of us believe in that."

Natalie glanced back at Jean. "Who says I don't?"

"Oh," said Jean. "Do you?"

For a second, even two, it seemed as if the answer to that question should make a difference. But even before Natalie gave her answer, which was squishy and equivocal, Jean had decided that, no, it didn't really. Age and pain affected everyone, regardless of their beliefs. And with Natalie's hypertension and penchant for sweets, it was only a matter of time.

"Ready? Eyes closed?"

"Ready."

Jean bent and picked up the paper bag she had placed by her stool. She opened it and took out a coiled wire. This was her heavy-duty cutting wire, a strand of thin stainless-steel cable, which she used to slice her twenty-kilo blocks of clay into manageable one-kilo hunks. Uncoiled, the wire was less than a metre long and secured at each end to a sturdy hardwood handle. At a cost of about four dollars, it was one of Jean's least expensive tools. And yet, after the storm, when she'd made her side trip into the shop to look at her wall of cutters and shapers, she'd known immediately that it was the perfect choice. Because it gave Natalie a fighting chance.

She stood up and pushed away her stool, unwound the wire, and got a firm hold of each of the wooden handles. After a delay to make sure Natalie was still holding her hands in a prayerful position, she reached out and eased the wire over her friend's head.

"Now you can look."

Jean didn't give Natalie time to gather the full significance of the situation before her – the shining grey wire twisting across her field of view, Jean holding it from behind the way she might have held a ribbon she intended to wrap around a present, the fact that the wire was vibrating an inch from her gloved hands, the gloves themselves and their greater meaning. Jean said, "Now you can look," and then she pulled the wire tight and cinched hard, hard as she could, as if Natalie were an old and very difficult block of clay.

As sure as she had been that this was the right choice for her friend . . . as sure as she was still . . . Jean found it very hard. Unbearably hard. Not the physical struggle, that was only to be expected. Indeed, it was the point. And she was strong, after all those years of working with clay, hauling the twenty-kilo blocks from the car to the back of the shop with no help from Milt, dividing them up into chunks, pressing and pounding and moulding the lumps into something unique, something worthwhile, and doing it over and over again after each failed attempt. Working in ceramics was an odd amalgam of artistry and dumb manual labour, and Jean was inured to it. So no, her muscles weren't the issue.

It was just that she would not have chosen this end for herself, and it was upsetting. Violence had never formed any part of the picture she'd imagined in that first ecstatic moment of inspiration. Thanks to her mother she was not afraid of blood, and it didn't bother her now, except that it suggested pain and pain had always been the very thing she'd wanted to avoid. But she knew that her own expectations and sensibilities were beside the point, and that her notion of joy and Natalie's were very different. She believed that with this deeply important, deeply Natalie-affirming conflict, she was honouring the true essence of her friend. And Jean knew too, so vividly, that there was no fighting a disease like the one that had taken her mother. There was no fighting age. It claimed you and pulled you and there were no ledges to grab, no wires to fend off. So you had to give in. And for someone like Natalie, that would just be a terrible way to die.

"This is better, Natalie," she said as she heaved on the wire. "I promise you, this is so much better."

When it was finally over, when she was done and sure there would be no Adele-like surprises, Jean collapsed back on the kitchen floor, wholly spent. She stared up at the ceiling, sucking for air, letting the muscles of her hands and arms release and unclench, enjoying the cold, unyielding compression of the tiles beneath her, absorbing the stillness around her, the utter silence. She lay back for the longest time, eyes on the stucco above, feeling the weight of Natalie's head in her lap, but most conscious, most appreciative, of the silence. It was a lovely silence, complete and clean and weightless. It was uncluttered by the distraction of misgiving or apprehension, the disquiet of expectation, of anger or guilt. It was nothing like the silence that surrounded her those three months of nights in her mother's house, when she lay awake in the spare room waiting for her mother to die. It was a silence without pain. It was a silence without hope. It was rare and full and perfect.

But after some time, as Jean lay quiet, she became aware of a sound pressing at the edges of this stillness. It knocked at the shell of the hush, tentatively, and gradually grew louder and more insistent. At first it was a sound without context, it agitated the air she breathed but had no connection to her. She was annoyed by this spoiling sound, and she tried to push it away. As far as Jean was concerned, the sound had no business being there and she refused to decode its meaning. Until suddenly she realized: someone was knocking at the door.

She raised her head off the tiles and looked. From where she lay, she could see the edge of the front door and a shadow coming through its bevelled glass window. Someone was there. And as she took hold of this fact, like plucking a grape from a vine, another few facts tumbled with it. The person had a voice. The person was calling her. The person was Milt.

"Jean!" he was saying. "Jean! Please, come to the door. I know you're there."

She sat up and pulled her robe tight to her chest. It was Milt, hammering on the door! Milt had come, and she didn't know why, but it thrilled her!

"Milt?" she called. The hammering continued. "Milt!" she called again, and it stopped.

There was a second's pause and then her husband – her *husband* – called out, "Jean?" He rattled the doorknob and began to knock even harder. "Jean? Are you there?"

"Milt, stop!" Jean called from the kitchen floor. She put a hand to her forehead. "Stop banging!"

Milt did as he was told, and the reverberations shimmered off through the house. "Jean," he shouted, "can I come in?"

Jean looked down at Natalie's body, her head still heavy in her lap. She touched Natalie's hair, the dark curls at her temple. "No," she said. She tried to lift Natalie's head and shift her body so that she could get out from beneath it.

"What?"

"No!" she yelled. "You can't come in!" Natalie's head was like a great, packed bag of bread flour, a brick, a bowling ball – already weighty in itself. But it wasn't just itself; it was joined to another, greater weight. It was a bowling ball yoked to a sofa, and so it was almost impossible to move. And from her position on the floor, Jean had no leverage. The only way she could get herself free was to set her hands on the bloody tiles around her and shift herself backward until eventually Natalie's head was between her knees, and when Jean tugged her robe free, Natalie's head skipped over the hem and hit the tile with a musical *thunk*.

"Please, Jean," Milt was saying. "I want to talk to you! Don't you want to talk?"

The pools of blood on the floor were turning sticky. As Jean moved away her palms made smacking noises on the tiles.

"Milt, this is not a good time."

The blood stretched from the far kitchen wall to the fridge and speckled the hallway beyond. Once Jean got to her feet she did her best, in her slippers, to step around and over it. Once in the hallway she could see Milt's fuzzy silhouette on the other side of a sheer fabric panel that covered the leaded glass of the front door. She stood back, at the edge of the shadow he cast on the floor.

"Milt," she called, "you have to go away."

Milt's fuzzy hand pressed against the glass. "I was wrong, Jean. I was wrong and I'm sorry. I saw you at the picnic today, talking to Welland, and right there I knew I was making a mistake. It wouldn't work with Louise. It was just a fantasy. It was stupid and I love you and I'm sorry."

Jean pulled her blood-damp robe tight. There were things she wanted in the world and a husband was one of them, and her husband was Milt, Milt who knew her, Milt who had confessed his sins, Milt who had come back. She knew that it was weak, and she hated her weakness, but after all she had been through she needed some comfort and she wanted this man. She didn't want to grow old, and she didn't want to die in pain, but worse than either of those was to die alone. Even her mother had not died alone. Even Marjorie had had someone. She'd had her. And now here, Jean saw, was her own answer, here was her own practical solution. Here was her Milt.

"Jean?"

She looked back at Natalie's body on the kitchen floor, the coils of the cutting wire looped lazily under her chin, the steel strand embedded here and there in the blood-glazed skin of her neck. She looked down the hall toward the door where Milt stood waiting. Was it even possible, Jean wondered, for a woman ever to be purely happy?

"Milt," she said as she went toward the door, "I'm afraid I've made a bit of a mess."

Some hours later, shortly after seven o'clock, Jean was sitting with her hands folded in her lap in the champagne-carpeted ostentation of Fran Knubel's living room. Fran was carrying in a silver tray bearing glasses of Chablis she'd bought at the liquor outlet on Primrose Street – or, as Fran had put it, "the best white wine I could find at that dinky little store." She ferried the tray to a mahogany tea table, which stood ready between a turquoise-upholstered wingback chair and a burgundy, flock settee, and with a free hand pulled out a sliding shelf on which to set it.

"Well," said Fran as she handed Jean her glass of wine, "wasn't this an eventful day?"

Jean, reaching for the wine, flinched.

"Arthritis?" asked Fran.

"No," said Jean. "I must have pulled a muscle somehow."

Chapter 19

"Don't you just love Céline Dion?"

It was a seven-hour drive to Bier Ridge, New York. And as Jean watched the strategic highway-side vegetation roll past, the thin line of brush and trees that suggested miles of wilderness but veiled untold atrocities of development – conglomerations of Big Boxes and strip mines and fields sown with corn that would never touch a plate – she still struggled to accept the reality of her predicament: that she was making this trip, spending these hours, venturing at last to see her long-lost friend Cheryl, in the passenger seat of Fran Knubel's Cadillac SUV.

"Don't you?" said Fran from behind the wheel. "Don't you love her?"

"She's very good," said Jean, her eyes on the lying foliage.

"She sounds like angels to me." Fran reached down and pushed Céline's volume a smidge higher. "I could die listening to her singing."

Jean turned her head slowly to look at Fran. Part of her knew that she didn't really mean what she'd said, because people joked about death all the time without realizing how close it was, and how final. Another part of her thought that if Fran expected her to do for Fran what she was doing for her friends, the woman was sadly mistaken.

They were skirting the limits of a town called Marshall, about the size of Kotemee, and here and there through the trees Jean caught glimpses of the rooftops of subdivisions, which didn't surprise her because there were few small towns that really wanted to stay small, but which made her sad for the same reason. Years brought change, some of it good but most of it bad, and there was nothing anyone could do about it. You couldn't stop the change; all you could stop were the years.

Fran seemed determined to share her whole library of Céline Dion, one disc after another, so she was occupied for a while and mostly quiet as she drove, which Jean viewed as the one true bit of grace granted her by Céline's stentorian talent. Unlike an hour ago – when Fran wanted to wrench Jean out of her thoughts every few minutes with a detailing of the extensive plans she and Jim had for their kitchen, master bedroom, and basement media-room/wine-cellar reconfiguration – Jean was able to concentrate. She was able to replay in her mind, as a car-accident victim might relive the seconds before impact, the events that had led to Fran's offer to drive Jean to Bier Ridge, and her own unthinking answer of "Sure," which had bound her to Fran as certainly as a pair of handcuffs had bound Tony Curtis to Sidney Poitier in that movie . . . what was it called? . . . *The Defiant Ones*.

She thought back to the moment when she'd picked her way

toward the entrance of Natalie's house in her bathrobe, intending to open the door. She had intended to, because she was shaken after her ordeal with Natalie, quite shattered actually, and needed someone to hold her, and like a miracle there was Milt, and he loved her and wanted to be with her, *her* and not Louise. Because he was her husband – by no means a perfect one, which hardly needed to be said, but her husband nevertheless. Because they had shared twenty-nine mostly happy years together, so that by now their memories were entwined like bindweed and neither of them could look back on his or her own life without thinking of the other, which was, this accumulation of reminiscence, the only, *only* benefit of age.

So Jean walked to the door as Milt stood waiting on Natalie's front step, his fuzzy silhouette visible through the sheer panel over the bevelled glass of the door. She reached for the handle, certain that Milt would be getting ready to swallow her in a big bear hug the way he used to, that he would look at her with love in his sad grey eyes and reassure her that whatever years he had left would be spent with her.

And then she stopped.

She looked down at the blood-soaked front of her robe, at Natalie's drying blood on her hands. She glanced back at the spray of red that reached into the hall like strewn cinnamon candies from all the flailing – Natalie had fought so ferociously! – and thought of her friend now splayed out on her own kitchen tiles. And she realized that Milt could not possibly be allowed to see any of it. He would not understand. He would not know how to cope. He would make everything so much more complicated. And Jean knew that seeing what she had done was sure to change how Milt looked at her, that it would erase the love in his eyes and put worry and confusion, perhaps even fear, in its place. And she knew that would break her heart.

So Jean did not open the door. With two clean fingers she pulled aside the edge of the sheer panel and peeked out at Milt, so that he could see nothing but her face. And though it was the hardest thing she had ever done, though it made her throat ache to say the words, she told Milt to leave.

"Go away, Milt," she said.

"But Jean . . ."

"I mean it. I don't . . . I don't want you here right now."

Milt put his pudgy face close to the window, so there was only a pane of glass and an inch of air between his nose and hers and she could almost feel the bristles of his beard against her cheek. "Jean, I don't understand. I *love* you."

Jean saw his eyes welling up and she bit her lip. "I want you to go."

"Let me in!" he begged. "Let me in or I'll break the door down!"

She closed her eyes and kissed the glass, and let the sheer fabric fall back into place. Milt was making so much noise at the door that she felt it was safe to cry, so she sobbed loudly as she walked back to where Natalie lay. On the front step Milt continued to rage about busting down the door, but Jean had lived with him long enough to know he would never do any such thing.

After Milt finally gave up and trudged off, Jean realized that she had barely enough energy and time to get herself ready for dinner at Fran's; she'd have to leave the cleanup of Natalie till later. Upstairs in the cramped bathroom she didn't bother with another shower but scrubbed her arms and neck clean, and washed the tear streaks from her face. She fixed her makeup and dressed. Then she had to call upon all of her reserves of willpower to walk out the door.

Fran and Jim's white-brick residence was located on Jolling Crescent in the same elevated section of Kotemee as Blanchard

Avenue, where Jean had grown up, although it had to be said that Jolling was an even nicer street, with even handsomer houses. Jean had walked along Jolling plenty of times as a child, but this time, as she made her way in the fading light, she noticed that many of the houses were new. A lot of perfectly fine older homes had been knocked down and replaced with houses that were bigger and grander, with larger garages. Jean usually found that offensive, but now she couldn't summon the indignation.

At the apex of the crescent she came to Fran and Jim's house, which was set back from the sidewalk to make room for the circular driveway where the Cadillac SUV sat as if it had been put on display just for her. The house itself featured a roof that started high and swooped low toward the street, and halfway down the slope of the roof two large gables jutted out, looking big enough to be sizable homes in themselves. Staring up at these gables, Jean didn't have to think very hard to imagine the spacious second-floor rooms behind the windows, and for a moment, she found herself wondering if Fran and Jim slept in their own separate bedrooms. Then she realized that was the very sort of thing Fran might wonder about *her*, and she pushed the whole unseemly subject from her mind.

At Fran's door she sighed and put her thumb to the buzzer, resigned to an awkward few hours before she would be able to make some excuse and leave. Her dramas with Natalie and with Milt had left her feeling rather fragile. It was that fragility, she decided later, that underlay what happened over the next couple of hours and, since she could never blame Natalie, that meant, more or less directly, that it was Milt's fault.

What happened was that Jean found herself drinking Fran and Jim's wine, and not really minding sitting in their formal living room, and enjoying, frankly, being a little pampered for once. Jim had a nice, manly presence about him, an aura of power deferred, and Fran just seemed so pleased that she had come, nothing was too much trouble for her. Another glass of wine? More nuts? Different nuts? How did she like her chicken cooked? Was chicken all right? Maybe they should have done fish. They could *do* fish. It went like that. Fran ordered Jim around so much, to get nuts and wine and check on the chicken and *the potatoes, the potatoes,* Jean briefly feared for his health. He was a large man, he had a torso like a loaf of bread, and he was sweating . . . .

But it was all right. And eventually the three of them sat down to dinner. Fran had set a lovely table, using heavy silverware and, as she put it, her "historic" china, which featured a delicate blue-and-gold forget-me-not pattern around the rim, and which she seemed to want to make a topic of conversation because of Jean's work in ceramics. Nothing about the china interested Jean, but she didn't say that, and she tried not to show it, because for once she didn't mind Fran talking. From the way Fran behaved all night, it was as if Jean was something of a star in her eyes. Perhaps that had always been true, but somehow it had never been apparent to Jean before. Fran spoke about how much she admired and envied Jean's artistic ability and, not only that, her courage in offering her work for sale. She admitted that she could never do that. "Isn't she brave, Jim?" Fran asked her husband. "And so talented." And Jim, who seemed to defer to his wife in everything, at least everything of a household nature, agreed.

The only awkward moment that occurred during the first part of the evening, and it was only slightly awkward, came when Fran bustled around the table to point out to Jean something about the china pattern – a flecking in the gilt that she considered significant for some reason – and then paused. After a second Jean realized that Fran was staring at something, and it was something in her hair.

"What is it, Fran?" she asked.

Fran frowned as she peered closer. "It looks like a spot of dried blood . . . with a piece of skin in it."

Jean reached up, feeling for the spot, and found it, and so wished at that moment that she had taken the time for a proper shower. She dragged it crumbling out of her hair and looked at what remained on her fingers.

"It's glaze," said Jean, wiping her fingers in her napkin. "And a bit of clay."

"The glaze is red, though. Dark red. You almost never use red."

Jean merely smiled at Fran. "I'm working on something new."

Things proceeded very amiably after that. The chicken Jim brought out was done in a nice oyster mushroom sauce that was obviously made from scratch, and it was accompanied with fiddlehead greens, which Jean loved, and buttered carrots and roasted new potatoes. Jean mentioned that she had once done a ceramic of fiddleheads sprouting from the fingertips of a half-submerged ceramic hand – *Fiddlehead Resurrection* she'd called it – which delighted Fran but left Jim looking rather mystified. Jim wasn't an art appreciator, that much was obvious. Or a conversationalist. He seemed perfectly content to let his wife run the show, just as Fran seemed quite content to run it. They appeared, all in all, to be a very happy couple.

And then, at a certain point during dinner, Fran got a little agitated. Somehow they had gotten onto the topic of friendships. Fran referred to Jean's recent loss of Dorothy and how hard that must have been, and then she turned the conversation to herself. She admitted that since retiring and moving to Kotemee from the city, she and Jim had found it hard to make new friends. "People in small towns aren't what I expected," said Fran, fussing with her linen napkin. "I thought we'd be part of a *community*. I had some silly idea we'd be *welcomed*. But it hasn't been that way. Everybody here is just as insular as they are anywhere, except for you."

She touched the napkin to her nose as Jim leaned over and put his big paw on her arm, and Jean became aware of a sudden weight pressing on her, which was obligation, and the need to assure Fran that friendships didn't always come easily to her, either.

And that was how she got talking about long-lost Cheryl Nunley, and her apparent trouble, and Jean's deep regret over losing that friendship, and her frustration at not being able to visit Cheryl. And that was what led Fran to exclaim, with an almost phosphoric burst of certainty and fervour, that she would drive Jean herself. She would drive her tomorrow. She would *insist*!

And Jean, realizing too late that her fragility from the day's events had lulled her, indirectly but inexorably, into a trap, said . . . "Sure."

It was her cellphone that finally brought Jean relief from Céline Dion. She heard the ringing in her purse as if it were calling to her from another room, reaching her through the wall of voice. She dug out her phone and waved it to get Fran's attention, then pantomimed placing it to her ear.

"Sorry!" said Fran. She leaned forward to kill the stereo. "I just get so caught up sometimes."

Jean could tell that it was Welland calling, from the picture she'd assigned to his number. It was her favourite picture of him, looking very handsome in his uniform, but also smiling in a brothery way and not like a police officer. "Hello, Welland."

"Jean?" said Welland. "Where are you?"

There was something decidedly off about the tone of Welland's voice. It was more police officery than his picture, and it made her back stiffen. "Why are you asking?" she said.

"Remember I told you yesterday the city detectives might want to ask you some questions? About Adele Farbridge? Well, now they're trying to reach you. Nobody said anything to me, I only know because I'm on the system."

The system, the system. Jean was starting to regret ever getting him onto it. "All right, Welland," she said. "Thank you for telling me."

"So where are you? I called your home number and Milt said you've been staying at Natalie Skilbeck's house, but there's no answer there."

An image appeared in Jean's mind of Natalie, dragged out of view behind the kitchen island and shoved up against one of the low cupboards, which was all Jean could manage to do with her because she was so heavy. And the blood had been almost impossible to get out of the grout between the tiles. "Don't go bothering Natalie, Welland," she said. "I'm not there any more." She looked over at Fran, who was happily driving in the fast lane of the highway even though she was not going very fast at all. Her whole life Jean had complained about cars that did that, and now she was in one.

"Right," said Welland. "So tell me where you are."

"Welland, don't be bossy." He was starting to sound not only like a police officer but also like Andrew Jr., which was even more off-putting. "At the moment I'm enjoying a nice drive and I don't want you to spoil it."

She hoped that would be the end of things, but it wasn't. Welland just kept pushing for her to tell him where she was, and whether she was with anyone, and where she intended to go. And if it was far away from Kotemee, Welland said, then that might be a problem for the detectives. They might consider that "suspicious," he said. Even listening through her little phone, sitting in Fran's slow-moving Cadillac SUV, Jean knew the code of Welland's voice well enough to hear what he could not actually say. That he was afraid for her, but didn't know why. That he was not even sure that he had a reason to be afraid, and was almost frightened to find out. That he loved her and wanted to be a good brother to her, but that he was also a little excited, because he was finally on the inside of a real police investigation. It was quite remarkable, thought Jean, the messages a voice conveyed.

And she understood too – although Welland's voice didn't tell her this, it was her own common sense – that she was rapidly running out of time. The detectives from the city wanted to talk to her, and once that ball started rolling you couldn't stop it. Soon they would want to talk to people who knew her and had spent time with her recently. People like Jeff Birdy. People like Milt. People like Natalie.

But that was all right. Because there was only one person left in the world whom she cared for enough to call a friend, and she was going to see her soon.

"Fran," said Jean, when she finally hung up on Welland, "I'm fairly certain this Cadillac can go faster."

They were heading along the interstate to Owasco Lake, and according to the little clock on the dash it was about five o'clock.

"Nearly suppertime," said Fran. "Why don't we pull off for a bite?"

Over the preceding several hours, Jean had come to understand a few things about Fran, apart from her Céline Dion obsession. One was that Fran was rather expert at reading maps. The Cadillac had a computer capable of providing directions, but Fran never used it. Instead she folded the state map into precise and easily accessible quadrants and had Jean hold it for her. She had learned that, she said, while travelling with Jim through southeastern Turkey, where "one wrong turn could have meant our heads." Indeed, it sometimes seemed as though Fran felt the same way travelling through New York State; without warning she would snatch the map from Jean's hands and check a coordinate before handing it back. After the second hour Jean was no longer startled by this, although she was not yet fully inured.

Another thing that Jean had learned was that Fran did not like driving for very long without stopping. Already there had been two pull-offs for a bite, and one fairly recent bathroom break. Fran had caught a glimpse of an Applebee's beyond the veil of trees and wondered aloud whether Jean needed to "go to the loo." Jean had assured Fran that she didn't, but found herself leaning hard to the left anyway as Fran swung onto the exit ramp. She thought there might be something wrong with Fran's bladder, but Fran explained that it was precautionary. Taking regular breaks, she said, allowed you to stay alert behind the wheel, and staying alert meant staying safe. She had learned that driving with Jim through Bolivia.

But this time, Jean thought she would take a polite stand. "Wouldn't you rather keep going?" she said. "I think we're almost there."

Fran snatched the map out of Jean's hand, gave it a once-over, and handed it back. "We're still an hour away," she said. "Also, as you said yourself, we don't know what we're going to find when we get there. And if we're just showing up at your friend's door, we can hardly expect her to feed us."

"I suppose," said Jean.

Fran glanced over. "I guess you're getting anxious."

Jean stared through the windshield at the highway that ribboned away from them into the distance, and at the licence plates and taillights of the cars zooming by in the slow lane. "I am a bit."

"It must be so wonderful," said Fran. "For Cheryl, I mean. To have a friend who cares about you so much that she'd drive hundreds of miles just to see you in your hour of need. I've never had anybody who cared about me that much."

Jean gave Fran the best smile she could manage. "I'm sure that's not true."

"Oh, no, it is true." Fran repeatedly checked her side and rearview mirrors as she spoke. She'd been doing this the whole trip, because for the driver talking was as bad for alertness as eating and you had to work extra hard to stay focused. Jean was no longer disconcerted. "When I was little," said Fran, "my dad took work wherever he could find it, and so we moved around all the time and I never had a chance to form a really close friendship with anyone."

"Do you have any brothers or sisters?"

"I have one sister," said Fran, her eyes on the right-hand mirror. "But she's six years older. And anyway, siblings aren't quite the same thing as friends."

"That's very true," said Jean.

Fran went quiet, and for a while there was only the hum of the tires against the road. "Well," she said finally, "I can hardly wait to see what real friendship looks like. I envy you so much. And Cheryl. Especially Cheryl, because she has you for a friend."

Jean felt her face get hot and she knew that she was blushing. She had the sort of skin that blushed bright pink, although since high school it hadn't often been a problem. She turned away from Fran as if something beyond the passenger window had caught her attention. "That's very sweet," she said. She noticed an exit fly past and realized it was the second Fran had missed since talking about getting a bite. "Didn't you want to stop, Fran?" she said.

"Oh, well, I thought it would be okay to keep going, just this once."

Jean glanced over and she could see that Fran was blinking away tears. "Thank you, Fran."

"No, it's fine," said Fran, with a small sniffle. "It's just so exciting."

The Finger Lakes landscape undulated around them like mounds and folds in a moss duvet, and here and there lay the chenille patches of vineyards. Whenever the road rose and the Cadillac crested the peak of a hill, Jean could see on the horizon strips of water that glinted pale gold in the early-evening light. Like a glass of Chardonnay, she thought. And she could read, in the highway signs they passed, place names by the dozens, so many of them "Hills" and "Mills" and "Corners" and "Springs." This wasn't wine country, it was small town country. She thought now that she knew why Cheryl had come here. It was a land with a hundred Kotemees . . . a hundred versions of home.

At about six-thirty Fran pulled off the highway, and they began to follow a two-lane blacktop that took them rivering between hills and fields, through acres lavish with fruit. After a while Fran plucked up the map and studied it, as Jean watched row after row of tall vines troop past her window, and when Fran announced that they were getting close, Jean felt a surge of exhilaration in her chest and had to take a deep breath. She tried to picture the look on Cheryl's face when she appeared at her front door. Would she smile? Jean wondered. Would she be joyful to see her? Or, in the middle-aged face standing before her, would Cheryl see thirty-seven years suddenly gone, and hate her for it?

Fran discarded the map because it was no longer detailed enough for her liking. Moments later they rounded a curve and Jean spotted, thirty yards ahead at the mouth of an even narrower road, a battered white sign announcing the village of Bier Ridge. The blue border that surrounded the sign seemed to have broken off in places, and the painted bunch of purple grapes that accented so many of the signs in this part of the state seemed to be missing its top half. Jean also noticed that the sign was held up, at a slight tilt, by two unpainted wooden legs, as if the whole assemblage had been clapped together in haste or frustration. But it was the sign they were looking for.

"There!" said Jean.

"I see it," said Fran, and she wheeled hard to the right. "Okay, what number am I looking for?"

Jean pulled the sheet with Cheryl's miserable picture out of her purse and checked the address the police had entered. "Three twenty-seven East Lake Road." She looked up through the windshield. "How are we going to find East Lake Road?"

"We're on it," said Fran. She was leaning over the wheel, scanning the road ahead as if she were on safari, scouting for lions gorging on water buffalo.

"But I didn't notice a street sign."

"There's only a couple of roads around here, and we're on the east side of the lake."

"Oh."

With nothing to do or contribute, Jean folded the paper away and stayed calm by watching the scenery scroll past. Some of the homes here were lovely: bright clapboard houses with pretty gingerbreading and accenting shutters; handsome stone edifices with wide, groomed lawns and carriage houses in the rear. There was love in these homes, she thought, or at the very least money. More money than most people in Kotemee had, except of course for Fran and Jim. Yes, Fran would certainly be in her element here, Jean thought. And she had a flash of worry. She wondered whether money might be at the root of Cheryl's current trouble. Perhaps her friend had aspired to some sort of life here that was out of her reach. Perhaps Cheryl was a nobody here, just a grocery store clerk with a farmhand for a husband. She wondered if Fran, unwittingly, was driving them in her shiny, late-model Cadillac SUV toward some sort of shack, a broken-down hovel scorned by other Bier Ridge residents as a local embarrassment. She hoped the best for Cheryl but, with that picture to consider, the worst was not beyond the realm of possibility. And as a girl she had never had the best of taste.

They passed through a brief density of buildings, a little clutch of shops and official-looking structures bunched against the road like aphids on a twig, and then the buildings again became more sporadic.

"And that was Bier Ridge," said Fran. She sat back in her driver's seat and looked over at Jean. "Maybe we should stop and ask someone."

"Maybe it isn't the right road. Where's the map?"

Jean checked the floor and between the seats, then craned around and saw the map tucked into the crevice of the back seat where Fran had tossed it. She reached for it, feeling herself tip slightly as the Cadillac took the incline of a hill, hearing the engine surge as Fran pressed on the gas. The map was a foot beyond the tips of her fingers.

"There was a little grocer's in the village," said Fran. "Why don't we turn around and ask there?"

"No, no," said Jean. "I'll get it." The last thing she wanted was for her reunion with troubled Cheryl to happen in the checkout line of some awful food mart.

"You know what Jim and I have learned?" said Fran. "Once you're in the neighbourhood of where you want to go, it's more efficient to ask for directions than to keep driving."

"I'm sure you and Jim have learned a whole lot of things," said Jean. She had unhitched herself from the seatbelt and now she was wedging herself between the two front seats, trying to stretch to reach the silly map, which was just . . . almost . . . she'd thought the seat leather would let her slip through more easily than it did . . . she felt her stomach lurch as they crested the hill and started almost immediately down . . . and the map began to slide toward her fingers . . .

"Got it!"

Jean realized now that she was wedged fairly tightly between the seats and her breasts were bunched up to her collarbone. She flailed for a moment with her free right hand searching for a hold to pull herself up, and, in the process, purely by accident, she whacked Fran somewhere on her face. The contact was so brief and sharp it wasn't clear to Jean where exactly she had hit Fran – it felt like an ear, though it might have been an eye – but she felt terrible and would have said something immediately except that before she could speak, Fran let out the most appalling scream. It was a sudden, explosive kind of scream, a scream of total shock, and Jean's first reaction was to think, well, that was a bit much; she hadn't whacked Fran that hard. But then suddenly she felt the whole car moving, swirling, she felt G-forces pushing her body frontways and sideways and she heard squealing tires and Fran making strange huffing sounds as though she was either working very hard or she was in shock, and it seemed to Jean that Fran was losing control and that any second they were going to crash. All because of a little whack on the ear. And the string of thoughts that whooshed through Jean's mind as she was tumbling forward and hitting her knee on the gearshift and her head on the padded roof of the car was that she was going to die before she'd given Cheryl her beautiful gift and that it was *just ridiculous* and that she loved Milt and that she did love her brothers and that she should never have let Fran drive.

And then the car stopped.

"Oh my God!" yelled Fran. "She just came out of nowhere! Are you all right?"

It took Jean a moment to realize that she was alive and not hurt, and another to fully grasp that she was sitting in the passenger-side footwell, with her rump on the floor mat, her limbs above her, and her head wedged against the glove compartment, as if she'd been folded up and tucked there like tissue paper into a gift bag.

"I'm sorry I hit you, Fran," she said, "but honestly." She tried to move but she was stuck, and she reached out her hand for Fran to give her a hoist up.

But Fran didn't notice. "I can't believe I missed her!" she exclaimed. And suddenly she was wrenching her head around and looking toward the rear of the car. "There she is!"

"Fran, help me."

But Fran, who seemed charged with some strange cross-current of jubilance and outrage, was now busy staring at something or someone outside the car. And then her head began turning – Jean could see all this happening above her at seat level, like a movie – and it seemed that whatever Fran was staring at was coming closer, approaching along the passenger side. Then Fran, giving herself fully to outrage now, jabbed a button in a console to lower the passenger-side window, and when it was down she pointed across Jean's field of view.

"You!" she shouted. "Why did you jump in front of us like that? What were you trying to do, get yourself *killed*?"

Outside the car someone, a woman, howled a single, mournful word before dissolving into sounds that Jean found incomprehensible. She cried, "*Yes!*"

Jammed into the passenger's footwell, Jean worked her head around to try and see who would say such a crazy thing, and into view came a woman. Bleary-eyed and swaying, obviously drunk, she peered in through the open window, followed the path of tangled limbs down, and squinted as if she were trying to make out some phantom in a fog.

"*Jean?*"

And so, not quite the way she'd imagined it, Jean was finally reunited with Cheryl Nunley.

Chapter 20

Some plans turned out to be more difficult to achieve than you imagined.

Jean had always known that she was taking a chance just showing up at Cheryl Nunley's door, but she'd always assumed it would be a normal sort of chance – the chance that Cheryl might be extremely busy with house guests, or the chance that she might be away on vacation, or the chance that she might be having an exceedingly bad day, like the one she seemed to be having when her police picture was taken. There was even the chance that after thirty-seven years Cheryl might have forgotten about Jean altogether and wondered what sort of insane person would drive all that way uninvited to see someone who didn't even remember her. Because she believed her cause to be loving and even noble, Jean felt those were chances she was willing to live with. She'd just never considered the chance that Cheryl might be a complete walking disaster. In a circumstance like that, practicality called for a bit of a rethink.

For one thing, Jean decided to hold on to her apology to Cheryl for just a bit. Cheryl didn't seem to be in a state to really appreciate the apology and how heartfelt it was. It was hard for Jean, because she had so much remorse to express. But it seemed best to just get Cheryl to a safe place, such as a couch, and not rush anything.

She tried to look at the positive: at least Cheryl remembered her after all these years, and even fondly so. In fact there'd been times, Cheryl said (as far as Jean could make out), when she'd seriously thought of calling Jean – at Christmas, for example, when she was really in need of a friend because she was so profoundly depressed. Apparently Cheryl was often depressed, and at Christmas it just got that much more crushing.

All that despair had certainly left its mark. She looked so old to Jean, as if the last thirty-seven years had used her up, sucked out the true Cheryl and left the loose exoskeleton of an old crab. She was overweight, and it wasn't a well-carried weight, hidden by fashion and offset by posture, it was sloppy and slouchy, as if she had completely given up. Her eyes were sunken and tired. She had a puffy drinker's face and her hair was a haphazard, burr-coloured snarl. And her housekeeping! Jean had not yet quite recovered from that first moment when she and Fran had walked in the front door of Cheryl's house, which had looked so sweet from the outside, and set eyes on the squalor and smelled the stench of piled up dirty dishes and discarded food containers and floors covered in seed husks and feathers and so many bird droppings the banisters seemed to be covered in stucco.

At that moment, as she was taking in the scene, Jean would not have blamed Fran if she'd turned around, jumped into her

SUV, and fled into the Céline Dion–fired night. But Fran didn't go. She gave Jean a look that suggested the two of them certainly had their work cut out for them, and then she just began cleaning up. She washed the dishes, for starters, while Jean did her best to get Cheryl to make some sense. When that proved a waste of time, Jean steered her upstairs and into the least soiled bed. And the next day when they came back, after spending the night at a bed and breakfast, Fran took it one chore at a time, never complaining, never tsk-tsk-ing as Jean feared she might, until, after a full day, the main floor of the house was almost presentable. There was only one condition that Fran imposed on Cheryl as she undertook all this work, and it was one that Jean fully supported: never, ever, not once, not as long as they were there, was that horrible, kettle-sounding bird to be allowed out of its cage.

While Fran worked away in the house, Jean gave herself two jobs. One was to keep an eye on Cheryl, because every time she wandered out of sight she came back more drunk. There was also a good chance she might at any moment dash off into the path of another oncoming car; Cheryl herself admitted that her leap in front of Fran's SUV had been her fourth attempt in two days. She felt she was close to getting the timing just right.

The other job Jean assigned herself was to try and understand what was happening at the winery, because it was apparently causing Cheryl an awful lot of stress.

It was such a pretty property. The land was rounded, like a plump woman's thighs, gradually sloping toward the lake in the distance, and over these long, gentle curves stretched rows of tall, fragrant vines dripping with young grapes. Jean strolled for a while between the vines, with miserable, stumbling Cheryl in tow, and she could almost taste the sense of hope and possibility that had drawn her friend here.

The house itself was a large split-level, probably built in the Sixties, painted the pale yellow of young corn and shaded by big trees – three maples and two oaks, all of them bright green and fluffy with leaves – and Jean could just imagine what it was like in the fall when the colours came, in that joyous October gush. Behind the house stood a tin-roofed barn covered in old, worn wood, and this barn was divided into parts: a work area, with two stainless-steel tanks each about the size of a garden shed; a storage room, containing hundreds of cases of bottled wine; and a kind of showroom, with big windows, a long counter, wood panelling, and Mexican tiles on the floor. This last part was the tasting room, or so Jean was told by a sweet, old, European man named Josef Binderman, who worked in the winery and spoke with a charming accent (Austrian, apparently, not German as Jean had thought), and who had a very wise way about him. It was Josef who took Jean on a tour of the facilities, told her about the vines, let her sample the wine juice that was aging in the steel tanks, and then sat her down at one of the big pine tables in the tasting room and filled her in on all the recent trouble.

So Jean had a sip or two of a white wine and a red wine, which were not bad at all, and she learned about Cheryl's second husband, Tam Yoon, leaving three months before and just about cleaning out their joint bank account. She was told that the employees, all except Josef, had left because Cheryl could no longer pay them (or because Cheryl had once or twice been inappropriate while she was drunk). And Josef explained that, as small as it was, the winery was far too much work for one man, that harvest time was only a few months off, and pretty soon the whole thing was just going to grind to a stop. The grapes would rot on the vines, and Cheryl wouldn't be able to sell the place for anything close to its value. And selling was Cheryl's only option; Josef was as clear about that as he was about being Austrian.

Cheryl's contribution during this meeting was to mutter over and over about Jesus, which surprised Jean because she had not known her friend to be religious. But then she saw that Cheryl was pointing at the light fixture in the ceiling, so she assumed she had misheard.

That night, after dinner, Jean and Fran relaxed on the balcony of their room in the little Dancing Brook Bed and Breakfast, which sat on a rise overlooking an old, arched iron bridge. What the bridge crossed – an exquisite, narrow gorge, with a waterfall that dropped like a silky tress of hair a hundred feet to the Lueswill Creek below, skirting the dark, jagged remains of this gouge in the rock, a majestic scar made by some vast, unknowable power that seemed to have torn away a hunk of the landscape deliberately, even in anger – could not be seen from Fran and Jean's room. But they could see part of the bridge, which had been painted black, and they took pleasure in that.

Jean poured two glasses of Bier Ridge Riesling from a bottle Josef had given her and handed one to Fran. The two women were sitting in wicker armchairs and dressed in their pyjamas and robes, having showered after a long day. Fran had worked particularly hard, Jean knew, which was why she had let her use up most of the hot water.

Fran took a sip of wine and pursed her lips in appreciation. "Oh, that's very tasty."

"And it's very well earned," said Jean. "My goodness, Fran, what you did with that house in one day. I couldn't be more grateful."

"Really?"

"I'd never have managed all that myself."

Immediately Fran looked away, toward the trees that blocked the view of the gorge and most of the bridge, and Jean could see that she was trying not to smile too obviously. There was nothing

superior about the smile, or triumphant. It seemed only that Fran
wanted to keep some part of her delight private. She wiped the
base of her glass against the edge of her robe and, having composed herself, turned back around.

"Something you probably don't know about me," she said.
"When I was younger, my family didn't have much money. So, to
help pay for university, I worked on weekends as a hotel maid."

"That *is* a surprise."

Fran gave Jean the full weight of her gaze and nodded gravely.
"I had to clean a few things worse than bird poop." She squeezed
her eyes tight for a moment, as if to shut out the memories.
"Anyway, I'm just happy to be a help to you. That's what friends
are for."

Jean heard that and let it pass; she was too relaxed to argue
about words, about presumption. She sipped at her wine. And
then, strange how the mind worked – a couple of women dressed
in bathrobes, the scene toggling a brief memory – she thought of
something. "My friend Natalie said that to me recently, that phrase."

"You mean . . . about friends?" said Fran. She shrugged. "I
suppose it's a common expression. Like, 'God moves in mysterious ways.' Something we say to explain something that can't fully
be defined. Because no one ever completely knows what friends
are for, but – they're for things like that."

"Doing the thankless work," said Jean. "Out of a sense of duty,
and affection."

"That's right," said Fran. "Except, you thanked me." She saluted
Jean with her glass, and took another sip, and seemed to glow.

Somewhere on the other side of the house, the sky burned
with the setting sun and, for the pleasure of Jean and Fran on the
balcony, faint suspicions of pink washed into view. And hundreds of miles away, in Kotemee, thought Jean, a neighbour was
undoubtedly beginning to wonder why Natalie's Monday and

Tuesday copies of the *Star-Lookout* had not been retrieved from her front step, and her customers would be vexed by the appointments she'd missed. And Welland, if he was any sort of policeman, if he had any hope, would be figuring out where Jean had gone. And in a hospital in the city, Adele might be rising out of her unfortunate coma. And even if none of those things came true, it was still very likely that tomorrow, detectives from the city would be knocking on her and Milt's door. Finding Milt. Events were sure to move very quickly after that.

Jean said, "I have to decide what's the best thing to do for Cheryl."

Fran gave a quiet sigh. "How to help her," she said.

"Make her happy," said Jean.

"Because she's in such terrible pain."

"Yes, exactly."

Fran nodded solemnly at this shared understanding of Cheryl, then shook her head in a way that Jean interpreted as only slightly judgmental, which she certainly felt Fran had earned. For a while the two women said nothing, as the sound of the unseen waterway, amplified by the hidden chasm, drifted up to them.

Chapter 21

Grape leaves were very relaxing. As subjects, they didn't hold much interest for Jean – they were just ordinary three-lobed palmates, with scalloped margins where the veins came to tiny points at the edges. They were wide and sloppy, lazy and limp, like floppy hats or old slippers, and would make, she thought, a terrible ceramic. And yet, despite that, or perhaps because of it, she quite enjoyed them. They were leaves that could just be, without her thinking about how she should incorporate them into her work. They placed no obligations upon her. Unlike her friendships.

It was about nine in the morning; Cheryl wasn't awake yet, and Fran was working outside the house. She had adopted as her new task the neglected strip of garden that lay beside the driveway, and when Jean had left her she was tearing out weeds with the fervour of an exorcist ridding a damned soul of its demons. So Jean was free to wander the eastern acres of the vineyard, among the Cabernet Franc vines, and let her mind roam without distraction.

There had been times in the past, as Jean was coming to the end of a very complicated and ambitious ceramic, and she had solved all the problems she had encountered, and her vision was all but achieved, that Jean had felt a sort of wistful, yearnful sadness. Pouring yourself into an effort so completely, the way she did, made finishing it bittersweet. Success could feel like a kind of death. And so that moment – when she closed the kiln door on her final attempt, the one she knew was going to work – was always a little dangerous for Jean, and for her project. It was tempting to change something, to add something, to push the project in an odd direction at the last second so as to give it a new kind of life. Once or twice, she had succumbed to the temptation and it had worked out just fine. More often, it had ruined everything.

Something like that perilous melancholy was settling on Jean now.

As she stood in the midst of the tall vines, Josef Binderman appeared in his overalls at the end of the row. He shambled toward her, taking his time. The sun was off to the left and the shadows from the leaves made a pattern of mountains across his face.

"You like it, yes?" he said. "In the sunshine, with the grapes?"

"With the leaves," said Jean. "Yes I do."

A little frown of confusion came and went over Josef's brow. He tapped his nose with a knobby finger and sniffed the air. "Now the grapes are young, you know. But coming close to harvest time, the air is thick with the sweetness."

"Have you worked here a long time?"

His eyes crinkled as he smiled. "Now I am one of the buildings, like the barn. Many owners have come and go, but I stay. That's why I say to Mrs. Yoon, don't worry. I am not going to leave you with nobody."

Josef lifted a casual hand toward a small bunch of grapes, hidden among the leaves. They were still a milky green, like the Riesling grapes in the western acres, and small, the size of blueberries. He pulled a few of them free, then popped one in his mouth, and Jean heard the crunch as he bit down.

"Isn't that sour?" she asked.

"Of course," he said, grinning. "But still it's good to me. I said to Mrs. Yoon, 'Right now your life is like these grapes you know. Very sour. But soon it will come the sweet.'" He worked his jaw for a moment and spat out the seeds.

In Jean's view, certain old people, and Josef seemed to be one, fostered an absurd and rather tragic optimism about the future. Perhaps it was denial, working its evil spell. She adjusted the strap of her shoulder bag and held her hand out for a grape, and after a second of uncertainty the old man dropped one into her palm. "Josef," she said. "What if Cheryl's life doesn't ever become sweet?" She squeezed the hard little grape between her finger and thumb. "What if you knew it would stay as hard and sour as this?" While she waited for Josef to answer, she put the grape between her teeth and bit down. The juice was tarter than lemon, and her face contorted so much that one eye closed. It seemed to sum up Cheryl's situation nicely.

Josef rubbed his bristly face and gripped his nose as Jean flicked the sour grape into the dust. "Some years, that happens, you know," he said. "Maybe the weather is not too good, the sun doesn't come. The grapes don't get ripe."

"What do you do then?"

Josef pressed his lips together in a way that looked schoolmarmish to Jean. "Then is a good year for compost."

Her other friends had been more or less contented. Looking

back over what she had accomplished, Jean had to admit that it had been easy to work with contentment. She'd simply had to find a way to bring that essential happiness to a final, poetic peak before trimming off the last unwanted part of life like some ugly porcelain fettling. But Cheryl's experience was entirely different. She was living a sour-grape life. It didn't require much sunny-vineyard reflection for Jean to decide that here she needed a different approach.

There were no children in Cheryl's life; even if it was impossible for Cheryl to articulate much of anything about her situation, that was obvious from the lack of pictures on the wall. There was clearly no longer any husband, either, and no friends near her other than Mr. Binderman, who didn't really count. For a woman in Cheryl's situation, needing real understanding and support, a fussy elderly man was as useful as a ringing bird. Jean thought that of all the emotions Cheryl must be trying to wash away with her desperate drinking, loneliness was probably the strongest. Jean had so much to make up for in her past with Cheryl, and the loneliness of her friend loomed very large indeed.

As they walked back toward the barn, with Fran visible in the mid-distance, on her knees, clawing at the earth, Jean's phone rang. She took it out of her bag expecting to see Welland's picture, but saw instead that it was Milt. Her face went cold and her hand trembled a little as she brought the phone to her ear.

"Hello, Milt?"

"Jean, where are you?"

She smiled at Josef Binderman and moved slightly away. "How are you doing, Milt? I'm so sorry about what happened at Natalie's. I've been thinking of you just about every hour since then and I –"

"Jean," Milt interrupted, "I'm not calling about that." He was using his stern voice, which he reserved for moments when he felt his concerns outweighed those of anyone else. But Jean didn't mind because it swept her instantly back to a time when the two of them were planning their wedding and Milt would be take-charge about something, like wanting to invite his slouchy cousin Hendrick from Lethbridge or refusing to pay for a proper professional DJ, and he would brook no resistance. It reminded her of an era when neither she nor Milt had even heard of Louise Draper, and Marjorie was so far from death that she was still a forbidding presence in their lives and her opinions of Milt and his career and Jean and her art lay like a shadow upon them. And this was what they had thought of as hardship.

"What, then?" said Jean.

"There are two police officers here wanting to speak to you."

"Oh." She wondered whether, for Milt's sake, she should sound surprised. Would that be less worrying for him, or more? "Well, right now I'm visiting a friend."

"Who? What friend?"

She hesitated.

"Is it a man?"

"Milt, don't be ridiculous."

"Well why won't you tell me?"

Jean smiled again at Josef Binderman, who was hovering as if he had something to say. "I just don't think I should have to share everything with you all the time," she said. "I think I should be allowed that privilege for once. Let's remember the months and months of you neglecting to tell me some very important things."

"But the police –"

"Milt," she said. "Just hold on." Her phone had beeped and, taking it away from her ear, she saw Welland's handsome picture. She pressed a button. "Hello, Welland?"

Her brother's voice boomed into her ear with all his earnestness. "Jean, I wanted to let you know that those city detectives are heading to your house to see you."

"Thank you, Welland. I already know that."

"How? I just saw it in the system."

She looked to the cloudless sky. "Obviously, Welland, that system is not the end-all and be-all. If you want to do police work you should probably do your own finding out of things also."

"Well, you should get back here or it's going to look like you're hiding something. And, oh, by the way, you should tell Natalie the same thing because they want to see her, too. I assume she's with you because she's not at work and she's not answering her door. And guess what, Jeanie? I found that out all on my own."

"You . . . went to Natalie's?"

"Yes, I did. Looking for you. First her grooming place, all locked up, and then her house. Stood knocking at her door for twenty minutes in case she was in the shower or something. Nothing. Zippo."

Zippo. He was trying to sound like Andrew Jr. "Well, Natalie is not with me."

"Then where is she?"

"Welland," said Jean, "I have to go. Thank you for being so sweet and worrying about me. I love you, and goodbye." She punched a button and gave a little wave to Josef Binderman, who was still not going away. "Milt," she said, "are you still there?"

"Jean Horemarsh?" said a strange voice. "This is Detective Rinneard speaking. Your husband –"

Jean snapped her phone shut. It was probably a silly thing to do but it was the surprise – she couldn't stop herself. She squeezed the phone in her hand and tried to picture what Detective Rinneard might look like, and the image came to her of a burly man in a dark suit and a fedora. Was that too old-fashioned? There weren't any detectives on the Kotemee force so she didn't know what to expect. Maybe these days all of them looked like Serpico. She imagined someone who looked like Serpico grabbing the phone out of Milt's hand, and her heart started thumping. Maybe he'd *hit* Milt.

Josef Binderman began to approach and Jean did her best to smile. As she did her phone began to ring again, and when she looked down she saw Milt's picture, which meant it was not Milt at all. The phone kept ringing and getting louder, so she just dropped the phone into her bag and chose to ignore it. Clamped the top of the bag shut with her hand.

"Josef," she said over the ringing, "did you want to tell me something?"

And Josef Binderman, looking very perplexed, told Jean his idea.

Cheryl was not nearly as big as Natalie, but she was remarkably leaden. The dead weight of the drunk, Jean thought as she hauled on Cheryl's clammy arm in her bedroom, and it reminded her so much of trying to move Natalie over the kitchen tiles that she half expected Cheryl's head to flop backward like a lid.

"You know what we should do?" said Fran. "We should put our shoulders under her armpits and use our legs to lift."

You wouldn't have thought Fran would have any insight into moving an unconscious body, but then there was no telling what she'd had to deal with in those hotel rooms. Together they slid Cheryl off the mattress in her underwear until her heels thud-thudded on the carpet, and then they carried her like a snipered soldier out of the bedroom and into the shower. Cheryl was not cheerful about it when she came to, and she flailed a bit, ripping down the shower curtain and giving Jean a nice smack on the forehead. But eventually she seemed to accept that it was two against one.

Josef's idea had been simple, but really very inspired (it was almost as if Austrian common sense was a higher calibre of common sense). He'd come to his idea, he told Jean, when he'd spotted Cheryl's truck in the parking lot. He explained how Cheryl had crashed her truck into the "Welcome to Bier Ridge" sign, not once but twice. And after the second time, the regional police had suspended her licence and confiscated her keys. And so she had no way to leave. She was trapped at the winery. His idea was for Jean to take Cheryl somewhere, anywhere, and give her a different view out her window.

"A change of scenes can do some wonders," he said.

Such a simple idea, yet Jean knew that he was right. She'd learned first-hand, after all, just how trying it is not having access to a car. And she could see also how it was the winery that was amplifying Cheryl's pain. It was an ever-present reminder of her disastrous marriage. It surrounded her with her own failure, like a cage built with bars of mistakes. Somehow this just made sense to Jean, because she had thought herself, a few times, about what life might have been like had she married a different man, or given birth to children, or even moved away from Kotemee. Gone to someplace where she was brand new and alone, a smooth pebble on a wide, wet shore. Someplace without any ties, without any friendships or family, no one who could remind her of how young she'd been once, how gorgeous and alive and full of promise. How eager she'd been to greet every morning. How long ago it had been.

After Jean and Fran had hauled Cheryl out of bed, after they'd scrubbed her and dried her and put her in clothes (Fran had been quite impressive in the way she'd held Cheryl's wrists and stuffed them down the sleeves of her blouse – "Like forcing stuffing into a chicken," she'd said), they fed her some coffee and porridge which, the porridge, they thought would be good for her stomach. Then they sat down with her at the dining room table, one woman on either side of Cheryl in case she should bolt or topple, and presented their plan. Jean talked about taking a long drive somewhere. To give her a change. To get her away from the winery, and the memories, and the incessant buzzing of that horrible, horrible bird; wouldn't that be nice?

As she spoke, Jean could see past Cheryl, through the window. A lovely breeze ruffled the trees that guarded the house, shaking the leaves like the pompoms of cheerleaders, urging her on. But she found that keeping a smile on her face was a little more difficult than she'd expected. Because she was trying to fill Cheryl with a sense of hope that she herself could not really claim. A trip could change Cheryl's immediate surroundings; it could even lift her mood. But Jean knew that it wouldn't change any of the awful realities of her life. No drive through the countryside could repeal the sentence of old age. No afternoon on the beach could grant her the companionship and love of friends that gave shape and breath to each remaining day. Cheryl was still a prisoner of the hard truths, no matter where Fran's SUV might ferry her. And Jean knew that she was now, herself, a fellow captive. This had been her sacrifice for her friends.

But as her gaze wandered while she made her case – Cheryl wasn't looking at her anyway – Jean could tell that Fran was quite convinced a trip would do Cheryl some good. She looked as firm and certain as a coconut. There was something sweetly naive about that. So, almost for Fran's sake, Jean kept on, kept talking, selling the plan to Cheryl the way she might sell a ceramic that was slightly cracked.

"So, Cheryl," she concluded, "what do you say? Let's go on a nice drive. We can go for a couple of days if you like."

"It'll be fun!" exclaimed Fran.

"All you need to do is tell us where you'd like to go."

Sitting between them, her face still shiny pink from the wash-cloth, her hair neatly brushed, and dressed in clothes without any trace of vomit, Cheryl stared forward in silence. She blinked a few times and waved a hand in front of her face, as if she were trying to clear away fog. And when she opened her mouth, she said just about the last thing Jean expected.

"I want to go home."

Jean glanced over toward Fran and back again. "What do you mean, home?" she said.

"To Kotemee."

"Well, that's *easy*!" exclaimed Fran.

"No, no," said Jean. She put two firm hands on Cheryl's arm. "I meant go for a nice day trip somewhere. Isn't there a lake you'd like to swim in, or a museum you'd like to see?"

"I want to go *home*," shouted Cheryl. She ripped her arm from Jean's grip and would have fallen out of her chair with the momentum if Fran hadn't been there to block her.

"I think she really wants to go home," said Fran.

"But Cheryl," said Jean, "it's been thirty-seven years. Do you even know anybody there any more?"

Cheryl's thick, dopy eyelids blinked at Jean. Her lower lip was quivering.

"I know *you*," she said.

It took about an hour for Cheryl, with Fran's help, to pack a suit-case. Fran, describing later how it went, alluded to a lot of Cheryl throwing things toward the suitcase from her closet, a lot of Fran doing her best to scrape together a few ensembles from the heaps, and a lot of Cheryl lying down on the heaps that Fran was trying to sort through. She spent a further twenty minutes saying goodbye to her bird, which, in Fran's account, involved Cheryl muttering incomprehensibly and passing slices of peach through the wires of his cage, while the bird whistled like a football referee.

Jean spent that time making arrangements with Josef Binderman, who seemed almost giddy at not having Mrs. Yoon to worry about for a while (though he was rather less thrilled about adopting the bird). He said that while she was gone he would talk to other winery owners in the area and see if he couldn't line up a buyer, and Jean had no doubt that he could. When she said goodbye, Josef reached out for her hand, brought it toward his white-stubbled chin, and kissed it. It was an old-man sort of thing to do, Jean thought. Possibly Austrian. And quite pleasant.

They hadn't been in Fran's SUV for two minutes before Cheryl was asleep in the back seat, and she stayed there, snoring, while Fran and Jean paid for their room at the Dancing Brook Bed and Breakfast, and had a quick look at the gorge. When they got back on the road, Fran reached toward the glove compartment and began to take out a Céline Dion CD.

"Fran," said Jean, "I know you love Céline. But would it be okay if we took a break from her very impressive voice for a while?"

"Of course," chirped Fran. She dropped the CD into the glove compartment and snapped the door closed. "Actually, I'm glad you said something. I think we know each other well enough now to be honest about things like that, don't you?"

"Yes," said Jean. "I do."

"That's part of being friends, isn't it?"

Saying this, Fran seemed to watch the road even more intently than usual. Jean heard the yearning hum of Fran's tires against the pavement, saw her fists tight around the wheel, and felt her own inner resistance crumbling. "I guess it is," she said finally. And Fran, eyes on the road, lit the Cadillac's interior with her grin.

A few minutes later, as they merged with the highway traffic and Fran secured her position in the fast lane, Jean's phone began to ring. She reached into her purse as if it were a mousetrap, and pulled it out gingerly. Welland.

"You're at Cheryl Nunley's!" he crowed when she answered. "And no, I didn't get that from the system. I just noodled it out."

"Very good, Welland. But we're not there any more. We're on our way home."

In the driver's seat, Fran gave Jean a cheery thumbs-up.

"But, Jean, I don't think that's such a good idea." Welland's voice became dark and hushed, and as he spoke a picture came to Jean's mind of her brother crouching down behind his desk, beyond the view of Tucker's Car Wash outside his window, like a small boy hiding from his parents behind the living room couch. "Jean, I'm sorry to tell you, Adele died this morning."

"Did she?" Jean allowed herself a small smile, even as her vision misted over a little.

"Yes, and there's city detectives all over the place here. There's some at your house, and some over at Natalie's, and there's even two of them in Andrew Jr.'s office."

"I see."

"There's all this crazy talk, Jean. You won't believe what they're saying. I don't even want to tell you it's so crazy. But just – maybe don't come home right away. Get a lawyer."

"Welland," said Jean, "do you think you should be telling me this? You might get in trouble."

"I'm scared for you, Jeanie."

He didn't have to tell her; she could hear the fear in his voice. She told him not to be scared, that everything was going to be okay. She said this not because she thought it was true, but because she was his big sister. She was the matriarch of the family now and it was her responsibility. And it worked; when Welland spoke again, she could tell he was a little calmer.

"I keep thinking about what Mom said. Remember what I told you at the funeral?"

"I remember," said Jean.

"You're strong, Jeanie. You're a strong woman. That's what she said."

"I know."

"I'm not making it up."

"I know you're not, Welland."

After she said goodbye, she held the phone in her lap for a while and watched the Buicks and the Toyotas and the Fords passing them on the right, rushing by in the slow lane like chosen people, and it didn't bother her because she had much bigger concerns. She turned and looked back at Cheryl, still asleep on the soft leather of the Cadillac.

She had so little time.

"Is everything all right?" asked Fran.

Jean straightened in her seat again and set the seatbelt like a sash against her chest. She stared out the windshield at the diminishing road and breathed in the Cadillac air. "Fran," she said, "do you ever think about getting old?"

"If I think about it I get too depressed," said Fran. "So I try to stay busy. Or I listen to Céline, and she just drives those thoughts right out of my head."

"I think about it all the time," said Jean.

"Well, you know what they say about getting old," Fran chuckled. "It's better than the alternative." When Jean said nothing,

Fran took her eyes off the road just long enough to glance over. "Don't you think?"

She had so little time.

Halfway home, with the afternoon sun hanging just above Jean's passenger-side window, Cheryl sat up, awake.

"I'm hungry."

When Jean looked back, she felt a surge of relief, because the woman she saw, even with sleep-flattened hair, was so much more like the Cheryl she'd known years before. Her eyes were clearer, she had more true colour in her cheeks – not just the grapefruity pink of washcloth abrasion – and she smiled at Jean, for the first time, as if she really knew her.

"Hi, Jean," she said.

"Hi, Cheryl."

"Is there any wine in the car?"

Fran said she was overdue for a pull-off, and so the women started looking for signs announcing a town that might have a nice restaurant. Fran also whispered to Jean that she didn't think it was wise for Cheryl to stop drinking all of a sudden, since it was the sort of thing that could lead to erratic behaviour, of which Cheryl had already proven herself quite capable. And they were, after all, in a moving vehicle.

"You're very practical, Fran," said Jean. "My mother would have loved you."

They were passing a sign for Priormont, population 23,896, and Fran was giving it a thumbs-up, when Jean's phone rang again. She looked at the picture and felt sick, because it was Milt's face. Which meant it probably wasn't Milt, it was Serpico in a fedora. It seemed to Jean as if those detectives had stolen her husband's face from her.

"Aren't you going to answer it?" piped Cheryl from the back seat.

"Not just now," she said, and slipped the ringing phone into her purse.

Fran curved off the highway at the next ramp, and as they drove toward Priormont in search of a place to eat, Cheryl regaled them with stories from Jean's youth. It was if she had risen from a sleep of decades and even the smallest event was fresh. She told stories about beloved boys, and broken bra straps, about reading Tillie Vonner's diary, watching Dorothy Perks kiss, and the time Jean got a mouthful of dragonfly when she was bicycling down the Conmore Avenue hill. There was never a moment in Cheryl's account of the past when the two of them were not friends, when they felt betrayed by one another, or abandoned, and when the stories were over and they were pulling into the parking lot of a tidy-looking steakhouse, Jean was more depressed than ever. Because all of her deep affection for Cheryl had come rushing back, and the thirty-seven years of friendship the two of them had lost stretched behind her like a petrified forest, agonizing in its near-beauty, its almost-life. And she wanted more than ever to do for Cheryl what she had done for Dorothy, and for Adele, and for Natalie, which time and circumstance now made impossible. She wanted to give her a moment of pure happiness that sank deep into the muscle and bone of her soul, and then save her from the pain that would surely come spilling in the moment Cheryl remembered that she was a disaster.

From the restaurant's parking lot they made their way up a flagstone path, past the log-look exterior and a wide, plate-glass window through which Jean caught a glimpse of a fireplace. Forever, it seemed, she had wanted a home with a fireplace – the smell of wood smoke coming from chimneys in the fall always sparked in her a great longing – but it had always been denied her, because when she and Milt were house shopping, the sorts of homes that had fireplaces were the sorts they couldn't afford. Milt had told her at the time that one day he would build her a fire-place, and of course that had never happened. Walking into the restaurant it occurred to Jean that she had lived the best years of her adult life without so many of the things she had wished for – her dear friend Cheryl, a fireplace, her mother's spoken respect – and the combined tragedy squeezed and packed the sadness she was feeling even deeper inside her.

At the little sign asking them to wait for service they stood politely. The restaurant was not very busy, because they had arrived before the dinner rush, but even so it took a while for someone to come and seat them. Beside Jean, Cheryl was rubbing her arms as if she were cold, and her breathing was becoming panty, like a dog's. Fran and Jean exchanged a glance that said they both knew what was happening, that it was the withdrawal and they'd better get a glass of wine into Cheryl as fast as they could. So when the waitress finally came, wearing a crisp white shirt and her hair tied back with a black ribbon, and led them to a booth with orange vinyl upholstery, the most important thing was getting in an order for drinks before she was gone. It took a minute then for Jean to notice that they'd been seated with a view of the fireplace she'd seen through the window. When she realized it, her throat became suddenly tight with emotion. Sitting near the fire, with Cheryl next to her in the booth, and Welland's reminder echoing in her head, it seemed to Jean almost as if she were being given a taste of the life that could have been.

"This is quite nice," said Fran, getting comfortable on the seat opposite Jean. "I think I'm hungry enough to eat a cow." She paused, and giggled. "Jim and I were in India once, and I said the same thing and got some very sharp looks."

Cheryl seemed unamused by Fran. She was sitting hunched and more dog-panty than ever, and in her lap she was rubbing the knuckles of her hands as if she had just punched someone. "Where's that waitress?" she said.

"She's coming," said Jean, "don't worry." She tried to use her most calming voice, and patted Cheryl's arm, and she could see the slightest easing of the distress in Cheryl's face. The thought passed through Jean's mind that if the two of them had remained close for all those lost years – if she had not abandoned her friend – it might have given Cheryl the support she needed to never become an alcoholic. She felt more protective of Cheryl in that moment than she had for any of her friends, and worse than ever about herself.

Jean's phone rang again as the waitress arrived, and she picked it out of her purse while the drinks were being distributed. Fran took a sip of the cranberry juice she'd ordered.

"You're very popular today," she said. "I only wish my phone rang half as much."

Cheryl, who was obviously not happy that her drink was the last to be served, half turned to Jean. "Well?" she snapped.

Jean said nothing. She simply stared at the ringing phone in her hands. There was no picture in the little display, which meant the call was from an unrecognized number. She never got calls from unrecognized numbers, and she was at a loss for what to do.

"Oh, for God's sake," said Cheryl. She put down her glass, which was already half empty, grabbed Jean's phone and opened it, then she shoved it against Jean's ear. "*Speak*," she said, and went back to drinking.

Jean opened her mouth, and a second later formed the word, "Hello?"

"Is this Jean Horemarsh?" said a man's voice.

"Yes?"

"This is Detective Rinneard again. You hung up on me before."

"I'm sorry," said Jean. She cleared her throat. "That was a mistake."

"I would like to speak with you in person, Jean. It's very important. Can you come to the police station right away? We can meet in your brother's office."

"Do you mean Welland's office? Or Andrew Jr.'s?"

"I mean Chief Horemarsh's office. I don't know any Welland."

Jean straightened in her seat. "I have two brothers," she said. "Welland Horemarsh is also a police officer. Which obviously Andrew Jr. forgot to tell you."

"Where are you now, Jean?"

"I'm on the road. About to eat a nice meal."

Beside Jean the waitress appeared and pulled out a palm-sized pad. When she saw that Jean was on the phone she turned to leave, and as she did, Cheryl lifted her glass and made pinging noises against it with her fingernail. "Actually, make it two," said Cheryl.

"Are you alone?" said Rinneard.

"No, I'm with friends."

There was a very deep silence at the other end of the phone.

"Jean, listen to –"

She snapped the phone shut and set it down on the table's glossy surface.

"Lose the connection?" said Fran. She shook her head sympathetically. "We're probably not close enough to a city."

"Why don't you just turn it off?" said Cheryl.

Jean looked up and smiled at them both. She realized what it meant now that the detective had called from another phone. "I might get a call from Milt," she said. Her husband's face had been returned to her.

"Milt?" said Cheryl. "Do you mean Milt *Divverton*?"

"That's right." Jean beamed. "We started dating after you left, and then we got married."

"But," Fran leaned in and spoke in a showy whisper, "they're not together any more."

"No, Fran, that's not true," said Jean. She patted the phone. "I think Milt and I are working it out."

Fran flopped back against her vinyl seat in a display of utter relief, like someone who had learned her house had not been crushed by a mudslide. "How wonderful!" she exclaimed. "That is the *best news*. Because those two," she directed this at Cheryl, "they are made for each other."

For a moment, the three women in the booth seemed to glow in the warmth of Jean's announcement, and Jean exercised forgiveness regarding the presumptuous thing Fran had said.

Shortly, the waitress returned with Cheryl's second and third glasses of wine, and the women made their orders. Jean didn't have much of an appetite, and she thought a spinach salad would be more than enough, because salads at steakhouses were always paradoxically large. Fran ordered a strip loin, cooked medium, in peppercorn sauce with a baked potato, and Cheryl chose a simple pasta. Jean thought she probably had a queasy stomach.

The waitress stopped at the serving station and picked up a grisly-looking bone-handled steak knife, which she set proudly beside Fran's other cutlery.

"I'm surprised you're only having a salad," said Fran.

Jean drew her fingertip through the condensation beading against her glass of white wine. "Not very hungry," she said. Her bright mood had been short-lived; in the last few minutes she had slipped from her lovely Milt thoughts to more of her miserable Cheryl ones. Because her mind had drifted back to the tragic situation, which was that the friend she wanted to help most in the world, the friend to whom she deeply wished to make amends, was the one friend she was going to disappoint yet again. You couldn't escape thoughts like that. They were like water finding its level, like sad condensation trickling down the side of a glass.

It seemed to Jean that the knowledge that she had failed Cheryl was going to be with her forever, like a puddle on the floor of her mind, and that whatever happened once they got back to Kotemee, and whatever happened with Milt, she could never be truly happy again.

And did she feel a tiny bit sorry for herself, as she sat in the orange vinyl booth? Probably. No one knew more vividly than her what a great blessing was the bliss that she had provided for Dorothy and Adele and Natalie, a joy that was pure and sweet and that would never dissolve into anguish and pain, the Marjorie sort of pain, just thinking about which made Jean shudder. And so as she dwelled on the misfortune of Cheryl, still drinking beside her, always drinking, she allowed herself to consider her own plight, which was almost as bad. Maybe worse in a way. Because as sad and disastrous as Cheryl was, she really had no idea how bad it was going to get. But for Jean, the knowledge was luridly clear. And in the face of it she was left to wonder, where was *her* moment of pure beauty, where was *her* gift of unalloyed bliss? Who was going to save *her* from the ravages to come? No one was, that was the answer. She was all alone. She was as alone, and as doomed, as Cheryl. Their fates were entwined. Indeed it seemed to Jean, as she glanced up and caught sight again of the logs burning gold against the blackened surround of the fireplace she could never have, that the only thing that could give her true joy now, a joy worthy of her own Last Poem, would be giving the same to her friend. And because Cheryl was miserable and there was no time to do anything about it, that could never happen.

And that was when Cheryl set down her wine glass, let out a deep breath with her eyes closed, and said the most remarkable thing. "Oh, God," she said with a sigh. "I'm so happy to be going home."

"I'm sure you are," said Fran.

The little hairs on the back of Jean's neck began to prickle.

"What did you say, Cheryl?"

"I said I'm so *happy*." She pushed her hair behind her ear and looked at Jean, and leaned over to wrap her arms around Jean's shoulders. "Thank you, thank you," said Cheryl, giving her a sloppy, urgent squeeze. "I don't know what made you come looking for me, Jean. But I'm so glad you did. I've been so miserable, for months. And now I'm not any more, because you're here, and . . . I'm going *home*."

When Cheryl leaned back again she used her napkin to wipe the tears from her cheeks. "Excuse me," she said. "I'm a little emotional. Maybe I should just visit the loo."

Jean was so lost in thought and possibility that she didn't twig, immediately, that she needed to move to let Cheryl out of the booth. It was Fran giving a little cough that prompted Jean to slide clear. And as she stood, watching her good friend, her rediscovered friend, making her way a little unsteadily to the washroom, Jean racked her brain and looked around, searching.

"Jean?" said Fran.

"Everything's fine," she said. Her eyes drifted, still searching, to the place setting in front of Fran, to the glass of cranberry juice with traces of lipstick on the rim, to the side plate and the salad fork and the bone-handled steak knife.

"Fran," said Jean, grabbing the handles of her bag, "you stay here. I'm just going to check on Cheryl."

"That's a good idea."

Three tables away, their waitress was busy taking orders from a young family with a black-haired infant in a high chair. A manager dressed in a stiff shirt and striped tie stood twenty feet away near the entrance to the kitchen. The serving station was deserted, so no one saw Jean pick up a steak knife as she walked past, and slip it into her purse.

It wasn't the perfect solution, she knew. But this was likely her only chance. Cheryl had actually said she was happy – for Cheryl, this was surely something of a peak – and the situation called for improvisation.

She pushed open the heavy door of the washroom. A short, dim passageway led to the main area lined with stalls on one side and sinks on the other, where the walls were covered in a mottled grey tile, and a cool, unflattering light fell from bulbs recessed in the ceiling above. A silver-haired woman – about Marjorie's age, Jean guessed – leaned against the sink counter with her face close to the mirror and applied a dark pink to lips drawn tight over her teeth. Jean scanned the rest of the echoey room, dipping her head slightly to check under the four stalls, and saw Cheryl's feet at the far end. Jean knew she couldn't just stand there, the old woman was already glancing at her through the mirror, so she entered the near stall, removed the serrated knife from her purse, and perched on the edge of the seat.

The old woman took an inordinate amount of time at the sink. And she made a lot of hum-humming noises as she finished her lips, noises that she probably couldn't, herself, even hear. Jean tried not to imagine the disease that had very likely already begun eating its way through the woman's insides, but it was too easy to picture her face, mere putty over bone, when the final days came, and the inhuman sounds she would make then. All Jean could do was hope for the woman's sake that whatever took her would be quick, and that her children would be spared the duty of witnessing her agony.

Sitting there, waiting, Jean girded herself. It was going to be different, the thing she planned. It was going to be quite tricky. She wished she'd had time to practise, because it was the sort of thing you didn't want to get wrong. Closing her eyes, she tried to do what athletes did, which was to visualize success in her mind.

Her stance, that was easy – a warm embrace from behind, her cheek pressed against the side of Cheryl's head. She tried to picture the motion she would use, the way a baseball player might imagine his swing. And her version of the ball going over the fence . . . *hurray!* . . . that was a vision of happy Cheryl, her eyes going suddenly wide, and the light within them dimming, softly but certainly, even as Jean's own sight – an instant, a stroke behind – began to fade.

Milt . . . she thought of Milt, even though he wasn't part of her vision, and her brothers, too, all of them saddened and confused. *What could possibly have been going through her mind?* Well, never mind. This was one time she didn't have to explain or justify. Nobody needed to understand but her. Was it too much to ask for a moment of pure elation, and then nothing else?

The old woman's heels finally sounded a diminishing clip-clip against the tile floor, and the heavy door's hinges groaned. And when a sudden roar of flushing water came from Cheryl's stall, Jean slipped quietly out of hers, hurried down the little passageway to the washroom door, and locked it.

When she returned, with the knife's bone handle in her grip, she found Cheryl already at the far sink. As Jean watched from a few feet away, she washed her hands and then bent to splash water on her face. That was the perfect opportunity, and Jean recognized it as such. She came up behind, squeezing the handle of the knife, her heart jumping in anticipation of what she was going to do, for both of them. To the sound of running water she ran through it all one more time in her mind, a quick replay of triumph – stance, swing, home run, *yay!* – and waited for her friend to rise.

When Cheryl finally lifted her head she came only partway, letting the water drip from her nose and chin onto the porcelain. And it was a close call for Jean. She tried to calm her breathing because she'd nearly blown it, nearly jumped forward at the first

Cheryl twitch. She told herself to wait, *wait* – swish, crack, over the fence! – she knew Cheryl would look up eventually.

And, eventually, she did.

Cheryl stood and stared into the mirror, and reacted with surprise to her friend looming behind her at the moment Jean swooped in. And everything went according to Jean's mental rehearsal. She wrapped her free arm around Cheryl's waist in a tight and loving embrace. She held her close as she pressed her cheek against Cheryl's damp ear. She looked into the mirror to watch the dying light in her friend's eyes. And then . . . well . . . then it all went crappy.

Before Jean could lift her knife hand to execute the twinned motion she'd planned – which, *zip*, *zip*, was sure to have worked perfectly – she took a last look at Cheryl's face, and saw just what Cheryl saw. The dark pouches under her eyes, the sallow sag of her cheeks, the general shadow of despair. There was no happiness there, Jean realized. Not one little bit.

"I'm really a mess, aren't I?" Cheryl said.

"Oh," said Jean, trying to hide her disappointment. "No, you're not."

"Be honest, Jean. I remember you being honest with me before."

Jean sighed and loosened her embrace. "All right, Cheryl. I admit that you've looked better. But I honestly think that's true of anyone our age."

Slowly Cheryl dipped her head, and her shoulders began to shake. Jean could hear the rise of her first, choking sobs. And so, before her friend's pain took irrevocable hold, Jean did what she had to do. She laid her knife hand on Cheryl's shoulder, turned her, and wrapped her friend in her arms. She held her and let the tears soak into her blouse and tried to absorb the shaking. And she apologized. She said all the things she'd wanted to say, about how wrong she had been to abandon her friend, from that day by the weeping willow, about how childishly she'd behaved, letting petty hurt and jealousy keep her from giving Cheryl all the love and support she deserved, and about how sad she was, how awfully sad, for Cheryl's terrible loss all those years ago. She said everything to Cheryl. In fact, she said it more than once, because Cheryl's extreme sobbing was making it hard for her to hear. "*What?*" she kept saying. "*What?*" It wasn't ideal, actually. But Jean just kept on apologizing, as often as she needed to, as loudly as required, even as she dropped her knife to the bottom of the waste paper bin. And she pledged to herself that she would always be there for Cheryl, for as long as it took, until the day she was deeply, unshakably happy. Even if that meant the two of them almost certainly getting old, which . . . well, looking at Cheryl, it wasn't even a question.

A moment later, as Cheryl was mopping her eyes with toilet paper, the washroom filled with the sound of frantic banging, and the voice of Fran, crying, "Jean! Jean! Are you in there? *Jean!*"

Jean went to unlock the door. And when she pulled it open, there was Fran. Or sort of Fran. Her face had been remade, as if by another artist, into an expression of exaggerated horror. In her hand, she held Jean's phone and, seeing Jean, she seemed not to be able to move.

"Have . . ." A whisper was apparently all the voice Fran could now muster. "Have you done something bad?" The noise of footsteps sounded behind Jean and Fran turned, her eyes fixed wide, to see Cheryl coming forward, wadding toilet paper into a tight, damp ball. She blinked and gaped again at Jean. "Milt called," she whispered. "I saw his picture so I answered it. I didn't think you'd mind. He told me I should run for my life."

"Milt said that?" said Jean.

"Why would Milt say that?" said Cheryl.

"He said . . ." Fran swallowed. "Well, he said that Jean was very dangerous at the moment. Or words to that effect."

Jean sighed and shook her head, and took the phone out of Fran's hand.

"Nothing at all is going to happen to you, Fran," she said. "I'm sorry, but you and I are just not that close."

Jean paid their bill and the three women left, although no one had eaten a thing. They climbed into Fran's SUV without a word. Fran in particular strapped herself in very gingerly.

As they made their way out of the parking lot and headed toward the highway, Jean thought about the people she was close to in Kotemee. Milt was first on her mind, of course, and not because she was annoyed that he'd upset Fran. Mostly she wondered whether this whole business would change the way he felt about her, because there were times when Milt was not very understanding and this was probably going to be one of those times. She thought about Welland, too, and worried about how this might affect his career, whether it would give him a bad feeling about police work, just when he was starting to get the hang of it. Andrew Jr. flashed through her mind as well, but she thought he would manage just fine.

As Fran merged onto the highway, Jean looked over her shoulder at Cheryl in the back seat. She still had the wad of toilet paper in her hand, and seemed confused but not distraught, as if she thought she might have misheard what Fran had said, or that she'd had some sort of alcoholic hallucination. At least she didn't appear to be jumping to any conclusions, which Jean thought was very fair of her.

In the driver's seat, Fran had the wheel in a firm grip. Her lips were pressed tight together, she directed a fixed glare at the road in front of her, and for once, Jean was pleased to see, she was driving in the fast lane at an appropriate speed. Jean thought the word that might best describe Fran just then would be *determined*. But she knew Fran well enough now to know there was probably a good deal going on under the surface. Fran had a lot more substance to her than she'd realized, and her mind was always working, and right now Jean figured it was probably swirling with all sorts of conflicting thoughts.

"Fran," she said, "if you need to listen to Céline Dion all the way home, feel free."

Fran turned her head slightly. "Really?" she said. "You won't mind?"

"No," said Jean. "It's absolutely fine." And she opened the glove box to let Fran choose.

EPILOGUE

PEOPLE LIKE TO KNOW how a story ends, so it seemed a good idea to say a few words about what happened to Jean, after she got back to Kotemee.

She was arrested, of course. That didn't take very long. Fran dropped her off at Jean and Milt's house, where the driveway and the curbsides were lined with police cars and dozens of silent onlookers, many of them people Jean knew. And when she walked into the house, Detective Rinneard, who had sharp blue eyes and a shaved head and didn't look anything like Serpico, arrested her for the murder of her three best friends. Jean didn't make any sort of fuss and "went along quietly," as they say, not even objecting to the use of the word "murder."

Jean's arrest, and the trial that followed, filled the Kotemee *Star-Lookout* for months. It was front-page news in the city for a day or two, and a bunch of TV reporters came and nosed around a bit, and did their reports standing on the sidewalk in front of Jean's Expressions. Milt kept the store locked, but they took some video of her display pieces in the window, and on the Internet there was lots of discussion of Jean's ceramics: "The art of the serial killer." Some people, including one prominent art writer from the city, said she was a genius, and if Milt had wanted to sell any of her pieces he could have made a small fortune. But he didn't seem to want to. Eventually, one night, someone put a brick through the front window of Jean's shop and tried to steal all of her ceramics. No one knows how many they made off with, but judging from the amount of dust and crumbled bits on the floor of the shop and the sidewalk outside, most of the pieces likely disintegrated as soon as the thieves picked them up.

For the trial, Jean said she didn't need a lawyer; she was content to plead guilty because she wasn't ashamed of what she'd done. But the court assigned her one anyway, a nice enough man who, because he was greying and had a bit of a belly, looked something like Milt, except with a nicer suit. He rounded up some psychiatrists from the city who testified as to Jean being temporarily insane at the time of the killings. But when Jean got on the stand she said that was all nonsense. She stood up and told the courtroom that after what she'd learned about growing old, if anybody thought she was crazy for giving her friends a fast, happy way out, then they didn't know much about friendship.

Cheryl Nunley stayed in Kotemee, and it was kind of funny how that worked out. She got herself into a twelve-step program, which seemed to do her some good. And when she sold the winery, she wound up with a parcel of money. It wasn't much, but it was enough to buy a cozy little house, and the house she ended up buying was Natalie's. She got it as cheap as could be, too, because nobody else wanted to buy a house where somebody had been gruesomely slain. Cheryl, however, bought it without any qualms whatsoever. She told people that whatever Jean had done, she'd done out of love, and so there weren't any strange feelings or vibrations in the house. The only problem was that it was a bit cramped. She thought she might put on an addition.

As for the men, well, let's see: Milt finally got a full-time teaching position, because without Jean's income from her art, he needed the money. And he didn't see Louise again; that decision stayed firm. Andrew Jr. carried on being chief of police at Kotemee, which was no big surprise. Nobody thought it strange to have a police chief with a sister serving time for multiple murders, because in a small town lots of people have relatives who do strange things that everybody knows about, and life just goes on. As for Welland, he quit the Kotemee force, applied for a patrol job in the city, and got it. The day he started, he enrolled in special training to become a detective constable. It meant coming in early and staying late every shift. But he was pretty determined.

Jean was sentenced to life in prison with a chance of parole after fifteen years. They trucked her off to the federal penitentiary for women in Mainsview, about a day's drive from Kotemee, and she took to prison life rather well, although she found it a little hard to make friends. She got lots of time for her ceramics, though, and after asking for nearly a year, she even managed to get the prison to install an extra-large kiln. There wasn't much greenery around the prison yard, of course, and her access to books was restricted mostly to what the prison library kept on its shelves, so the inspiration for her pieces had to come from her imagination, and from whatever her visitors might bring. And that's where Fran Knubel came in.

One day, a few months after the trial, Fran kissed her husband, Jim, on the cheek, climbed into her SUV, and drove up to see Jean. The two of them had a good long visit, or as long as the guards would allow, which was about twenty minutes the first day. Eventually they snuck that up to half an hour. And now Fran drives up about once a month. Usually she takes with her a little package of leaves, plants she's picked from the garden or weeds from the roadside, or even greenery she's cut from supermarket produce, like kale and celery leaves and basil, because these days Jean is happy for whatever she can get. Fran wraps them in a damp cloth laid inside a Tupperware container to keep them supple, as per Jean's request, and presents them proudly after the guards have given them the once-over to make sure they're not drugs.

Of course, people want to know why she goes up there. "Why are you going out of your way to see that killer?" people ask her. Fran just holds herself very tall and says it's hard to make friends these days, and anyone in her shoes would do the same thing. "Aren't you afraid?" people ask her. And Fran assures them she's not. Jean killed only the women who were closest to her, she explains, and she would not presume that level of friendship, certainly not on the basis of monthly visits. But then, Fran will become lost in her deepest thoughts, and she'll get a peculiar look in her eyes. It's what you might describe as a sad and hopeful expression.

Tina Dooley
Acting President
Kotemee Business Association

ACKNOWLEDGEMENTS

At times, the novelist is a scavenger, rooting among the weathered memories and dog-eared details of other people's lives in search of the piece that will fit his imagined construction, or the bean that will sprout something wholly new. My heartfelt thanks to those friends and acquaintances who, by sharing the stuff of their lives in conversation, seeded important elements of this story long before there was a story.

I'm grateful to the Canada Council for the Arts and the Ontario Arts Council for their crucial support. Thanks also to Tara for her ceramics knowledge, to Miranda and Krista for their reading and insights, to Lara Hinchberger and Ellen Seligman for their encouragement and guidance, and to Bruce Westwood and Carolyn Forde for joining me in the leap of faith.